"Fun, fast, and fascinating. *Girl Like a Bomb* hooked me and held me."

— —PETER CLINES, NEW YORK TIMES BESTSELLER, AUTHOR OF *PARADOX BOUND*

"*Girl Like a Bomb* is a book like a bomb— explosive, heavy and dangerous. A must read by an exciting new voice."

— BRIAN KEENE, AUTHOR OF *THE RISING* AND *PRESSURE*

"Like its characters, this thoughtful take on self-assertion, sex, and healing, shines."

— PUBLISHERS WEEKLY

GIRL LIKE A BOMB

AUTUMN CHRISTIAN

Copyright © 2024 by Autumn Christian

Cover by Joel Amat Güell

ISBN: 9781955904919

CLASH Books

clashbooks.com

Troy, NY

He was now in that state of fire that she loved. She wanted to be burnt.

— *ANAÏS NIN, DELTA OF VENUS*

PART 1

1

We took his truck out to his secret place, near the creek littered with beer cans. He parked in the trees and together we climbed out onto the rocks. Their shadows hunched over the fire of his lighter as he lit another stolen menthol. He chuckled while he told me a story about pawning his sister's antique dolls and his mother's Tiffany lamp for weed money.

He wouldn't let me drink his Four Loko. Not at first.

"You're just a baby," he said, refusing to look over at me as he smoked. "You'll blackout and I don't feel like carrying you home."

He didn't look at me even when he said I reminded him of Daenerys, from Game of Thrones – the Mother of Dragons. I thought at first he meant because of my pale hair, long and unkempt, but then he said:

"You have a face that's so soft, but it's a softness like fire."

* * *

He finally let me take a sip of his Four Loko. I grimaced and had to struggle to swallow.

"Told you," he said. "And don't roll your eyes at me like that."

"Tastes like fermented gasoline," I said, handing it back to him. "My favorite."

I needed to lose my virginity. I was already fifteen, and I wanted someone bad. I knew Spider was bad because he had a spit cup in the cab of his truck and thin white scars on his forearms he refused to talk about. We locked eyes for the first time in fourth period, his teeth hard-set, his stare like the sensation of chewing ice. He was older than me but still stuck in sophomore classes. I asked to borrow a pencil. He reached into his duster jacket and handed me one while time slowed and focused to a point in space between me and him.

"You might look pretty if you wore your hair down," he said when I took the pencil, and his tongue touched his front row of teeth.

I couldn't stop thinking about him since.

There were perfectly nice boys at Montamount High I could've lost my virginity to boys who would tell me I look perfect with their chests about to cave in, who would straighten my hair on the pillow afterward, smiling at the way my shoulder clenched. But they didn't have the bruised knuckles burnt with stories or a duster jacket with the arms held together with pins.

I didn't look at those other boys and felt like at any step, I'd sink underwater, backward, bound in chains.

I read once that humans can't help but seek out excitement — it's why we first made fire and invented the printing press and slept with foreigners on the other side of large bodies of water.

I liked that idea because it made me think that even a terrible mistake like Spider was cosmic destiny. Something imprinted into my DNA.

Something calling to me across the waves — through the window, after my parents had gone to sleep. Outside, wearing nighttime like leather, his neck lit up in oily porch floodlights.

He looked good in starshine, in 2 A.M time, even with his stick and poke tattoo of an eye on his neck, his combat boots held together with duct tape. The way he tried not to smile made me smile, and after I pulled on my hoodie and my sneakers and climbed out the window, his hand twitched, as if he wanted to reach out to me.

But he didn't, and this made me smile even more.

Breathe in. Air feels cool. Breathe out. Air is cooler. That night my chest felt like a cavern and I could fit the whole world inside.

"How'd you find this place?" I asked.

"It's my secret place," he said.

"Do you bring girls here a lot?"

"You're the only girl here," he said.

I stretched and scooted a little closer to him. I yawned as an excuse to try to show him the cute outfit I wore, but he continued to stare straight ahead as he lit another cigarette.

I crawled across the rocks and slipped my hands in between the chain of his crossed legs. He opened his knees when I leaned into him as if inviting me in.

I kissed him in a halo of nicotine smoke.

He gave me another sip of his Four Loko as he cradled my waist between his knees. I felt high off our proximity, like the smell and sensation of him would make me float away if the wind blew in the wrong direction.

"I know why you don't have a boyfriend," he said.

"Because I wear my hair up?" I asked.

"No," he said.

It became silent, and I knew he wasn't going to tell me why.

"I brought condoms," I said.

He gave a terse nod.

I didn't realize it'd be so awkward with both of us fumbling for our clothes in the dark without speaking, without touching, breathing out cool air like shiny oil slicks. Nobody ever talked about that moment before the act, when zippers got stuck and your lipgloss rubbed off on the inside of your sweater, when you laughed nervously because you had to do a weird shimmy to get out of your tights. And finally, when all the clothes were off, and all that was left was the interminable space between two bodies, there was the holding of breath like the next noise should be something tremendous, and not just the crinkling of a condom wrapper.

* * *

"You're a virgin, aren't you?" he asked.

I spread my jacket on the rocks and laid down. I shivered and the creek noise grew to a roar. I hadn't noticed before how cold it was.

"No," I said.

"Yeah you are," he said. "I can tell. You think you're being cool, but I can see it."

I fumbled with the condom. He plucked it out of my hands.

"I'll take care of that. Just touch me," he said.

"Where?"

"You know where. At least, I hope you do."

He didn't take his eyes off my chest, although he had such an intense stare it was like he looked through me instead of at me. My nipples hardened and I felt the rocks underneath me.

I reached out, unable to control my trembling, and began touching his cock.

A swallow stuck in my throat. I thought at first that he'd remain limp, that I couldn't get him up and I'd remain a virgin forever, but then after a good half minute I felt his cock harden.

His hands traced my ass and my hips. Then he touched me between my legs, and I flinched at his cold fingers.

"What are you doing?" I asked.

"Trying to get you to relax," he said. "Virgins. Have to teach them everything."

He pushed his cock inside of me in one fluid motion. One second I'm a virgin, and then suddenly I'm not. It didn't hurt like I thought it would. It was more like a pressure, a fullness, stretching inside of me. He went slowly at first, in and out, and I found myself holding breath.

I couldn't see his face in the dark, but I could see the place between my hips and his that I thought resembled an abandoned alien landscape.

"Here," he said. "Get on top."

He rolled me over. I felt awkward and unsure of how to move. All the videos I'd seen couldn't really prepare me for the moment I was looking down at another human being, his cock inside of me, feeling split in two but also sewn together, conjoined.

"Like this," he said, and guided my hips. "Like dancing."

But it was really nothing like dancing.

Something began to build in me.

I thought it must've been an orgasm but this wasn't like any orgasm I'd ever had. It started in my stomach and swirled downwards, heated, a little warm bundle of nerves inside the bracing cold. There was an intense pressure, and even when I clenched my hips together or shifted it didn't relent. And strangely, Spider felt it too.

When I tried to stop he grabbed me again by the hips. The whites of his eyes grew like cracks of light through a darkened gate. Tears welled in my own eyes, although I wasn't sure why. I saw the moon in double, shimmering through water, reflected off his pale chest.

I'd fingered myself before. I had my first orgasm riding a washing machine and I even bought a few sex toys off the Internet. Although sex-ed in middle school was all bananas in latex and warnings about STDs, I watched enough porn to fill in the gaps. I'd even read part of a PDF of the Kama Sutra, although I didn't really get it.

I wanted to be ready for this moment.

But there was no way I could've prepared for this. This

definitely wasn't a normal orgasm. This was an unbearable friction, a dry plain about to catch fire, a swelling, growing, heaving, pulsating, liquid swell inside of me that was louder and bigger than everything I'd ever experienced before. Nothing could've prepared me for the feeling of my body rumbling like an earthquake, turning my bones into tectonic plates.

I held my breath.

And I exploded.

A depth charge of intense pleasure ran through me. It spiraled out in all directions, not just into my vagina, but up through my heart, my throat, and down into my toes, moving in pulsing, frenetic, golden waves. It buzzed on the top of my skin, but also deep in my organs, my pressurized blood. It froze in my throat like black ice and seared my eyeballs. It licked the edges of my hair, curling through my scalp like fire.

Could someone die from having sex? Had I pushed a button that was the bomb inside of me, currently making its way to my vulva and my heart? I'd never heard of anything like that happening. I thought I was breathing but I couldn't be sure. Maybe this was a rare form of sex-induced brain damage. If at that moment someone had asked me my name, my address, my birthdate, I wouldn't have been able to answer. I'd become a frisson ball of nuclear-level sex energy that couldn't contain a single coherent thought for longer than a fraction of a second.

God, surely I should have heard about something like this.

Yet for a few moments, I couldn't hear anything except the rush of my own blood. I looked down, expecting to see my organs leaking out of my vagina, or a hole blown straight through my stomach. Maybe I'd even see Spider's corpse below me, his cock still erect inside of me, his eyes dissolved into glowing goo and his tongue swelling in his mouth like a slug.

But I was intact, and Spider was intact. There was nothing missing, no injury, just smooth skin and moonglow.

Spider grabbed one of my wrists, and I realized he was speaking to me, trying to reach me through the hissing scream of my body.

After a few seconds, the noise subsided, and the flush of lightning went down to a low tremble.

"What was that?" I asked when I could finally hear again.

He spoke, his voice thin.

"Don't stop."

2

Janna and Heather and I went swimming in the creek after school. Summer was almost over, and our bare limbs were dotted with goosebumps in our swimsuits. Janna stole a few bottles of beer from her dad's "Fun Fridge." We poured them into water bottles and sipped them as they grew warm.

"You didn't want to keep him, right?" Janna asked, flipping her hair back. "You wait at least a month to fuck if you want to keep them."

"Nah," I said. "The universe can have him back."

Janna was sixteen and considered herself experienced because she was a sophomore and had a long-term boyfriend on the varsity football team. Although nobody was really sure how a tiny, dark-haired girl who played tennis had landed teenage Channing Tatum. Mostly everyone was in agreement she was a little too loud, her chest a little too small, her dark burnt hair a little too big.

"We could scare him for you," Heather said in her quiet voice. "What's he afraid of? Spiders? Flying? Getting a job?"

She headed to the edge of the water, looking like some kind of lagoon-eyed nymph in her too-tight bikini.

"Nah, we don't have to scare him," Janna said. "Bev is just

practicing, right? So she'll be ready when she gets a real boyfriend."

"You know what they say. Practice makes perfect."

Although *practice* was a word that couldn't really cover the aching, twisting, heaving, magma-filled *need* seizing me.

"Well, he probably deserves to be punished anyway," Heather said. "Think of all the girls he's fucked over."

"That sounds boring," Janna said, right before jumping into the water.

Heather patted the back of her curly hair. "Great. My hair's frizzing. It always goes crazy in the heat."

"It's fine," I said.

"Maybe I'll shave it."

"I like your hair," I said. "It makes you look like a mermaid. Or one of those paintings, you know?"

Heather made a wistful sigh. "Oh, our little Bev is growing up. We should've hooked you up with someone better than Spider."

"It wasn't really like that," I said. "I'm fine, really."

As far as I knew Heather never had a boyfriend, but she'd lost her virginity one summer night to a wannabe pilot. Because of the wistful way she talked about him I imagined a boy coming down from the sky on a beam of light — like the angels that used to have sex with women in the twilight, their wings stretching a dome over both of their heads.

He might as well have been an angel, or dead. I heard he lived in another state and had to leave when school picked up again. After that Heather started painting her nails black and listened to death metal and never really recovered. As far as I knew she hadn't even really looked at a guy since.

Janna emerged from the water.

"I'm not going to fall in love until I'm 23 at least," Heather said.

"I'm never going to fall in love," Janna said, squeezing the water out of her hair. "That's how you get pregnant and fat."

"What about David?" Heather asked.

She shrugged. "He's sweet, I guess."

Heather took another sip of beer and passed it to me. It tasted almost like warm mud.

"You guess? You don't want kids?" Heather asked.

Janna laughed. "I'm going to have the doctors rip my uterus out."

"Ouch," said Heather.

"Desperate times call for desperate measures."

I tried to keep from smiling so big that my face would break. I wasn't broken up over Spider because I never wanted him. Not really.

I wanted a feeling.

I wanted a singular, frozen moment.

I wanted that sticky burning sensation. I wanted that pleasurable rush. I wanted that so-good pulse of an electric hair trigger acid machine just underneath my skin.

I didn't understand what happened that night, but I liked it.

I wanted to burst and sizzle and liquefy. I wanted the colors of the whole earth to bleed again, and I wanted my blood to get so hot and loud it'd block out the noise of airplanes, trains, my own irrepressible sex sigh which seemed louder than a rocket.

I wanted the bomb inside me to go off and I wanted my skin to scream. Again and again and again.

I wanted "Don't stop."

I wanted to fuck.

* * *

A rumor went around that Spider and I were a thing, so the *nice* boys wouldn't have much to do with me after that. They heard stories about how he held a kid over the scaffolding of an unfinished bridge and threatened to drop him for talking to one of his girlfriends. I had to find what I wanted elsewhere.

Gene Conroy, infamous high school dropout and chaser

of freshmen, often hung around the gas station parking lot. He'd listen to his iPod and chain smoke cigarettes while he watched the high school girls walk into the gas station to buy sodas and sugar-free gum. Some people said he worked at an illegal distillery a few miles outside of town. It wouldn't have surprised me, he always had a golden, sour smell to him. I dreamed of that smell, and as I slept it grew like a jeweled garden around me, enveloping me in its resplendent cradle.

I knew others could smell it too. It was like a bad boy musk that always attracted girls like me.

Whenever he did lure a girl into his locus, he'd disappear for a few days or a week. Poof. Gone. I imagined he'd take them to a retreat on the moon so that they could bounce on beds in zero gravity.

But the girl always left and he always returned to the gas station, to his cigarettes and iPod and recalcitrant bad boy pout.

One day I bought him an ice-cream Snickers to share, and we finished it together while barely speaking. He pressed his thumb against the dab of ice-cream on the corner of my face I left there on purpose, just like I knew he would.

I grabbed his wrist.

"I'm Bev," I said, and licked the ice-cream off his thumb.

I dreamed of him the night before hovering over my bed like a glittering cloud of cigarette smoke. Everywhere the mist of him touched me I tingled and hummed, and eventually I became so absorbed in him I too became a cloud, white to his dirty yellow tinge. I woke up to a half-gasp of an orgasm.

I wasn't really sure if I actually liked him, but I figured dreams of desire don't lie.

"Let me take you somewhere," he said.

"I like somewheres," I said, which I immediately felt silly for saying.

He rubbed his hands against my fingers. His fingers had a crooked bend, they'd been broken so many times, and when he spoke I could sometimes see a burn scar marking his tongue. Like most bad boys, he refused to talk about how he got his injuries.

I leaned into him, and we kissed. Just a little tease of a kiss, a peck followed by nervous laughter. His mouth seemed to be the only soft thing about him.

He opened the passenger door of his busted up Toyota Camry and ushered me into a seat littered with coke cans like I was a junkyard queen. He drove us to the Dairy Queen, and we dipped out behind the parking lot into the copse of trees.

And there he undressed like a tiger shedding its human disguise, standing in the dip of light that bent through the leaves. I realized this was his natural environment, not leaning up against a gas station but deep in the woods with the dusk settling over his dark skin, like a black curtain draped over a blazing meadow. In the distance the neon ice-cream cone of the DQ blinked, but we might as well have been a thousand miles away from civilization. This was our new kingdom.

He lay me down on his jacket in the pine needles. I was ready. I'd spent my whole life waiting for moments like these, and I felt the backed up juices of heady blood and adrenaline waiting to gush through my entire body.

Even he seemed surprised by how ready I was. He stroked his cock while looking at me. His eyes became factories, building machines of dreams that were engineered to imagine all the things he'd do to me.

He put his condom on and his cock entered me. It wasn't anything like the way Spider fucked me; the rhythm was different, the smell and physical sensations were different. Even the way he positioned his hands, the noises he made, was different. Still, I wasn't a virgin. I'd already done this before, and the basic mechanics were the same. I could experiment with how I positioned my hips, where I placed my hands, which part of my body I chose to focus on.

"What do you like?" I asked.

"This," he said, as he thrust further into me, sending little frissons of sensation all the way up into my stomach.

"What do *you* like?" he echoed me, almost as an afterthought.

The word came lazily out of my mouth, and even I was surprised by its smokiness. It was a word like a serpent flicking its tongue.

"This."

It started to happen again.

A shift, a pressure, squeezing its way through my body.

A jungle seemed to grow in my periphery. The living rubies and emeralds of my dreams, panting with my nerves. And as the colors shone brighter and brighter, again I felt pressure increase in me, an earthquake of sensation building scaffolds of haloed light inside my blood.

I clenched my knees together.

When Gene Conroy pushed my knees apart again I exploded.

It went off in my stomach and spiraled down into my vagina. Then it shot out of me and into him. His stoic expression melted. His eyes bugged. His mouth widened. My ears rang. I felt like I was bleeding, burning, being stabbed with ethereal energy stuck on vibrating pins. I was not a body anymore, I was skin spun on top of a new heaven.

"Fuck, girl," he said.

We stopped as the ringing in my ears swelled and my sweat dripped into his mouth. We examined each other's bodies as if to see if we were still whole.

He pulled out of me.

"Where'd you learn to do a thing like that?" he asked, his voice trembling.

One of his fingers brushed against my arm. He breathed heavy like he couldn't get enough oxygen into his lungs. Sweat ringed his forehead like a crown.

"I don't know," I said. "It just kind of happens."

He braced his arms against the dirt as if he thought he might fall. His sweat halo made the smell of whiskey even stronger.

"I'm serious, Bev," he said. "I've never felt anything like that. There's something real freaky about you."

He drove me back into town. He gripped the steering wheel tight, his body locked almost as if he didn't dare move.

He seemed frightened of me and refused to look at me the whole way back. When he pulled over to let me out, he made a half-hearted attempt to say that he'd call me, but I didn't even bother to get his phone number.

Not because I was afraid, not because I didn't think he was boyfriend material (although, he wasn't).

I just wanted more.

* * *

After Gene and Spider, I set my sights on another boy with an animal name called Badger. He was a repeat senior. I only ever saw him entering or leaving the principal's office, with his burly body almost too big to fit through the doorway. He hunched as he walked, with big heavy steps like he wanted to burn holes through the floor.

He wasn't always such a fuck up, though. He used to be skinny enough you could see the veins in his sunken wrists. He was a model student. He won the spelling bee and first place at the science fair every year. We all thought he was going to be a lawyer or a businessperson or someone important.

Except, one day his girlfriend Sam disappeared. Rumor had it she got pregnant and was whisked away by her religious mother, sent to a Catholic school that was all reciting verses and genuflections. It might as well have been an iron tower, a surface that Badger could not scale.

After that, Badger started acting out in class — putting his boots on top of his desk and refusing to do his homework. Also, he began to eat. A lot. I sometimes saw him at Jimmy's Cafe, eating two of the breakfast specials and drinking a giant pot of coffee all by himself. He ate like a demon who wanted to devour the earth's supply of waffles and bacon, who had a vendetta against every farm and field. He ate like a conqueror, who'd laid rights to polish off every sausage link, fried egg, and bag of Cheetos in existence.

Once during school I brushed against him in the hallway, touched my hand lightly against his chest, and his hands uncurled.

"Do I know you?" he asked.

"Not yet," I said.

He looked at me then, trying to place me.

"Beverley," he said, testing the word out. "You're Beverly, right?"

"Just Bev," I said. "See you later."

I brushed my hand against him again. My heart jolted and struck me like a lightning bolt.

I knew that I'd gotten his attention when I caught him looking back at me.

I lurked around the principal's office for a week, waiting for him, feeling like a witch casting a spell whenever I spoke his name. I wore my silky pink lip gloss like a charm. I sprayed on Victoria's secret perfume like an enchantment.

My skirts got shorter and my tops got tighter. I couldn't convince my mom to throw away the money on a Brazilian blowout, but I started curling my hair and painting my nails. I'd practice my sexy look in the mirror before class, jutting my hips out, showing off the good angles of my face.

Janna said I looked like a teenage siren waiting for some hapless victim.

"Hey Badger," I'd say every time he came out of the principal's office.

I practiced different variations of his name, from a husky growl to a coo, trying to figure out the right way to express the syllables so that he'd be drawn to me.

Most days he kept on walking, but I was persistent.

Finally, after a week of this, which was an eternity in

school days, he came up to me. He asked me if I wanted to study with him after school, while looking down at his feet.

"I hate studying," I said, my heart kicking fast.

"I never study," he said.

"It's a date then."

* * *

I got a ride from Heather out to his trailer park that evening. She dropped me off with a "Good luck, babe," and a wink. I felt like maybe I shouldn't have gone out this far, but the excitement of the possibility of sex always pushed away all of my common sense.

There'd been a flood in that trailer park several years ago, and the water line where it rose was still visible.

I found his trailer where he said it'd be, rusted on the outside, the windows busted and taped over. The steps leading up to the door were painted red and black like blood and dirt.

Inside I found him mopping the baseboards. The kitchen shone like one in a model home. The carpet had been freshly vacuumed, and all the knick-knacks — baby angels, dogs with halos and Faberge eggs — had been recently dusted.

His mother sat on the plastic-wrapped couch like a bony doll.

"Hello Beverley," he said, and then corrected himself, "Bev. This is my mom."

"Hello!" I said, sounding overly-cheerful.

She slurred a hello.

"Thirsty?" he asked.

"Very."

He opened the refrigerator to grab me a soda. The refrigerator too was immaculate — all of the food neatly arranged in gleaming rows like a store display.

"My mom," he said in way of explanation. "She's got some autoimmune thing. Have to keep the place clean."

I pulled coupons for Dominos out of the sparkly red purse that my mom bought for me last Christmas at Nordstrom Rack.

"You hungry?" I asked. "I got coupons for half off a large, with some free breadsticks."

* * *

"Mom," he said. "Pizza's here."

She'd fallen asleep watching some kind of game show, her head lolling back, mouth open. She got up and rubbed her eyes, then slurred something incomprehensible before taking the plate and sitting back down.

Badger and I ate at the cramped kitchen table amongst the kitten salt and pepper shakers.

We took our time, but I was ready to fuck the moment he opened the pizza box, his eyes dancing like the lights of Times Square.

I barely ate anything because I was so focused on watching him eat. Nobody ate like Badger, like they had a vendetta against existence, like the very act of needing sustenance was an abominable one.

Yes, anger king, yes, eat like you're going to destroy the world, eat like you're the conqueror of the galaxy. I want to watch you trample the meatpacking plants to the ground, burn down the fields of wheat, annihilate the dairy farms that brought the milk to your doorstep.

"Let's go to your room," I whispered as he chomped down the last of the breadsticks.

"I don't have my own room," he whispered back.

We both glanced over at the couch. His mom had fallen asleep again, her plate still half full.

We went into the bathroom. I turned on the flickering light and there was a brief moment where we stood beside each other, awkwardly waiting. I knew we'd both been expecting this moment, felt it drawn taut like an invisible line between us, but we now stood as if unsure how to grasp it.

"You're nothing like Sam," he said.

"Thanks," I said, although I wasn't sure if he meant it as a compliment or as an insult.

I reached up and kissed his enormous chest.

He kissed my neck. He began to pant, although we'd barely moved. I helped him undress in that small space. I unbuttoned my shorts and I leaned against the sink as he helped me wriggle out of them.

He pushed me against the sink, and I felt the leaking faucet cold against my ass. He kissed my thighs, once each, and then in a clumsy way he was on my clit with his tongue.

I was always finding new ways to shake.

I got close to orgasm but didn't quite make it. I was still learning how my body worked. It was more about the exploration than the resolution.

"I want to do you," I said, gasping. "I want to put your cock in my mouth."

He indulged me, let me kneel in front of him, in front of his thighs so big I thought I could lose myself in them. I touched his cock with both hands. It was bigger than I was used to.

"How do I—?" I asked, feeling nervous for the first time in a long time. "I've never—"

"I'll show you," he said.

I took his cock into my mouth. I discovered I couldn't fit it all in the way, and I gagged a little when the tip touched the back of my throat.

"Just go up and down," he said, gentle, and he touched the nape of my neck.

My entire body sparked like his hand was electric. I could feel the strings of his desire vibrating between us.

"Tighten your mouth a little," he said. "Use your hands."

By the way he breathed in little gasps, it seemed like I must be doing something right.

"You're too good for me," he said.

"I'm not good," I said when I was able to speak. "Now fuck me."

His face was covered in a sheen of sweat by the time he put a condom on, and I felt the pulse-pounding of his need as he gripped my shoulders. He pushed himself so far into me I thought I might burst.

It was coming fast then, without warning. It was coming and I—

The explosion hit us.

It rocked us so hard that the outline of the faucet imprinted itself on my back. He groaned. I swear I felt the trailer shake. When I looked up at his face it was vibrating like an insect's and my own insides were trembling so fast I felt like a spaceship in warp drive.

His mother called him in the next room.

"I better check on my mom," he said.

He put on his clothes and left the bathroom. I grabbed my bra, wrestled it on and left quickly.

I wanted to leave while the flush of the moment was inside of me, so I could enjoy it unhindered.

I danced a little as I walked. I felt like I was holding a ball of spastic light inside of me.

* * *

I called Heather and she came and picked me up alongside the road. Her windows were down, and she blasted Eminem, tapping her black nails against her pink furry steering wheel cover. Her cousin Patrice was in the backseat, playing a Gameboy.

The passenger side door wouldn't open, so I climbed through the window of her car.

"You seem happy," she said. "You must've done it."

"Got a cigarette?" I asked.

"Not in front of my cousin, I don't."

"Oh shit, sorry," I said.

I glanced back at Patrice, who seemed completely absorbed in her Gameboy.

I didn't even really want a cigarette. I just wanted to taste the moment. Savor it. I leaned back in my seat, unable to keep from smiling.

"Yep," she said. "You totally did it. You're glowing."

She cackled.

I unrolled the window, and stuck my hand out the window to feel it bounce against the air currents.

3

The next day in the cafeteria Heather came up to me and nudged my elbow, bumping my tray full of chicken nuggets.

"You're getting a reputation," she said.

She stood with both feet planted, slightly apart, and stared at me wide-eyed, holding a diet coke with a bendy straw in both hands.

"A reputation for what?" I asked, even though I already knew.

"You know," she said. "Being bad."

I tried to keep a straight face, but I couldn't help but smile. And when I smiled, she did in return, breaking out in a grin behind her coke can.

"It's kind of cool, right?" she asked.

We sat down at a nearby table. A buzzing swept through my head as I looked around at the boys in the cafeteria, imagining them all naked.

"You look hungry," Heather said.

"Not for chicken nuggets," I said, and we both laughed.

"You should come to Jane's party tonight," she said.

"Another one? My mom's getting worried about me staying out late all the time."

"She'll get over it," Heather said. "You're not a little girl anymore."

Janna walked up to us, wearing sunglasses. She stumbled a little as she reached for the chair.

"Hungover?" Heather asked. "Where's David?"

"Fucking dead, I hope," she said and slid into the chair.

She took out a water bottle and fumbled with the cap.

"That's not water, is it?" I said.

"Of course it's not," she said.

"Come to a party with us," Janna said.

"Get your mind off of it, right?" I said. "I mean, remember all that stuff you said about love?"

She tipped the water bottle into her mouth and swallowed, wincing.

"Bev's got the right idea," she said. "Fuck love, right Bev? There's just fuck."

* * *

I told Mom I was going to study with Heather and Janna, and she told me I was a bad liar, but she let me go anyway. I changed out of my jeans and sneakers into my party outfit in Heather's car.

Janna was still drunk. I brushed out her hair a little, and put some blush on her cheeks to give her some color. She took off her sunglasses and examined herself in her phone's camera.

"My eyes are all red," she said. "I look awful."

"Nah, you look badass. Like Medusa or something," I said.

Heather parked in front of Jane's house, lit up with cotton candy-colored lights. Top 40 Pop blared from the windows, but the silhouettes with red paper cups behind the curtains never danced. A fog machine outside pumped gray clouds across a lawn littered with abandoned glow sticks.

We get out of the car, and I let Janna lean into me as we headed for the door. I felt the eyes of everyone turn toward us as we made our entrance. I wasn't sure what those stares meant, not at first, for all I knew we were on a red carpet heading toward our debut or walking through a jungle about to be devoured.

When we entered the party, I realized they weren't looking at Janna, with her drunken swagger, or at Heather, in her into gothic party dress and Cleopatra eyes.

They were looking at me.

They knew something in me had started to change. Something that I didn't quite have a name for, not yet. It wasn't that I was more confident, or more knowledgeable. It wasn't that I was no longer the embarrassed virgin, shoulders shy, trying to hide non-existent flaws in my hoodie and baggy jeans, behind my hair, behind my fingers.

It wasn't just that people looked at me differently now when I walked down the hallways at school or when I showed up at parties, in my Forever 21 gold-sequin mini skirt and tiny crop top. Or that I now wore crooked eyeliner and a lipstick with the name "Harlequin," or had exchanged my sneakers for platform booties.

It wasn't just "There's something about that girl," or "I heard she'll have sex with anyone," that roamed through huddled circles of conversations.

It wasn't just that whenever I walked through a doorway it was like bursting a bubble, eyes turning, bodies turning, acknowledgment like a flood, like a new kind of food. Attention like a tangible thing, that could be seized and devoured.

A coiled heat grew inside me. It melted my nervous skin.

When I woke up, I no longer tiptoed across the floorboards, afraid to wake my mother.

When I looked in the mirror, I did not flinch from my own eyes.

You have a face that's so soft, but it's a softness like fire.

Maybe I wasn't changing at all.

Just, for the first time in my life, I was.

"What's Furby doing here?" Heather whispered to me.

"Who knows," I said.

His real name was Fitzgerald but everyone called him Furby. He kept touching the silver cross wound around his neck. He had a smile like a poster of an American dream, with too-whitened teeth and a jawline like a wheat combine. But still, there was some kind of dark voodoo about him that made no sense to me, a lurid enchantment that made girls lose their heads in his proximity. He was telling some terrible joke about a casserole his mom baked, but still, they laughed like they'd never enjoy anything else ever again. Lucy Fountain kept touching his leg and Mary Forester kept running her fingers alongside his shoulder.

"Hey! Bev!" Furby called out to me.

All of the girls surrounding him turned to me, wide-mouthed and wide-eyed, like all of the joy had just been ripped out of each orifice.

He bowed, like we were in Victorian England. "Good evening."

He might've been a good Christian boy, but that stare he gave me wasn't.

I imagined then that he had a demonic, enchanted portrait of himself in a cobwebbed basement somewhere, growing more gnarled and red as he remained smooth-skinned.

"Good evening?" I found myself mouthing as Janna and Heather pulled me away.

"No way," Janna whispered. "No way. Not him."

"I don't feel like going to hell anyway," I whispered.

We went into the kitchen where Joe Realm was pretending to be an MC with a broken microphone. He was ultra-skinny these days, without any muscle on him, and wore what looked like his dad's too-big leather jacket. He had his hair slicked back with too much product, and kept fingering a rose-gold pin on his lapel.

He stood in front of a table covered in 2 percent beer and little plastic cups full of Jell-O shots.

He spoke into his microphone as we approached, his eyebrows waggling.

"And here comes three lovely ladies! Heather, Janna, and is that a newcomer?"

He lowered the microphone a bit as he scrutinized me.

"Wait. Beverly? Is that really you? You look different. I'd say, transformative even."

"She's a beautiful swan who's transformed into an even fucking sexier swan," Janna snapped. "Now give me a fucking shot."

I turned to Joe and tried to put on my most charming smile.

"My friend would like a shot please," I said.

"Be my guest," Joe said, returning the smile as he motioned toward the shots.

Heather, Janna, and I each downed one. The Everclear burn shot up into my nose, despite the strawberry Jell-O.

Janna slammed her cup down and gasped like she'd just come up from underwater. Heather grabbed her by the elbow when she staggered a bit.

"Joe, make out with me." Janna said, lurching forward, "I think I saw David in there. I want to make him jealous."

Joe slicked back his hair like he was an extra for a 1950s rock band.

"You're pretty, babe, but you're like a sister to me," Joe said. "Also, you're drunk. Like, really drunk."

"Useless," Janna said, rolling her eyes.

She pried herself from Heather's grip, then spun on her heels and disappeared into the living room. Presumably, to go after David.

Heather sighed, "I better go make sure she doesn't kill him. Take my purse?"

She headed after her.

I downed another Jell-O shot.

"Nice tights," said Joe. "They're sparkly."

"They look better off," I said.

"You've got a boyfriend you want to make jealous too?" Joe asked.

"You mean you don't know?" I asked. Then I remembered, Joe was homeschooled. I only knew him because his mother was friends with Janna's mother. That meant he hadn't heard the rumors about me and Spider, or any of the others. Unlike the boys that I usually fucked, he didn't have dirty fingernails and a death wish. He had a nice smile that didn't hide a sinister, sharp crescent. He probably didn't even swear. This was a rare opportunity.

"I don't really do boyfriends," I said.

I picked up another shot.

"Careful," he said. "Those are strong. You don't want to end up like your friend."

I handed it to him. "This one's for you."

"I don't mind you trying to get me drunk," he said.

He knocked the shot back.

I took his hand and we headed upstairs. Music pulsed up through the floorboards. We tried a few doorknobs until we found an open room lit blue by a bubbling aquarium. I set Heather's and my purse down at the foot of the bed. We spent a few moments watching the starfish, and orange striped clownfish, and broad angelfish. Blue light from the tank rippled across Joe's face in soft waves. The Jell-O shot warmed my body and my blood, making my limbs feel stretched and far away from my head. He said, "You have gorgeous hair, you know. I'd like to keep it. I mean, not in a creepy way."

"Sure, that's not creepy at all," I said.

I sat down on the nearby bed. It sloshed underneath me.

"Ooh, it's a waterbed. So retro," I said and patted it beside me.

"As much as I like the aquarium preshow, I think we should head to the main event," he said, grinning like he might lose his mouth if he didn't hold it upright.

"Yep," I said. "You're definitely homeschooled."

"I think it gives me a certain charm," he said.

"Stop talking," I said. "I'm not here to talk."

I felt silly talking like that to homeschooled Joe, but then again, all talk about sex seemed silly to me. I didn't quite know how to speak about the primordial origin of everything, without coming across as awkward and clumsy.

He moved closer to me and reached out for my face with both hands outstretched, then stopped.

"Dang, I forgot to ask. Can I touch you?" he asked, his hands wavering a few inches from my face.

I rolled my eyes. "Don't be an idiot."

I grabbed his head and pulled him in for a kiss. A growl rose in my throat like I could bend down and tear his throat out. We fell into the bed together. He was sinewy and soft in my arms. He shed his leather jacket and I thought of a baby panther, its teeth growing in, its fur untarnished velvet.

I took my crop top off. When he stared at my breasts, his eyes seemed to shoot to the moon.

"I said you could touch, remember?"

"Right," he said.

He kissed my stomach in a rapturous way that the bad boys never did. His hands hovered over my breasts, barely touching them as if he was afraid to squeeze. He looked like he was having a religious experience. When he spoke his voice was breathy like the words had spiraled in his throat.

"I want to see what you can do," he said.

"What do you mean?"

Someone knocked on the door.

"That better not be you in there, Charlie!"

"Wrong bedroom!" Joe called out.

A pause. The door opened a crack and someone peeked in. Joe moved to cover me with the sheets.

"Shit, are you in there with Bev?" the girl said.

"Privacy, please!"

Tara from my physics class busted through the door. She stumbled into the room on her mother's heels, swinging around a bottle of rosé. Her frizzy hair was piled up on top of her head like an animal, and it cast shadows on the walls like eagles and cranes fighting each other.

"I can't believe you're hooking up with Bev."

"Does privacy mean anything to you?" Joe said. "And why are you so surprised?"

"No, it doesn't, not when you're hooking up at a party," she said. "And you're a certified geek. To answer your questions in order."

Tara landed on the edge of the bed, bouncing a little.

"I want to see her do the thing," she said.

"What thing?" I asked.

"Oh come on!" Tara said. "Everyone knows!"

She took off her jacket, revealing her rainbow-colored necklace on her freckled neck, and began babbling so fast I could barely make out what she was saying – something about how everyone said free love ended in the 60s but love was forever and would always be free, that her mother went to Woodstock and blessed her chakra necklace with good vibes, that she knows she's talking too much but she just can't stand the quiet. Joe and I couldn't get a word in edgewise. And as she kept talking, she leaned in further, twisting into us. She kicked her heels off and wriggled in between us, separating Joe and I.

Finally, she paused for air and blurted out.

"Bev, have you ever been with a woman before?"

I shook my head. I'm already imagining what she'd be like naked, all rough like some kind of desert animal, imagining what she'd be like wrapped around my tongue and my fingers, the way she'd writhe, how she'd taste from her frizzy head to her toes.

I glanced at Joe.

"Whatever. Go ahead. It's hot," he said, and shrugged.

"Hold on a minute," I said, turning back to Tara, blinking away my fantasies. "What thing are you talking about?"

"The people at school. They say you can do this thing," Tara said. "It's better than an orgasm."

"Yeah, but, I don't know if it'll work on another girl," I said. "Who told you?"

"Well, let's see," she said. "You can experiment with me."

When she took her shirt off she revealed cuts all up and down her chest, waist, arms. Cuts like a second skin, or like she was trying to create a new skin. Some were old, whitened into scars. But some were fresh, like red welling thin mouths.

She caught me looking at them and said, "Don't make a big deal out of it."

"I wasn't," I said.

When she kissed me, she pushed her gum in my mouth. I spit it out and she giggled. My fingers traveled from one scar to the next. Joe lay back and watched us, bouncing slightly on the waterbed, and I could tell by the way he quivered, by his spastic motions, that he was trying to keep cool.

"Oh come on, Joe," Tara said with a sigh. "Just don't lay there. Join in, it's only fair."

He glanced at me, then at Tara.

"Well, what do you want me to do, kiddo?"

"Don't call me that, for starters," Tara said.

Joe and Tara began to kiss, then I'm kissing Joe while she's running her fingers up all and down my body, then she's kissing me in between my legs. The waterbed made us all move in slow motion like we were gelatinous. I couldn't tell who was touching me, which limbs belonged to which person, even my own.

I thought maybe this was what being fucked by a laughing god was like, shapeshifting in your arms, growing an arm in the center of his back, growing extra fingers just to tease and disorient you. An extra tongue, double mouths, sex multiplied and fragmented.

We hadn't even started having real sex yet, but the friction, the thing with no name, started to grow inside my stomach, increasing in pressure.

Someone knocked on the door, but Tara shouted at them in Spanish and they left. We all thought this was hilarious, and we couldn't stop laughing. We caught our breath, and then we took turns drinking Tara's rosé. When we finished that she produced a flask of whiskey from her pile of clothes on the floor, as if by magic, and we drank that as well.

Tara and I began to roll around on the bed together. Joe laughed and played with my hair. All the while my blood vessels were chanting and my muscles were knotting into chains and the pressure was growing, growing, spiraling all throughout me, urging me to push forward, to spill over.

"You really never have been with a woman before?" Tara asked. "You should do it more often."

"Probably," I said.

"Let's scissor," she said. "It's a bit awkward at first, but I think you'll like it."

She showed me the position to get into, each of us facing away, our legs intertwined so that our vulvas touched. I felt like we were making a beautiful sculpture, our bodies no longer recognizable as individual parts, turning our bodies into a sum greater than its parts.

"Sorry," I said to Joe, who was sitting on the edge of the bed with Tara's flask. "Don't mean for you to be left out."

"No," he said. "Shit, this is great. Like a dream, right?"

Joe tipped more whiskey into my mouth, and then Tara's, as if anointing us.

"Okay," she said. "Now move like this." We ground against each other, the flesh on our skinny asses and thighs rippling with the motion.

We ground against each other's legs. The friction got tighter. The whiskey and rosé and Everclear bloomed in my stomach like a burning garden. I glanced up at Tara. Her scars glowing in the blue light seemed like upside down smiles.

I exploded.

Tara went white. Then I turned white, like static, like a porcelain angel in the center of a volcano. White noise poured into my throat and into my brain. The pleasure was loud enough to liquidate our skin. I didn't just feel my own pleasure, I felt Tara's as well. I was inside of her skin, pushing down on her heart.

"Wow," she kept saying. "Wow."

She disentangled herself from me, and then we were two again.

I managed to turn to Joe. My own voice came to me far away, like I was speaking on a low volume television.

"Get a condom out of my purse," I said. "It's the red one."

"Why?" he asked.

"Because I want you to fuck me too, duh," I said.

"Oh, right."

Joe fumbled around in my purse for a few seconds before finding it. He stood at the edge of the bed with the condom, breathing hard, balling his fists as if trying to work up his nerve to come closer.

I spread my legs.

And I said, as seductively as I could:

"Hurry up."

He came back over to me, put it on, and guided his cock into me, while Tara still shook on the bed with the revelation of the explosion.

I knew it'd been less than half a minute, but I could go again and again. The thing inside me was tireless, and I was close enough to the edge that it wouldn't take much to push me over again.

"Wow," Tara said when the color returned to her cheeks. "They weren't lying about you."

Tara opened a window and smoked a cigarette, still shaking. In between puffs she kept mouthing, "Wow," and nodding like a drunken baby as she fingered her rainbow chakra necklace.

As Joe and I fucked, it came inside me again. Fast and sudden. Bang! Like a gun made out of thunder. It shot through the center of him, spiraled outward as if twisting him into a new skeleton. He jerked forward, his mouth flew open. I was surprised I didn't see sparks coming off his tongue.

Wow and wow indeed.

"You're some kind of witch you know?" Tara said, her voice floating like mist.

"Holy hell," Joe said, pulling out of me, "Definitely better than a witch."

"Did you cum too?" Tara asked.

I shook my head. "No, that's a different thing."

She gestured at Joe.

"Eat her out, Christ," she said. "Be a gentleman."

Even after having exploded twice, having been shuddered through with a depth charge of pure energy, I was ready for more. I grabbed fistfuls of his hair when he knelt down, and murmured something like a prayer.

Just when we've got a rhythm going, Janna and Heather burst through the door.

"Oh my god, we've been looking everywhere for you. Janna already threw up twice and I'm too sober for this," Heather said. "Let's get out of here."

We left the party in a whirl of lights. My blood felt like unicorn blood, light and airy and full of silver.

* * *

When I got home I collapsed right into bed. My skull rang with music from the party, with the scent of strawberry Jell-O flavored Everclear. My body thrummed with Joe and Tara's skin-to-skin contact. I was exhausted with bright sensations.

But I was still horny.

So I slid a hand inside my skirt and began to masturbate.

I fantasized about one boy after another, coming through the windows, walking through the door. They're like fauns as they tiptoed across my carpet, small and oiled and suntanned, with lithe muscles and green eyes. They've got horns like rams, and they came to me naked as animals, smelling of grape and warm grass.

They brought flowers to leave at the altar of me.

As I neared orgasm the flowers piled up so high around the edges of my bed that I couldn't even see the door anymore.

The fauns surrounded my bed and touched me with fur tipped fingers.

Thud!

The fantasy, and my impending orgasm melted away.

Thud!

I bolted upright in bed.

A boy stood outside my window with a rock in his hands. He pulled his hand back to throw it right before I opened the shutters. I didn't recognize him at first, and when I finally did, I thought that maybe I'd dreamed it up because I couldn't fathom why Fitzgerald Monty, the pastor's son, would be outside my window.

"Furby?" I asked.

He dropped the rock. "Bev!"

I didn't know what to say, so I went with the obvious.

"What the hell are you doing?" I asked.

He planted his feet in the grass and threw his arms open wide, a little bit like Jesus.

"I want you to be my first," he said like he was reciting lines for the theater.

"Before tonight I didn't even think you knew my name," I said. "And you know my mom's home, right?"

"It'll be quick," he said.

"Not what a girl wants to hear."

He stammered. "It'll be slow. And quiet. I've been preparing."

"Did you seriously follow me home?"

"I can't stop thinking about you," he said.

"You heard the rumors, didn't you?"

He stammered again, searching for words. "You're special. You're really special, Bev."

I hesitated. His preternatural charm seemed to have melted away in the night as if on the way to my house he'd shed it while he walked. Fitzgerald was just a boy like any other. And a virgin.

Fuck it though, I was still horny, and he'd interrupted my orgasm. He owed it to me.

So I let him inside.

"I can't believe you're still a virgin," I whispered when he came into my room.

He had on a dark, woodsy cologne that made him smell like an old man.

"I was saving it until God gave me a sign," he said.

I stared at him, waiting for more of an explanation. He just shivered.

"Are you serious?" I said.

"He—"

"Whatever, just get naked."

We both undressed. He took everything off except his cross necklace, which glinted in the dark.

"Get on the bed," I said.

"I wanted it to be special," he whispered. "You're the one who can make it special."

"Stop talking," I said.

I grabbed another condom from my purse and made a mental note that I needed to get some more next time I had the chance.

Furby lay supine on the bed, still except for his fingers drumming against his sides. I had to admit he looked good, really good. The low light brought out his best features, and his body was tight and strong. I didn't even have to touch him, and already his cock sat nearly upright.

I tasted electricity in the air.

"Can you really do what they say you can do?" he whispered.

"Feel for yourself," I said.

I straddled him and he winced. Not from pain, I realized,

but from the guilt of pleasure. He actually grabbed the cross around his neck.

I paused.

"Do you want to do it or not?" I asked.

"Yes," he said, and swallowed. "What do you want me to do?"

"To be quiet."

I rubbed my ass against his cock, and his breathing shifted.

"Don't throw rocks at my window ever again," I said as I continued to rub against him, as I watched his body twitch and fold into a new rhythm. "I'm fucking serious. You could've woken my mom up."

He had that half-lidded eye look that made boys look like snakes. He opened his mouth to respond.

"No talking," I hissed.

"Okay," he whispered.

"Your cock isn't bad, though," I said.

Again he opened his mouth to speak but then thought better of it.

"Good boy," I whispered.

As I rode him I closed my eyes and I pushed my pillow against his mouth to keep him from moaning aloud. The fauns returned. They were lighting black pillar candles in my honor, bringing sacrifices of rum and Skittles, my favorites. No, they were building me a temple, with the pillars carved into the shape of nude women and the sanctuary filled with orchids. Fuck. They worshipped me day and night, trembling at the sight of me. They worshipped me on their knees, with shoulder blades like perfumed knives. Oh. They're afraid to touch me because I beamed like the sun. Oh yes. Yes, just like that. Fuck. I've become a goddess, as I was always meant to be.

Fuck, they trembled just to touch me.

Fuck.

Their tongues were like winter pools, melting in the center.

Their nails were like black witch's glass.

Fucking hell, fuck.

I exploded for the third time that night.

And until that night, I never knew a girl could collapse like a broken red star.

Maybe this was what dying felt like, or being born, if one could retain consciousness while being reknit into the fabric of the universe. For a few blissful overwhelming seconds, I was a body unwound and wrapping around itself over and over again. I weaved through metaphysical wormholes between nothingness and existence.

When I managed to open my eyes, Furby seemed to be in that same space, his eyes beaming messages from an unknown celestial body.

I had to shove my hand to my mouth as the involuntary laughter shuddered through me.

When I was able to control my limbs again, I threw Furby his clothes.

"Get out," I whispered.

"Bev—"

"Was it good?" I asked.

He nodded.

"Get out then!" I said. "Before I get grounded for a thousand years."

After he left, I collapsed into bed and smelled the sex in the sheets, his old man's cologne. I found his crucifix underneath the pillow. I imagined that he'd ripped it off during sex and left it. He was always touching it as if to remind himself of its presence. I thought there was no way he could've left it behind.

To me, that meant something important and symbolic.

I dangled the crucifix in the moonlight to watch the way it glittered.

This was how religions started, with a cataclysmic bang loud enough to make you believe in God.

4

My mom asked me to run errands with her but I knew it was just a convenient excuse. I couldn't remember her taking such a huge interest in my daily life before. It must've been some kind of latent Mom gene that blossomed forth the moment I turned fifteen. Lately every chance she got she wanted to discuss my future.

It didn't take more than a minute and a half after I got in the car for her to ask, "Have you thought about what you're going to do after high school?"

She ripped open a granola bar with her teeth and munched on it as she drove.

I sighed and lay down across the length of the backseat. She looked like she hadn't slept at all again, with mascara flecks on her cheeks and dark circles like record grooves underneath her eyes.

"I don't know. I haven't really thought about it."

"Well you should start thinking about it, summer's almost over and you'll be a junior," she said. "Get your feet off the window, please."

"What's happened to you? You sound just like a mom," I said.

I took my feet down.

"That's because I am a mom," she said.

"Maybe I'll worry about my future if I don't flunk Algebra again."

I was never good at numbers. I couldn't even keep track of how many people I'd had sex with. I knew I should've been thinking about exponents and imaginary numbers because finals were coming up soon, but all I could think about was Mitch from last night. He told me he was a werewolf, and he needed to have sex to cure his bloodlust. We'd hiked out into the woods, and he made me hold a silver ring to keep myself safe while he wrapped his arms around my waist and pressed his fingernails against my bare belly.

I tried not to shiver at the thought of it.

"Or maybe you could worry about it now?" my mom said.

"Huh?" I asked, shocked back into reality.

"Your future."

I didn't know it was possible to slump even further down into the car, but I did.

"I'm not really good at anything," I said.

My mom snorted. "Of course you are. You're resourceful and very brave. And also you're witty, just like your father was."

"Are you saying I should be a comedian?"

She laughed a little at that, although she seemed annoyed that she found it funny.

"No, Bev. I'm saying you can be whatever you want."

Most of my friends joined a band, or volunteered at soup kitchens, or wrote books in ruled notebooks. They had dreams they knew how to position the arc of their bodies toward so they became reality. They wanted to be engineers, doctors, or movie stars. Veterinarians, football players, and lawyers. And they worked toward it.

I just spent my time saving my favorite man crushes to a board on Pinterest and dreamed about riding across a planet of perpetual sunsets in a shiny red car with a lollipop in my mouth.

I'd been so busy the last few months learning the subtle shifts of the human body, the way people wriggled and squirmed, the physics of taking clothes off, all the different variants of how eyes could say 'fuck me,' that I hadn't thought much about school or what I wanted to do afterward.

As if she could read my mind my mom asked me,

"Bev, are you having sex?"

My stomach plunged.

I pressed my thighs close together where Werewolf Boy left bite marks.

"Bev?" My mom prompted me.

"You don't want an honest answer, do you?" I asked.

"Honey," she said.

I sat up again and pressed my head against the glass. I acted as if I was distracted by the passing whir of buildings and cars, the boots store, the McDonalds.

"Hey," I said. "Can we make tacos tonight? It's been awhile since we had a real dinner. I'll even make guacamole."

"Don't even try it. You know I don't want to have this conversation either," my mom said.

I groaned.

"Why do you even care?" I asked.

"Bev," she said, her voice a little softer. "What have I said before about conversations like this?"

I sighed.

"We have to be honest with each other."

"And why is that?" she prompted me.

"Because we only have each other," I said.

"And?"

"And no matter what, we need to trust each other."

I thought again of Werewolf Boy, howling at the moon while I sat back on a log, naked and laughing. He pushed me against that tree, gently, nibbling at the skin on my neck like he had enough savage in him to gnaw me down to the bone.

I really just wanted my life to be one long drawn out moment of fun, scratching an itch that always moved just underneath my skin, but I knew you weren't allowed to say things like that aloud.

"Are you having sex, Bev?" she asked, this time her voice more gentle.

I bit my lip. "Yeah."

She pulled into the grocery store parking lot. "It would've happened sooner or later."

"God, this is embarrassing."

She set the car into park but didn't reach for the key in the ignition.

I reached for the door but she said, "Hold on Bev. Are you being safe? Using birth control?"

"Yes."

"What kind?"

"Just condoms."

"We'll get you an appointment for some birth control, okay? You can get the shot or some pills. The last thing we want is you getting pregnant."

"Mom, why do we have to talk about this?"

"We have to talk about this because if you're going to do adult things, there can be some real adult consequences. You've still got the emergency watch app on your phone?"

"Yes."

She went to night school to get her bachelors several years ago, back when we were poor, and now she was working on her master's. Between that and work, there wasn't much time for anything else. The lines on her face got wider every year, and her lips thinner, like trying to do everything at once had made her skin pull apart in every direction.

But when I caught her eyes in the rearview mirror her usual tired face seemed to have been replaced with a cool precision and a focus that'd erased all the usual lines. "Do not ever let a boy do something to you that you don't want, okay?" she said. "I know you'll feel pressured to, especially if you want him to like you, but trust me, honey, the price you pay for that will never be worth it."

"I don't do that," I said. "I mean, I won't."

"Do you have a boyfriend?"

"Hell no," I said.

"If you get pregnant, if you get an STD, you can't rely on a boy to stay around. You have to be prepared that they may leave."

I realized then that this conversation must've been in the back of my mom's head for years. That's why she had such an intense look. She wasn't just thinking of me, she was thinking of herself, sitting in back rooms with dirty wallpapers, making scrap soup, trying to keep me warm, all because she'd believed in the romance promised by a man who didn't care if he burned the world, burned her, just to get what he wanted.

"Like Michael," I said.

I didn't want to call him Dad.

She nodded.

"We have each other for now," she said. "But I tried to teach you to be self-reliant because really, the only guarantee in life is that you have yourself."

"I know."

"I know you know," she said.

"Are we good?"

"Yeah," I said and sighed. "We're good."

She turned off the car and opened the door. My legs felt heavy as I swung out of the car I swallowed, my throat dry.

"Still want to make tacos?" she said.

"Who doesn't like tacos?"

We headed into the store.

"Don't think this means I've forgotten about this whole thinking about your future thing, okay, Bev? You'll have to start sending in college applications before you know it."

Again, I groaned.

* * *

As we were carrying our groceries out to the car a boy waved at me from the window of the nearby pet groomers.

"Friend of yours?" Mom asked.

He'd been grooming a Lhasa Apso on the table in front of him. The Lhasa whipped its head around toward me as well and sniffed the air experimentally.

"I don't think so," I said.

"It seems like he knows you."

He turned away from the window, talked to what looked like a manager, and then headed out into the parking lot after me.

Only when he got close, and I saw the sloping line of his eyes, and the way his teeth were set in his face, and that Italian nose, did I recognize him.

"Spider?"

He looked so different in the sunlight wearing his green uniform and clean boots. He'd shaved too, and cut his hair. He wore a name tag that said "Andy," and I realized I'd never actually known his real name.

"It's so good to see you," he said. "You look beautiful."

"You look different," I said.

He hugged me, crushing the bag of bread and tomatoes against my chest. He still smelled of weed, but also of woody cologne, and dog biscuits, and dandruff shampoo.

"I'm going to put these groceries in the car, sweetie, meet you there," Mom said. She took my bags and headed off.

"You look really nice," I said. "What the hell happened?"

"I am really glad I got to see you again. I wanted to thank you."

"Thank me? For what?"

He clasped my hands in his.

There was something newly transparent about his face, like I could almost peer through his chest and see his heart throbbing. He didn't seem to be the same person who could give me a look that made me feel like I was falling underwater, bound in chains.

"You changed me," he said.

"I... changed you?"

"After that night at the creek, something happened. I got home and I just felt like such a piece of shit, you know? It was like some hole opened up in the back of my head, and all the black shit poured out."

"Come on," I said. "You're not that bad."

It sounded lame, but I didn't know what else to say.

"I felt so awful about what I stole from my mom. I thought about what an embarrassment I was to her. How I wasn't setting a good example for my sister. I was becoming just like my dad. And I fucking hate my dad."

"You think I had something to do with that?"

If he heard me he didn't react. He just kept talking.

"Everything changed after that. I got a job so I could help pay for my sister's therapy and some of my mom's doctor bills. And my new girlfriend, she wants to be a lawyer. You'd like her, she's real nice. She's good for me. I'm going to community college in the fall."

He glanced back at the window, where the Lhasa Apso was staring back at him, wagging her pom-pom tail.

"I'm going to study animal science. I think I want to help dolphins. Or be a zookeeper. I always liked animals. I just kind of, you know, I forgot about it. Isn't that crazy, forgetting you like something?"

"Bev!" My mom called. "The ice-cream's melting!"

Spider, or should I say, Andy, glanced back at the store once more. His manager was trying to clip the dog's nails, but the dog kept dancing and yelping.

"Sorry, I got to go back," he said. "HoneyBucket will only let me touch her."

He hugged me.

"It's so good to see you," he said. "Really."

He ran back into the groomers, leaving me alone with the rush of sudden questions I had.

* * *

I forgot about the Spider incident when Heather messaged me in our group chat with Janna.

U coming to the party tonight with us?

Yes.

Wear the red dress. The cute one, Janna texted.

K boss.

And I forgot about the encounter with Spider.

The three of us arrived at the party together, along with Heather's cousin Patrice. There was a band in the backyard playing shitty Pink Floyd covers. And although there wasn't any alcohol except a small bottle of Curacao, there were plenty of red cups to go around. Elliot Varger from gym class made a Sudafed cocktail that nobody would touch, but we drank plenty of diet Pepsi in the sticky heat. The boys took their tops off and played frisbee. They were cute, but nobody I was interested in. Patrice spent most of her time in the corner playing on her Gameboy, kicking her legs in her frayed flip flops.

Tara brought an Ouija board and as the sun went down we ended up talking to the spirit of Johnny Depp, who's divine message from the beyond was for everyone to eat more cheese fries.

I was bored until I saw the new kid. I elbowed Heather and whispered.

"Hey, do you know who that is?"

"That's Emershan, your new boyfriend," Heather said. "He's from South Africa."

He somehow managed to make sipping a diet Pepsi look elegant. I thought about licking the sweat off his neck. I imagined he tasted sweet. Not sickly sweet, like Hershey's chocolate, but like dates or plantains. Earthy, like something that came up from the ground.

"Go talk to him," Heather whispered.

"You don't have to tell me twice," I said.

I sat beside Emershan and said the first thing that came to mind.

"I'm Bev. You hungry?"

"Very," he said.

We ended up in the kitchen together, rummaging through the fridge and cupboards to search for something we could eat.

"So, what's Africa like?" I asked.

"It's a big place," he said. "People here think I lived in some kind of tribe. They forget we have cars and cities just like you."

I found a package of bread and we decided to make sandwiches. Somewhere in between deciding on whether to eat peanut butter or to slice up a ham, we started kissing.

He said, "You are the only girl here who has a fire inside of her."

He almost sounded like he believed it.

We never finished making the sandwiches. I led him down the hallway by the hand, the both of us giggling, and we snuck into a back bedroom.

I closed the door behind us.

He massaged my face with his hands and said, "Surely you have a boyfriend."

"No," I said, and he acted amazed.

His fingers hovered across my nose, my cheeks, ever so gently brushing down like he was creating me himself out of thin air, conjuring me out of the magic of his gaze.

The Pink Floyd cover band wrapped it up, thank god, and someone started playing techno. The orange and red sunset splayed across Emershan's skin. I thought it made him look like his own landscape, a place where gazelles and tigers could dance upon his back and drink from the dregs of light.

But when it came time for him to put on a condom, he stepped back and stared at me. That cold stare made my thighs snap together.

"What's wrong?" I asked.

"I heard what you do," he said.

"Seriously, already?" I said. "But you just got here."

He grabbed my legs and peered down at my naked body. Like he was inspecting it. He touched my vulva and peeled back the folds with his fingers.

I thought of the way Spider looked at me in that parking lot.

All the black shit poured out of me.

"What's your secret?" Emershan asked, touching me not like a lover would, but like I was a dead pig in a lab.

"What are you doing? Get off of me," I said.

"What are you?" he said. "I'm going to find out what's so special about you."

"I said get off!"

I kicked him in the chest with my bare foot. He stumbled backward. When he regained his footing, he lurched forward and tried to grab my leg again.

"Stop!"

"Are you saying you don't want me?" he said. "I heard that you'd fuck anyone."

"Well I'm not going to fuck you," I said.

A cold gong went off in my stomach.

Wham. Wham. Wham.

"You're not right, you know," he said.

He grabbed my clothes.

"Hey!"

He slammed the door shut, leaving me alone and naked in the room. I got up, still shaking. I spied a paisley robe on a hook on the back of the door. I grabbed the robe and slipped out the window into the new dark.

* * *

"Do you remember me?" a boy asked me one day in the school courtyard. "It's Maurice."

I blinked, trying to place him in my mental map. I was pretty sure I didn't know a Maurice.

"I mean, Badger?"

"Oh!" I said. "Of course. I remember you."

He looked nothing like the Badger I remembered from six months ago. Not just that he'd thinned out, or that his facial features were more visible, his chin reduced, his haircut softer. He no longer hunched over as he stood, or walked with a stride like he was trying to hide from the satellites.

"How have you been?" he asked.

"Good," I said, unsure of what to say. "Great."

"You left one of your socks behind," he said. "And an earring, I think."

"Not mine," I said.

"Oh, that's okay," he said.

He looked down at his body. He touched his stomach as if he was unsure it belonged to him.

"I stopped eating so much."

"I can see that."

"And I started doing my homework," he said.

"Well, uh, that's good too," I said. "I won't tell anyone. I know you have a reputation to maintain."

The joke fell flat. Badger didn't laugh.

Someone kicked a soccer ball that rolled to Badger's feet. He bent, picked it up, and tossed it back. Another awkward silence ensued.

"Thanks, by the way," he said.

"For what?" I asked.

"You know," he said, and shrugged a little. "For that night."

A blush rose to his cheeks. He was already turning away, into the cafeteria.

"Hey!" I said, but he didn't stop.

I followed after him. I thought of Spider.

A hush descended on the cafeteria when I entered.

They were looking at me.

All of them, with the silence loud as a bang.

There was Timmy Sorrells, the banged-up motorcycle boy who liked to jump from high places. And Heather Nova, who'd dyed her hair a bright pink. There was Miriam with the lip piercings and the clothing like a trash-bag. Jimmy Terrance, Joe the MC, Werewolf Boy, Terrance McClure, and more. A ripple of recognition passed between them and me.

Even Heather and Janna stared at me.

Was it just me, or had my blood and the sunlight gotten brighter?

Badger stood on the other side of the cafeteria, looking back at me.

The bell for 4th period rang. The spell broke, and the crowd stood up and my heart was pounding so fast that I thought it might turn into wings and I'd begin to levitate.

* * *

I found them on Facebook, or Twitter, through text messages, Snapchat, Google searches. I found them all, every person I'd ever fucked.

Gene Conroy moved to Tennessee to help his brother start up his bar. He took out a loan and got surgery to fix his broken fingers. He actually posted pictures of him on Snapchat smiling. Smiling with the sunlight in his hair just so. There was a picture of him at the bar with his brother too, the both of them with their dark hair and dark eyes, like two sunsets.

Werewolf Boy shaved his beard and stopped going out at night under the full moon, chasing (so-called virgins). He'd taken up taxidermy and fishing and picked up women in mini-skirts who never heard him howl at the moon. On his Tumblr he'd gone from posting gory pictures of women in distress to pictures of undisturbed nature — owls, bubbling creeks, sunsets instead of blood moons.

I found Furby's Snapchat and added him. Furby threw away his sacred icons and quit the church. He spoke out about his childhood abuse and started going to therapy. He worked part-time at a taco truck and had actually gotten accepted to an Ivy League school.

Thanks, by the way, he messaged me, without any other explanation.

Thanks for what? I texted back, but he didn't respond.

I paced around my room. I touched my stomach as if it'd have the answers. I undressed and found a hand mirror. I lay down on the bed and looked at my own vagina with the mirror to see if there was something wrong with it.

It looked completely normal, like any other vagina I'd ever seen. And the gynecologist Mom took me to told me I was healthy.

Anyway, why would there be something wrong? Nobody I fucked had anything bad happen to them. They weren't saying I'd cursed them.

They were thanking me.

I looked up some of the others.

Tara had pictures up on her Instagram with #noharm written in marker on her wrists. "Please," she wrote in golden gothic emboss. "It's never too late to get help."

She dyed her hair a soft pink and wore crop tops to show off her puckered scars.

Even Joe, who had seemed rather harmless and well-adjusted, picked up his life. He had gotten a girlfriend, and posted pictures of the two of them fishing, riding horses. He'd taken up weight-lifting and lost the reedy, nerdy look about him.

Mom called to me from the other room. I jumped at the noise.

"I'm exhausted as hell tonight," she said, "Do you want pizza for dinner?"

"Yeah," I said. "No mushrooms."

"Mushrooms? I would never," she said.

I turned back to the computer, wracking my brains to remember some of the others.

Some of the people I'd fucked had adopted cats, started volunteering at soup kitchens, left abusive relationships, started working out more, reading more, getting gainful employment. Some cleaned up, but also others stopped caring about how clean they were. Many changed their hairstyles, which Mom always told me was people's way of trying to show that they'd changed.

Their Instagram's and Facebook's turned radiant. It wasn't that they were all rainbows and unicorns now, but like a light had been turned on, illuminating the darkest corners of their self which then disintegrated in the heat.

I tried to convince myself that I was imagining it.

I went back to the date. I remembered sleeping with Gene Conroy and scrolled back through his Instagram feed.

The day before we'd hooked up, he'd taken a selfie scowling at the gas station, with a cigarette in the corner of his mouth and dirt on his fingernails.

Then, nothing for a week, although he'd been posting daily up until then.

Then the next week, he'd began posting again. It was a gif of him laying in bed, with the light slicing through the overhead fan. He was only 17, but he seemed to have sliced years away.

#newdaynewme was the hashtag.

There's something about that girl.

Fuck.

All the black shit poured out.

Double fuck.

The pizza arrived. I went downstairs to grab some when Mom came out of her office and noticed my face.

"Something wrong?" she asked.

"I don't want to talk about it," I said.

She looked at me for a moment, held me in her gaze. I hated when she did that. She had some kind of psychic, penetrating stare that seemed to suss out all the interlocking mechanisms inside me.

"You're making me nervous," I said.

"You're pushing me away."

"No, I'm not," I said immediately, and then, "I mean, hasn't it always been like this between us? You've always had to work so hard and been so busy and—"

"It doesn't matter what's happened between us before. I know I've made mistakes," she paused. "But something is going on with you, and I want to help."

"What are you talking about?"

"You're my daughter. I know something is going on with you."

"Mom, I'm fine," I said, in a way that sounded like I truly wasn't fine.

"Do you want to talk about it?" she asked.

"No," I said. "No, mom. I'm sorry."

She sighed.

"Okay, Bev," she said. "But I just want you to know, whatever is going on, there's nothing wrong with you."

"Why would you say that?"

"Because I can tell. You think something is wrong with you."

"I'm fine," I said. "Mom, I'm serious. I'm fine." I went back upstairs with my pizza and texted Janna. *There's something wrong with me.*

Besides being a huge slut? LOL.

I'm serious. Haven't you heard rumors?

I watched the ellipses on the phone that meant Janna was writing back to me. This went on for several minutes as if she was hesitating, rewriting, erasing.

...

...

...

I heard you change people.

Change people?

You know. Don't you? Surely you've heard.
Heard what?
It seemed to take forever for her to respond.
...

...

When people have sex with you, they're never the same again. But in a good way. Like a curse in reverse. Haha.

5

I was failing algebra again.

Mr. Ainsworth asked me to come up to his desk after class one day. I thought he was going to send me to the principal's office again for having a too-short skirt, but instead his intense, small eyes softened like pools when he glanced up at me.

He pushed my latest test paper across the desk, marked with vicious red ink. I'd gotten an F.

"You're too smart for this, Beverly," he said. "What's been going on?"

I shrugged. "I hate numbers. They never stay in one place."

"You need to pass this time, or you won't graduate. Perhaps you just need some personal attention."

"Uh, maybe," I said, mostly just glad he wasn't yelling at me because I was wearing a top with spaghetti straps.

"How about you meet me this evening to go over it?" he asked.

I said yes without thinking it through, and so I ended up having to cancel a date with a boy from King Country. That evening I arrived at the near-empty school with my book bag, and had to play Kesha on my phone just to combat the eerie silence as I headed for the math wing. Mr. Ainsworth called to me from the hallway with his throaty voice, and I cut the music and entered the room.

I sat at a front desk while Mr. Ainsworth loomed over me and talked me through the algebra problems I'd gotten wrong on the last test. Despite his explanations, the numbers on the page in front of me squirmed.

It didn't help that all day I'd been thinking about—

There's something about that girl.

And I was thinking about—

You changed them.

Sex wasn't supposed to be a big deal. But this was a big deal. I never heard about a bad boy who fucked a girl one night on a full moon and then decided to turn his life around.

I never heard about an inner explosion, like a celestial orgasm, that seemed to transcend human shape.

The sun sunk down, and the moon floated upwards. The barred window pulled its shadow across my desk. Mr. Ainsworth went over the latest formula one more time, and I scraped together some kind of answer, but I'm pretty sure I hadn't done it right.

"Is this right?" I asked.

I glanced up when he didn't respond. Mr. Ainsworth stood square to my desk. His hair was slicked back. He wore a musky cologne that reminded me of an animal coming out of hibernation.

Had he ever worn cologne before?

"Mr. Ainsworth?" I asked.

"You have a lot of potential," he said. "You know that, right?"

I hated how nervous my laugh sounded.

"I don't, but thanks," I said.

"You're smarter than you try to let on, and well," his nostrils flared, "you're beautiful."

He always had a doughy look about him, but now his face was stretched taut.

"I know you came here for my help," he said. "But in exchange, I'd like your help with something."

He pushed some papers away and sat down on the top of his desk. Absentmindedly, he fingered the top button of his shirt.

"Will you come here, Bev?" he asked.

I tightened my grip on my pencil.

"Come here, Bev," he said.

That time, it was a command.

I felt like I should stay where I was, but I stood. This was Mr. Ainsworth, my teacher, after all, and he spoke with an authority that seemed to make me lose volition of my own legs.

"What do you want my help with?" I asked.

"I heard what you do," he said.

I swallowed. I became aware of a painful lump that suddenly appeared in my throat.

"I need you to do for me what you did for the others."

I hated the thinness of my voice.

"Those rumors you heard," I said. "They're not true."

"Please," he said.

I glanced out the window at the empty parking lot. We were alone.

"It's all gone to shit," he said.

"What do you expect me to do?" I whispered.

"Fix it."

"I can't!"

All human kindness slipped from his face.

"Come here, Miss Beverly Sykes," he said. "If you do not come here, there will be consequences."

I reached for my phone in my pocket. I needed to use the emergency app to alert my mom.

He lunged at me faster than I thought possible. He grabbed the phone and threw it. It smashed into the wall.

I grabbed the pepper spray that I kept in my back pocket. I'd been carrying it ever since that night with Emershan.

Mr. Ainsworth wrenched my hand and forced me to drop it. It rolled underneath the row of desks.

He pushed me down into the chair. He pulled fistfuls of my hair and forced me to look upwards with tears in my eyes. With his kiss, he swallowed the little fragments of my scream.

"Don't," I said. "Don't do this."

He wound his hands tighter into my hair.

"Just help me," he said. "All you have to do is help me."

"No!"

I tried to pull away with one violent thrust, but he held onto me. The desk tipped over. Papers and books crashed to the floor along with me.

He pushed me to the floor. Pain erupted out of the back of my head as it hit the tile.

"I shouldn't have expected a child to understand," he said.

He flipped me over, pressed his knee into the small of my back. When my fingers scrabbled against the tiles, trying to get away, he bashed my forehead against the metal siding of the chair and stars exploded in my vision.

He pushed my skirt up and tore my panties off. My head swam. All the blood seemed to drain out of my body. I heard a keening, heavy noise, like a machine crying.

Somehow he got his pants off. He forced himself inside of me, shoving my bare stomach against the cold tiles. I tried to push myself away from him, but I couldn't. He was too strong.

The noise got louder. Brighter. Hotter. Swelling. Growing. It was growing inside of me. Somewhere far I was still saying, "I can't," and "Stop," but that too became buried in the noise.

That familiar pressure came. And that pressure was building.

I could barely breathe. He was so big and I was so small.

And it fucking hurt.

Help, I thought. Help me. It was the loudest I could think to scream inside of me.

I exploded with his hand over my mouth.

The world erupted between my legs.

The force went straight to my heart and my lungs. It burst through every tunnel of blood. It screamed so loud inside of me that all of my organs shuddered. I thought my brain might shoot out of my skull and hit the ceiling.

I'd never felt it so heavy before, so strong.

So angry.

*   *   *

I don't know how long I lay there with the noise ringing in my ears.

Mr. Ainsworth sat a few feet away, staring down at me. He looked shell-shocked, almost innocent, like a child who'd seen the horrors of war and was unsure of how to comprehend them.

"What did you do?" he whispered.

He pulled up and fastened his pants, and stumbled back to his desk. He sat down.

He picked up a pencil and inspected it as if he'd never seen one before. Then set it down. He picked up another. Set it down. He shuffled the papers and straightened them.

I got to my knees. I pulled my skirt down.

"I understand what the problem is now," he said.

He picked up a pair of scissors and crossed the room toward me. I flinched and fell back onto the tile, covering my face with one hand.

"Please," I said. "Don't."

He stopped and I lowered my hand. The scissors glinted in the moonlight.

"I could justify my dalliances because I tried to be a good teacher to you kids," he said. "But inside I'm festering with rot."

His throat was tight like he was being choked by a phantom. He moved with a new rigidness, like if he moved like a normal human being his bones might pop out of their joints.

"Whatever you've done," I said, tugging on my skirt, "it can be fixed. You don't have to do this."

"No," he said. "It's too late for me. I realize that now. My wife already found out what was on my computer. She asked for a divorce this morning."

He put the scissors to his throat.

"Don't!" I said.

"You're a sweet girl, Beverly," he said. "You're concerned about me, after what I just did to you?"

I pushed myself up into a seated position. He turned and gazed out the window.

"Thank you," he whispered.

His arm tensed, and I looked away so I wouldn't have to see. I heard him fall to the side of his desk and I bit my tongue.

I never understood when people talked about being unable to keep themselves from screaming, but I understood then.

It was an awful kind of noise that came out of me.

Trying to not look at his body, I ran to the door and into the empty hallway.

I shouted for help, but the echo trembled through the hall unanswered.

I ran toward the exit like something was chasing me.

* * *

It was Spider who found me trying to stumble home in the middle of the road, my hands clutching my stomach, my head low enough to roll off my shoulders.

He pulled his truck over and opened the door. He was wearing his pet groomer's uniform, with black boots. A rush of familiar dog biscuit and shampoo smell wafted toward me in a cloud.

"Bev! Are you okay?"

He climbed out of the cab and ran toward me. He took my shoulder, steering me out of the way of a sedan driving home.

"I think so," I said, right as another shudder of pain ran through me.

"Your legs—"

I glanced down. Two thin streams of blood had dripped down my thighs and dried a crusted black.

"Oh," I said. "Don't worry. It's just blood."

"Bev, you're crazy. Do you want me to drive you home?" he asked.

"No," I said. "Mom's going to kill me if she sees me like this."

Despite my protests, he lifted me up. He was strong and I found my muscles dissolving into him as he carried me back to his truck.

I refused to give him my address, and he'd never been to my home, so he began to drive in circles around town.

As we drove, the pain seemed to lift out of my body. The road seemed to become a plane's runway, and each headlight became an angel's halo. I felt like a symphony of buzzing noise was pulling my spirit above my bones, and there it hovered, just above the skin.

I thought at first it was because I was going numb.

But it wasn't numbness, because something juicy and precipitous was flowing through me, a surge, a metaphorical flood of chemicals.

"Why are you laughing?" Spider asked.

I hadn't even realized I had been.

We continued to drive around and Spider remained mostly silent. Until finally:

"Well, if you don't want me to take you home, I'm going to get us some food."

He drove us through a McDonalds and ordered us both a burger and fries.

"And a milkshake," I said, leaning over toward the center of the cab so they'd hear me through the intercom. "Strawberry."

We went to the next window and when the food came I

dove into my milkshake. I sucked greedily on the straw, only in that moment realizing just how thirsty I was.

Spider continued to drive around, his bag of burger and fries untouched between his thighs.

"This is so good," I said.

"You seem better," he said.

I finished the rest of the milkshake, and took a giant bite out of my burger, before responding.

"How does it feel now?" I asked.

I didn't have to say what I was talking about. He knew.

At first I thought he wasn't going to tell me, but after a few moments of silence he began to speak, in that low, gnarled way he did.

"I don't have a good way to describe it."

"Try," I said, my voice soft. "I want to know."

"It feels like first time I took acid, and the first time I got drunk on whiskey, and the first time I kissed a girl, and the day I first won a basketball game, all in one."

"That sounds pretty amazing," I said.

"Except I'm focused. Clear. And I think when I wake up every day that eventually I'm going to fall back into my old life. But it just keeps going. Every day."

"You think I had something to do with that?

"I know you did," he said.

"Yeah," I muttered. "I do too now."

"Beverly," Spider said, "I can't just drive forever. You don't have to tell me what happened to you, but let me take you home."

I'd pushed Mr. Ainsworth into the back of my mind, but the thought of falling asleep made my heart pound and my stomach clench.

I knew when I closed my eyes Mr. Ainsworth with his rough skin and hard eyes would be waiting for me. The pool of blood that used to be my teacher would be waiting for me. And once they found his body, they'd search through the security cameras and see that I was also at the school that evening. And they'd bring me in for questioning. Maybe they'd even accuse me of murdering him.

"Just a little while longer," I said. "Please. I don't want to sleep yet."

He pursed his lips.

"Okay," he said. "A few minutes. But only because you saved my life."

I smiled. He didn't. I polished off my hamburger and fries, and my eyes became heavy like concrete. As if caught in a state between waking and sleeping. I looked out through the window I didn't see the darkness around us anymore. I saw a thousand sunsets, one after the other. I saw the light like strawberry syrup staining the night, erasing the stars.

I saw a road that could stretch on forever, if I had the imagination for it.

I spoke suddenly.

"I figured out what I want to do with my life."

"Oh?" he asked.

"Yeah," I said. "But it involves me leaving town."

He said nothing.

"So can you take me to the bus station?" I asked.

"You mean now?"

"Yeah," I said. "Now."

"Are you even going to say goodbye?"

"No," I said. "I don't think I can."

A few seconds passed. I thought he'd just end up taking me home, and I tensed my hands, waiting.

But then he just gave his signature terse nod, and turned the truck around in the right direction. I sighed and sunk further into my seat.

He didn't ask for an explanation, and I didn't give one. I just clutched my throbbing thighs as the earth vibrated straight through my spine.

PART 2

6

I stood backstage in my six-inch clear platforms, baby powder on my feet, white G-string, blonde hair extensions down to my ass, waiting for the music to start.

The air shimmered with glitter, and the walls were lined with mirrors like sewn-together disco balls. I caught my reflection a hundred times over, and I still didn't quite believe it was me – eyebrows shaved off and white half-pearls glued in their place, lipgloss, white feathered wings.

I wasn't Beverly Sykes anymore.

I was Angel.

I glanced back at the other girls. Trudy snorted cocaine at her vanity and Lindsey balanced a medical textbook on her knees. Candy's shift had just ended, and she was peeling off her garters and counting her money. Raven was putting on black lipstick like a superhero, eyes narrowed with deep concentration.

It was Lindsey who gave me the name Angel because I came riding into town alone, seemingly with no future and no past, with a face too sweet to be scarred with ordinary human pain.

Her words, not mine.

The music came on — Rihanna's "Pour it Up." That was my cue.

I strode onto the stage and into the blue light, my wings fluttering. It's Friday night at the Aquamarine, so the club's actually crowded. Once Raul took me off the day shift, I actually started to make money.

And I even got used to bruised thighs from the pole, sore feet from dancing in heels, chafing from rubbing on jeans during lap dances all night. I was a terrible dancer at first, but Raul didn't care about that. And Lindsey taught me a few tricks on the pole, nothing too fancy, just enough to get by.

There was something excitable in the air that night, a frenetic kind of pheromone that made the air hum, although the other girls would use words like, "sad" and "depressing." They saw lonely men, horny men, jostling boys, alcoholics who sat in the back like dark shadows, disgruntled girlfriends dragged there by their oblivious boyfriends, a sticky floor with spilled drinks and stray dollar bills.

But I saw opportunity.

The magic inside me pulsed to the beat of the music. I resisted the urge to hold my stomach as I danced because I felt like the grind and the pulse coursing through my blood might burst out of my skin.

I looked out across the stage as I danced and saw a dark-haired man in a navy suit, drinking alone from a bottle of champagne.

He'd been there every day for the last two weeks, but from the first day he'd come into the Aquamarine I knew he was a barely-contained scream wearing a human suit.

When he lifted the bottle of champagne to pour more into his glass, his arm shook as if he was lifting a huge weight. I knew it wasn't because he was weak, but because he was working so hard at keeping himself together, containing the ferocious heat inside of him, that it was using up all of his strength.

When you work in a strip club you become good at

reading people. Ex-strippers would make great therapists, they get plenty of field time.

Candy strode up to him and asked if he wanted a dance. He shook his head without even glancing up, and she walked off.

After my dance on the stage, I came up to him.

"Hey sweetie," I said.

"No thank you," he said before I could ask, again without looking up.

I turned around, but then he glanced up and took a sharp intake of breath.

"Wait," he said, and grabbed my wrist. "It's you, isn't it? I've been waiting for you."

"I'm here," I said.

I knelt in front of him, my wings brushing against his knees, and his eyes shone with reflected white light. I leaned forward and pressed my breasts against his knees.

"You can help, can't you?" he asked.

He began to shake.

"Yes," I said, squeezing his thigh. "I can help."

"I'll give you however much you want."

I rose, and held out my hand for him to take. "Just pay me for a lap dance."

He handed me two twenties. I showed him my garter, and he placed the bills there, gingerly, as if he was afraid to make contact with my skin. When he was finished, I smiled, and I took him into one of the private rooms in the back.

The light in the backroom was even darker, an almost sinister shade of blue, and our bodies seemed to be sliced in the darkness, our features distorted.

"What's your name, sweetie?" I said as I led him to the bench that ran crossways across an entire length of wall.

I urged him to sit down. He didn't answer.

I gyrated my hips, moving slow to the music pumping fast, as if I could slide in between the beats. He leaned back and tried to look like he was relaxing, but he squeezed his hands into fists.

I'm beginning to learn that sadness is like a smell, a cloud that plumes upward from the depths of a being and expands outward, affecting everything it comes into contact with.

"Did she leave you?" I asked him as I let my top drop to the floor.

"I don't want to bore you with a sob story," he said.

"There's a sob story all over your face," I said.

"Angel," he said, breathing my name out.

I let my brassiere drop, came close and wrapped my arms around his chest, pressed his face into my breast. He turned his head away at first, but I took his chin in my hands and redirected him back.

"I have more than enough room for your sadness inside of me," I said.

He shuddered and suppressed a deep sob.

"Angel," he said. "have you ever been so sad that you thought the world was going to collapse?"

"I can fix it."

"Not like—"

"Yes," I said. "Exactly like this. And I've fixed worse than this. Take my underwear off."

He reached out with shaking hands, and he did.

"It's still going to hurt," I said. "But that hole you feel? That hole that's sucking out your entire being? Like you're losing little pieces of you through a filter in all of existence? That's going to go away."

I unzipped his pants. His erection swelled. I found myself holding my breath, feeling my body pulse inside the music, pulse with the anticipation. The bomb inside of me began to count down.

Without ceremony, I climbed into his lap and drove his cock deep into me.

He gasped.

I've been waiting for this moment all night, so it only took a couple thrusts for the explosion to rock through me. It started in my vagina and extended outwards in both directions, to the top of my head and the tip of my toes.

Every time it happened, I thought I'd be ready for the sensation.

And every time, I was wrong.

I felt my body trying to fold in on itself, a rocket peeling itself away from the cells.

His eyes rolled back in his head and his body tightened.

But afterwards, when he was able to gain composure, he looked at me and said, "You're smiling."

"Yeah?'

"I've never seen a stripper smile like that," he said. "Ever."

* * *

A couple weeks later a bachelor party paid for a private room for the night, and they wanted both Lindsey and I to entertain them.

Lindsey was like the devil to my angel, and when we were on stage together we created a drama between dark and light, an eternal struggle of the composites of the universe.

She's stick-thin from the stress of constantly trying to keep up at medical school, and she tried to hide the stress in her face with sharp winged eyeliner and blood-red eyeshadow. She liked to prance onstage to German industrial music with a bullwhip. I tried to imagine this pale, thin, painted girl wearing a doctor's coat, telling people to bend over and cough, prescribing medications for blood pressure. It's difficult.

The man of the hour, the groom-to-be, was a little blonde guy who clearly never set foot in a strip club before. I bet he was probably something like a photographer, or a bartender at a craft brewery. His friends probably pressured him to get in one last hurrah before marriage locked him down forever. He walked in wearing a white blazer and a nervous smile. They bought a lot of overpriced champagne and went back to the private room with its high-energy music and dark lights.

He took to Lindsey right away, who came out dressed like Dracula in a little black cape, her hair done in tight dark waves. She was so thin, and so pressed with dark energy, that if she turned to the side I thought she might disappear, but it was her that the groom-to-be kept his eyes on, her that he smiled for.

Lindsey had been off for the last few days. She showed up at work with puffy eyes, danced a little slower, had moments when she stopped as if she'd been set on pause. In those last few months at the Aquamarine I'd learned the difference between being tired, and being sad.

Something happened to her, I knew for certain, but nobody at the Aquamarine talked about those things. Most of the girls that worked here didn't want to talk about their lives on the outside, they came here to dance in fantasy personas, make money, and then get out.

But as we danced together in that private room, Lindsey whispered to me, "Want to get crazy?"

"Show me what you got," I whispered back.

She grabbed my hips. The boys murmured and called at us as she danced up on me. When she came closer, I imagined that she'd be like fog and black licorice, but instead she smelled like a green candy apple.

I thought for a moment I saw something scaly flickering under her tongue, but I knew it was just my imagination, the intersection of dark lights and suggestion. Lindsey climbed into her devil persona just a little too well.

When she kissed me I imagined her swallowing up the light inside me.

The boys cheered.

It was in that moment, in the shift of her body, in the heat that seemed to steam off her navel, that I knew she wanted to fuck me.

Lindsey didn't do "extras," unlike me, most of the pretty

girls didn't — and it's not something we ever talked about. If asked explicitly for sex, we denied that we did such a thing.

But I can't save those who want to be saved just by dancing.

Caught up in the new excitement, the bachelor party ordered more champagne. The blonde groom crossed his arms and leaned back against the wall, but I could tell that he was excited too.

"Go get my bag," she said, and pointed toward the wall where she kept her velvet backpack full of tools.

Usually I'd say, "Get your own damn bag," but Lindsey's devilish eyes made me obey that night.

I grabbed the backpack and handed it to her. She pulled out a pair of pink fuzzy handcuffs, tossed the backpack, and turned toward me square.

Lindsey grabbed me and pulled me over to the pole in the middle of the room.

"You've been a bad angel," she said. "And now I'm going to punish you."

She winked at me before handcuffing me to the pole.

"You must pay for your sins, little angel," she said.

Then she ripped off my wings.

They fell slow to the ground in two crumpled fistfuls. My heart began to pound in my ears.

"I'm sorry," I said. "Whatever it was, I'll never do it again, I'm sure."

I bent over as I spoke, arching my back and wiggling my ass at the boys, but crumbled wings and the sickening doubt, like a bright bloom in my stomach, told me that this wasn't a game anymore.

I knew she was retrieving her flogger from her little velvet bag of goodies. Unlike the bullwhip, which she'd actually bought at a tractor supply company, that one was more suited for kinky sex.

Thwack!

The first strike against my ass cheek didn't hurt, but I still felt a burn flush through my entire body.

Thwack!

I writhed a little, as if pretending to be in pain.

But the third strike *did* hurt.

A lot. And the sensation ripped all the way down my back. My ears rang and pulses of adrenaline shot through my body. I craned my neck back to see Lindsey holding the little crop in one hand, and the bullwhip in the other, trying to guess which one she'd hit me with.

The boys of course, loved it. They clapped and cheered.

Just as I'm about to protest she reared her arm back and hit me again.

I nearly fell with the force of it. My arms strained against the fuzzy handcuffs. I struggled to stay upright in my heels, and when I glanced down I saw a bright spot of blood drop onto the floor. She'd broken the skin.

"Lindsey!" I shouted.

She reared her arm back again. I flinched, waiting for the blow to come down, but she paused.

"Do you think you've had enough?" she asked.

Do devils dance between eyes? I would've believed it, seeing Lindsey's face that night.

I knew that if I wasn't careful, I'd be carrying home new scars.

"No," I said, trying to push down the pain, gritting my teeth a little. "I haven't had enough. No punishment is enough for me."

"That's because you're a miserable little angel!" Whoever she was directing that anger toward, it obviously wasn't me.

"You're right," I said. "I am miserable, Lindsey!"

"Worthless," she said, pushing air forcefully through her teeth. "Worthless, lazy, good-for-nothing, bitch!"

"Hurt me then," I said. "Punish me. Come on!"

She relaxed her grip on the bullwhip, and inwardly I released the tension in my body.

"No, I'm bored of punishing you," she said.

When she unlocked the cuffs I wanted to slap her.

But then she kissed me again, and sparks shot into my stomach and my throat. My muscles seemed to melt into the music.

Then we began to dance again.

Light and dark, merging into one divine being.

We headed toward the boys. Lindsey danced in the groom's lap, and leaned down to whisper something in his ear. He laughed. I paid attention to his friends, dancing and talking – about what, I couldn't remember, as a stripper it'd become second nature to make mindless, flirty small talk and I was so focused on the strip of pain in my back and Lindsey, that I did it without thinking.

Somewhere in between that, our bras came off. And our underwear.

Lindsey lay cross-wise against the men's laps, completely naked. She beckoned me to her.

I knew that I only imagined her tongue was forked, that her transformation into Satan's daughter was now complete.

With encouragement from the boys, I climbed on top of her.

We merged, grinding against each other, kissing, a white light falling into a black hole.

The gash on my back pulsed like a portal into a new world.

My body buckled. Lindsey's hair was in my mouth and her black lacquer nails were at my throat. I could feel the men's jeans underneath me and their excited breath and once more, the pressure building.

It's coming. Fuck.

It's coming.

It's—

She whispered in my ear, almost mockingly.

"Give it to me, sweet angel," and I knew right then that she'd planned this all along.

I knew exactly what she wanted me to give her, and I couldn't stop myself.

I became a prism of light, a honeycombed spaceship of pleasure. I arched my back and my knees pressed into Lindsey, into the men's legs underneath her, and I swear I heard a choir of angels singing.

I didn't remember much after that. We finished up the party soon afterward, and the boys left big tips and empty bottles of champagne.

Lindsey brought me a glass of water as I leaned against the bench, sweat melting the thick foundation off my face.

It took a huge amount of effort just to take a single sip.

"You know," I said to Lindsey, my voice exhausted. "You could've just asked."

She shrugged.

"You going to tell me what that was about?" I asked.

"I'll tell you later," she said, and kissed me on the forehead.

Lindsey was the only girl I knew who could make a kiss feel condescending.

And of course, she never did tell me.

* * *

Outside in the parking lot, my customer's women, wives, and mothers waited for me.

I suppose I should've known that they'd come for me eventually. I just didn't expect all of them at once.

They leaned against their cars, or crouched down on the pavement, or stood with crossed legs and purses crossed over their bodies. One of the women wore light-up sneakers, and she kept shifting from foot to foot, making the green lights shoot off. Another reminded me of a mermaid, with her dark red hair swaying in front of her face and her emerald green dress fluttering in the wind.

They all glanced up when I came out of the club.

I stopped, sliding a bit in my platforms, and reached for the taser in my coat. I'd been keeping one on me ever since that night with Mr. Ainsworth.

A blonde woman in a tweed jacket stepped forward.

"Are you Angel?" she asked.

"What's going on?" I asked.

"Oh honey," said the blonde-haired woman, "You're just a kid. Are you even old enough to work here?"

Truthfully, I was turning 18 next week, but they didn't need to know that.

"What is this about?" I asked, glancing from one woman to the other.

"We wanted to talk," the blonde woman said. "About what's been happening to our men."

I took a step back, and tightened my grip on the taser. I glanced around the parking lot — but there was nobody else. It was 3 A.M, and I'd been one of the last people to leave the club. The Aquamarine stood by itself at the edge of town, on a slick stretch of road as lonely as the apocalypse. There was a camera near the back exit, but that wouldn't do me much good right now.

"Look, you can't fool us. We already know what's been happening," said the woman in the light-up sneakers, still shifting from foot to foot.

"Give it to her, Janie," said the blonde woman.

"Don't come any closer," I took a step back.

Another woman stepped forward holding a package with a red, sparkly bow on it.

"What?" I asked, and my grip on the taser loosened.

"It's a gift. We all wanted to pitch in. To say thank you."

I took a few steps forward and took the package.

"Unwrap it," they urged me.

I pulled the bow apart. It fell slowly to the pavement. I opened the box to reveal a tan trench coat. Thick, of nice quality. I'd never owned something that nice.

I stood, stunned, holding the coat out in front of me.

"I know, it's not nearly enough," one of them said.

"Uhh. This is more than enough. I don't need anything, really."

They urged me to try it on. I pulled it over my thin jacket. It really was a nice coat.

An Indian woman wearing red shoes stepped forward.

"My husband, Morris, he came back from the war broken. Broken bones, I could've handled, but I couldn't handle this."

"My boyfriend," said the blonde woman. "I knew that he'd stopped loving anything a long time ago, let alone me." The other women began to speak.

"My son, Gerald, he'd gotten deep into a heroin addiction. I thought he was beyond saving."

"My husband stopped touching me."

"I was so sick of his shit, we were going to get a divorce."

"Then his eyes began to change, as if they were letting in light for the first time."

"He had stopped touching me, but one night he came home and we made love for the first time in six years."

"He started playing with our baby, and he smiled while he did it. He was actually smiling."

"He got clean, went to rehab, started eating healthy and helping around the house."

"He built the kids a treehouse, and took me out on dates again. He even started talking about starting up his old business again."

"Eventually I pried it out of Morris what had happened, although he didn't want to tell me."

"A girl at the club. Came from somewhere out of town, out of nowhere."

"A new girl with white wings and pearls for eyebrows. She did things that the other girls wouldn't, couldn't do."

"That's what Albert said too. A girl named Angel, who'd taken his old body and given him a new one."

I held the coat out, unsure of what to say.

"So, how do you all know each other?" I asked.

"Honey, everyone knows everyone's business in this town," said Janie. "A whisper could stretch from one end to the other without breaking a sweat."

"Will you fix me too?" one of the women blurted out.

I opened my mouth to speak, but for once I wasn't sure what to say.

"Oh, look," Janie said. "We're embarrassing the poor girl."

She held out her hand.

"Come with us," she said. "Won't you? We're having a party. Terrance is watching the kids."

I hesitated.

"It's okay, Angel," she said, in a way that reminded me of my mother.

"I can help you," I said. "All of you. That's why I came here. To help."

"You've helped so much already. Just relax for now."

I found myself climbing into the back of a Camry, wedged between two middle-aged women, my knees drawn up. It smelled the way cars that belonged to mothers always did – of baby wipes, dog hair, and Play-Doh.

"I can't believe how goddamn young you are."

"When I imagined what you'd look like, I was imagining a witch. A pretty witch. But you've got such a baby face."

"You really do look like an angel."

"Not innocent, though. Most of the girls your age, they always look a little lost. But you don't look lost. Your eyes aren't sad and scared."

"They're confident. Certain."

"They're—"

"Purposeful."

7

As she drove, the red-haired woman handed me a bottle of whiskey from the glove compartment.

"I'm Ariel, by the way," she said. "I know, like the Little Mermaid."

"Ingrid," said the woman to my right, in her light-up shoes.

"Destiny."

"Lily."

I wasn't about to tell them my real name. Ever since I'd left home, I hadn't been Beverly since I left home. I was simply Angel, and I wanted to keep it that way.

"Don't be shy. Take a drink," said Ariel.

I tipped the whiskey back.

"Look at you," she said when I winced at the burn. "Just a child."

"Where did you say we were going?" I asked.

"You'll see," she said.

Not that there were many places to go in a mid-sized town at three in the morning. And the town itself had mostly gone to sleep. Except for the lonely street lights, there was mostly just long swathes of darkness extending past the little housing complexes.

We pulled into the parking lot of The First Sacrament Methodist Church.

I hadn't been to a church since that sleepover with Mary Mae, when her mother had called me a little heathen and dragged me to get baptized. When Mom found out, she was pissed, and there were no more sleepovers at Mary's house after that.

"What are we doing here?" I asked. "After-hours praying session?"

"Nah," Ingrid said. "It's just one of the few places we can actually fucking relax."

"There isn't even a damn coffee shop in this town that we can go to and relax, so we come here," Ariel said. "I guess it's kind of like our strip club."

Ariel got out of the car and unlocked the back door with her key, just as the other cars drove up. The women piled out, and we all went inside.

"I'm one of the Saturday teachers," Ariel said, by way of explanation as I headed in.

We walked into the sanctuary and one of the women flicked the low lights on. I found myself breathing differently, as if the air here was of a different purity. The red carpeting, wooden pews, and stacked bibles gave the place a sort of musty, hushed atmosphere. A kind of reverence that was the total opposite of what I was used to at the Aquamarine.

The blonde-haired woman, who I learned was named Nessa, went into the storage room behind the altar and came back with a box of wine.

"Anyone got a bottle opener?" she asked.

One of the women fished one out of her purse and tossed it to her.

"Is that the communion wine?"

"Yep," said Nessa. "Drink up."

Without much protest, they opened up a few bottles and passed them around.

"Mmm," said Ariel. "Heretical."

"Be a little respectful, Ariel. Jesus Christ," said one of the older women.

"Respectful? That ship sailed a long time ago," she said, and took a long swig before passing the bottle to me.

One woman found a box of candles and began to light them with her zippo. She placed them on the floor around the altar. We gathered nearby, sitting on the pews or on the carpet.

"Shall we start?" I asked, taking a swig of wine. "Who wants to go first?"

I rose wobbling to my feet. These plastic heels didn't do so great on carpet. The women fell silent as I turned to them.

"That's what we're here for, isn't it?" I asked.

Silence.

"You do know how my power works, right?"

More silence, somehow even quieter than the silence before.

"Sex," I said. "We have to have sex."

After another second of heavy silence, Ariel began to cry.

"Oh, honey!" said Nessa.

She pulled tissues out of her purse and handed them to Ariel. Her tears were big enough to blind her, but she just clutched the tissues.

"I didn't want to do this! But he's going to leave me!" she said, nearly wailing. "After that night at the Aquamarine – he became so vibrant and cheerful. A decade of depression, gone in just a few weeks. But now he never comes home! I'm just too dull and miserable to follow him into his new life!"

After a pause, another woman spoke up. She held one of the wine bottles in both hands, and bent down as if whispering into the mouth to keep the words a secret.

"I think my husband is cheating on me," she said, but didn't elaborate.

They turned to me.

"What did you do to them?" said Ariel, wiping the tears from her eyes, smearing mascara across her cheek.

"I make people better. Happier. More, well, more like themselves."

"Can you make Lily's husband stop cheating?"

I shook my head. "No, I can't control what happens afterward. That's up to you."

"More like ourselves? What if I don't like myself?" said Ingrid.

"I think you will," I said.

Ariel's tears continued to streak down her face.

I thought of the story of Jesus turning water to wine, and tried to remember if he'd ever been able to turn tears into joy. I knew that he'd fed people bread and fish, cured the blind and crippled, and come back from the dead – but was he ever able to transform a miserable life into one worth having?

I didn't know if he could, but I could.

I had that power.

I held my hand out to Ariel. She glanced up at me with her face glimmering.

"But what are you going to do?" I asked. "Are you going to miss taking this one chance, and regret it for the rest of your life?"

She sucked in a sharp breath.

"No," I said.

I held out my hand.

"Let's go. I can take care of you."

"No," said Nessa.

I cocked an eyebrow.

"In here," Nessa said. "In front of all of us. We're in this together."

I hesitated. I'd fantasized about having an orgy, of course, shedding my clothes and being surrounded in a rolling ecstatic wave of naked bodies, but not inside of a church, breathing staid air and surrounded by women with barely-contained anger and tight shoulders.

"I'm not much of an exhibitionist."

She rolled your eyes. "Aren't you a stripper?"

I felt the *fuck you* forming on my lips.

But I stopped myself at the last moment, and I forced myself to shut up and breathe.

"Okay," I said on the exhale. "Fine. We'll do it here."

Ariel stood with her arms crossed over her shoulders.

"Should I take my clothes off now?" she asked, not making eye contact.

I glanced around the church with its bright starkness, crosses nailed to the wall, stacks of bibles, and dusty tapestries depicting Noah's Ark and Daniel in the Lion's den. And then I looked back at the women, who shifted uncomfortably, or avoided making eye contact, or squirmed as if their clothes didn't fit right.

"No. Not yet. The mood isn't right," I said. "Do you guys have speakers in here?"

"Yeah. The controls are in the other room."

"Put something on," I said.

"Like what?"

"I don't know. Something sexy," I said.

One of the women disappeared into the backroom. We waited for a few seconds and then techno began to blare across the room.

Good enough, but something else was missing.

"Hit the lights too," I said.

All that was left was the low light of the candles, making flicker-shadows across the women's faces.

I went to the front of the sanctuary, in front of the altar, and began to dance.

I shimmied out of my trenchcoat, and then my second jacket. I still wore my brassiere underneath from work. It was white, almost sheer, and caught the glow of the candlelight, shimmering like diamonds.

I'd become used to dancing in front of men, but I'd never been looked at quite like I was being looked at by these women — their avoidance had transformed into fascinated, transfixed, intense stares, waiting with an almost violent expectation.

I danced out of my juicy sweatpants, revealing my lace underwear and thong. The heavy beat thudded between my ears. I felt myself nearly disappearing inside of it.

Some of the women began to hum, and others started to clap.

Ariel began to dance. It was first an awkward shuffle, but then she started to she really get into it, moving her hips, raising her arms above her head, touching her dark red hair.

Other women got up and also began to dance.

Soon, everyone was dancing.

I beckoned Ariel close to me, and she came toward me almost vibrating.

The women still looked hesitant and nervous, despite the new mood.

I looked out the window and saw the Church's name glinting on the sign outside, and started riffing.

"Do you know what the real First Sacrament is?" I asked.

I grabbed a candle off the floor and handed it to Ariel.

She seemed confused, but took it in both hands anyway, her hips still swaying like a hypnotist's pendulum.

"It's what we're going to do. Right here. Right now. This is the First Sacrament."

I grabbed another candle, and passed it to another woman. Then another.

They leaned forward, as if trying to reach to the end of the candle's flicker. The candlelight pressed yellow ghosts into their eyes and cheeks.

"The First Sacrament isn't wine or bread," I said. "It's sex."

They came closer, leaning in, pressing in. The music and

dark light transformed the entire room into my theater, and I felt the new energy squeezing my rib cage.

"So we're going to take the real First Sacrament," I said. "An old ritual to create a new world."

They swayed, not to the beat of the techno music but to the breath that exhaled those words.

"We're not beholden to our men and children. We don't have to be miserable. Or depressed. Or lost. We can take control. Be happy. Feel alive. In the new world we're going to create, you'll see that all of this is true."

I wasn't Beverly Sykes in that moment, I'd fully stepped into the costume of Angel so that the seams of my true identity were invisible.

"The origin of life, the origin of civilization. The origin of everything in existence."

And Angel knew exactly what to say.

"So do you want to join me in this new world?" I asked. "Do you want to become more than you ever have before?"

I held my hand out for a wine bottle, and when one was put into my hands I took another huge swig.

I handed the wine back and I kissed Ariel with the candlelight bathing our chins and lips. At first, I felt her stiffen with surprise, but then her shoulders relaxed.

When her lips parted for me I knew the spell was complete.

I took the candle from her and passed it off.

"Okay, now you can take your clothes off," I said.

I was speaking to Ariel, but they all undressed.

They took off their coats, scarves, gloves, sweaters, earrings, necklaces. Everything fell to the floor and they stood shining, naked, basked in both powdery darkness and yellow flickering glow.

Several women grabbed blankets from the nursery. When Ariel and I sank to the floor they created a soft landing space for us.

"You really are so beautiful." Ariel whispered as she looked up at me, her red hair splayed out around her.

She giggled, and a bright blush came to her cheeks.

I wiped away her last remaining tear with the back of my finger.

But I knew it wasn't me that she was talking about. Like I said, I'd gotten pretty good at reading people working in a strip club.

She was talking about that moment, that expectant hope, transfixed in the glow that made all of us beautiful.

Our bodies pressed together. Our hips and vulvas touched.

I slid my hand in between our legs, and gently worked a finger into her. To my surprise, she was already wet, as if she'd been waiting for me.

Another finger went inside of her easily.

She gasped in a quiet way, holding in her breath, holding onto my shoulders, as I rocked my fingers inside of her.

I felt close to exploding even though she'd barely touched me. Pleasure like a gentle electricity shot into me. I felt as if each individual vertebrae of my spine was pulling itself apart.

I'd been so pent up, so ready, that all it took was for her to grind her vulva against mine, and I was gone.

I exploded and Ariel cried out. Her voice echoed throughout the sanctuary. My vision distorted the room. The ceiling twisted. The candlelight bent. The woman's faces rippled like tidepools. I clung to the blankets as my entire body seemed to tear with the force of the power barreling through me.

And there was Ariel on top of me, head bent back, mouth open, hair as if she was suspended underwater, her face glowing with the flush of blood-red light pulsing to the surface of her skin.

"Wow," she said, exhaling as she collapsed beside me.

When Ariel was able to get up and breathe properly, they

gave her water and swaddled her in blankets as if she'd been reborn.

"How was it?" Ingrid asked. "What do you feel?"

"It looked hot," someone else said, and then came nervous laughter.

Ariel couldn't respond at first. Her tears had been replaced by thick droplets of sweat. She leaned back in the pew, opened her mouth, closed it, opened again.

"See for yourself," she finally said.

Nessa came to me next. She knelt in front of me with her eyes as sharp as lightning.

"Great tits," I said, breaking character for a moment.

But she didn't seem to mind. In fact, she smiled.

"They're fake," she said. "But thanks."

She climbed on top of me and leaned down, grazing her breasts against mine. She was softer than she looked, with fingers like velvet and thighs that smelled of baby oil. I made a mental note to ask her what moisturizer she used, but I forgot about it the moment she slipped her fingers inside of me, and kissed me with a wet and open mouth.

A hedonistic orgy would've been unthinkable to most of these women, but a religious experience – that was something they could get behind.

Again, it didn't take long before I exploded into Nessa. We shuddered and she fell to the blankets. The other women swaddled her and whisked her to the pews.

"Jesus fucking Christ," she said, her hair wild, her eyes even wilder. "That was amazing."

Nobody chastised her for the blasphemy.

I twitched with little aftershocks of pleasure as I glanced around the room at the women blooming in candlelight. Some of them chanting or murmuring, others whispering amongst each other.

"Who's next?" I asked.

When I opened my legs I felt like the whole world might spill out.

Then it was Ingrid's turn. And Lily's. Bang. Bang. One explosion after another.

I became giddy with laughter. I kept expecting someone to ask me what I was laughing about, but they didn't. Maybe because they were laughing too. We'd all become delirious.

My arms were almost too heavy to lift. My stomach clenched. My vagina was sore. I reached up to wipe the sweat pouring down my forehead, but my limbs felt like they'd been scooped out so I was nothing but nerves.

I'd never done this with so many people at once before and I thought I might be torn apart with the pleasure and the stress.

But still, I didn't stop. I would not stop. Not until every .woman in that room saw God.

* * *

The parking lot was completely full the next night at the Aquamarine. All the girls stared at me when I walked into the backroom.

"What's going on?" I asked.

"I don't know," said Trudy, rubbing her white nose. "You tell us."

"They're all here for you," said Candy, motioning toward the door to the stage.

Lindsey was leaning into her reflection, applying her usual blood-red eyeshadow. She was smiling, but pretended not to acknowledge me.

I tried my best to dress and finish my makeup while ignoring the stares.

When I walked out onto the stage that night the crowd cheered like an explosion. The room was nearly wall-to-wall packed, definitely a fire hazard. The bartender slung drinks as fast as she could, and I noticed that some of the other strippers on the floor were being pushed to the edge of the room. The bouncers tried to keep order, but they could barely get their arms out in front of them the room was so crammed.

And it wasn't just the usual customers – it was all sorts, both men and women. Rich, poor, young, old. I spotted a woman carrying twin babies on her hips with milk stains on her chest, and a man who appeared to be homeless with gloves made out of trash-bags. A group of boys wearing Metallica t-shirts underneath oversized suit jackets, stood near the front of the stage. They were obviously underage and I had no idea how they'd gotten in through the door. An old man who appeared more like a mountain than a living being, with his layered brown coat and shaggy eyebrows licked his lips when we made eye contact. An old woman wheeled around a desiccated woman hooked up to an oxygen tank.

And they all wanted me to fix them.

As I danced, the group surged forward to the edge of the stage to meet me, their arms outspread.

Angel and *First Sacrament* rolled like a wave through their lips.

They reached out to touch me with desperate grasping fingers and pleas. And every time I moved, their eyes moved with me, hungry with hope.

They reached out for me like they thought I could heal them with a touch or a look.

I made more money that night than I did in the last three months.

Hours later when I headed backstage again. Raul was there in the center of the dressing room with his arms crossed. His hair stood straight up in a shockwave as if he'd been grabbing it all night.

"Angel. This is your fault somehow, isn't it? What the hell is going on?" he asked.

I was about to speak, but then Lindsey, sitting at her dressing table, sighed and rolled her eyes.

"Angel went and started a religion," she said.

Raul glanced back at me, accusatory. I didn't know what

to say, so shrugged.

Lindsey turned back to the mirror, and went back to taking her makeup off.

* * *

It only took about a week for that fresh religious fervor to die down, and soon the crowd at the Aquamarine went back to normal. But word must have spread outside of the town because one night I talked to a doctor who offered me the works to 'study' me back at his clinic in L.A.

One night around 3 A.M. I put on my new trenchcoat and stepped outside into an empty parking lot. No cars at all. No people in wheelchairs, and small children with cancer, no debt-riddled, divorced, overweight, depressed people desperate for a change. Just the sky, which seemed to have taken liquid form, undulating softly above me, and the pavement beneath my platform heels.

I took a few moments to breathe and then checked my phone. Holding it made me feel less alone. It'd been weeks since I called my mom. For many months after what happened with Mr. Ainsworth, I had effectively disappeared from my old life. And when I did finally contact my mom, she was so furious she almost hung up on me.

I couldn't bring myself to tell her about Mr. Ainsworth until nearly a year after it happened.

And although she said she understood we still didn't talk to each other much.

When I called her she answered on the second ring.

"Bev?" she said, as if not quite believing it was me.

"Hey, I just got off work," I said. "Sorry, I know it's late, but I know you never sleep."

"Are you okay?" she asked.

"Yeah," I said. "I'm okay, but things have been crazy around here."

It was too late for the bus, and nobody was around to give

me a ride. I walked toward my apartment, one hand on the phone and the other on the taser in my jacket.

"Is someone giving you trouble at the club?" she asked.

The image of the club, crowded with people mouthing my name, eyes peeled for a miracle, flashed into my brain.

"No, not really," I said. "I miss you though."

The next thought made me feel like there was a fist in my throat.

"I miss home."

There was a long pause.

"You can always come home, baby," she said. "You know you're always welcome back."

I swallowed the seconds between us.

"I don't think I can," I said. "Not yet."

I expected her to argue with me. Instead she just said: "Okay, baby."

On the other side of the line, I heard Mom rummaging around in the kitchen.

"What are you making?" I asked.

I hated the strained way even small talk sounded.

"Chinese take-out," she laughed a little.

"I should've known," I said. "I can't remember the last time you cooked us something."

On my side, it was still quiet, that 3 A.M. quiet before the complete, breathless dark of 4 A.M. As I walked, I didn't even hear a dog barking. My heels clicking against the pavement sounded like rockets.

"Have you talked to Janna or Heather at all?" my mom asked.

"Sometimes on Facebook," I said. "But look, I wanted to tell you I might be going to L.A. soon. A man talked to me a few days ago. I thought it was a scam at first, but I checked him out. He's legit. He's a scientist who—"

I struggled to find the right words.

"He wants to figure out how I affect people like I do. He said he could help me get a therapy license afterwards. So maybe I could set up my own practice and even understand what it is I am."

"Does this have to do with your math teacher?" she asked. "What he did to himself wasn't your fault."

"I showed him something terrible inside himself, and he couldn't live with it anymore. And well—"

"You should go to L.A.," my mom said abruptly.

"Really?" I said. "I thought you'd try to talk me out of it."

"No. I wouldn't. Do what you gotta do, babygirl."

I headed into my apartment complex, with its gray walls and cricket silence, and climbed the concrete stairs up into my unit.

I had to step over four vases of roses and a pile of love letters to get to the door.

I walked around the plaid couch and coffee table and television that belonged to my roommate. The beige walls were bare, except for a single wooden sign that said "Eat, Laugh, Love!"

Ugh.

I headed into my windowless room, with its mattress on the floor and single cactus plant and computer with a fold-out desk and chair, the color of taupe foam.

"You still there?" my mom asked.

"Yeah, I'm here. Can I ask you something?"

"What is it?"

"Are you still mad at me?"

She hesitated.

"No," she said.

"You took too long to respond," I said. "That means you're mad."

She sighed.

"I'm trying not to be."

"One day all of this is going to make sense," I said. "And then you'll understand, and you'll be proud of me."

I flopped onto the mattress, belly first.

"I just want to fix the world. Is that too much to ask?"

PART 3

8

On my 21st birthday my bodyguard accompanied me to a fancy cocktail lounge in Manhattan, the type where the bartenders were called mixologists and jars of herbs lined the walls and the drinks cost $18 each. I couldn't go anywhere without being recognized these days. I had just turned 21, and the paparazzi had been waiting outside of my apartment to wish me a happy birthday as they snapped my new outfit. My social media was blowing up with birthday wishes. An audible hush descended upon the Friday night crowd as we entered the bar, and I imagined a spotlight shining down on me, turning my hair golden and my eyes into fire. Tonight was my night. I ordered a dirty vodka martini. The bartender didn't ask for my ID, but I tried to give it to him anyway.

"I'm 21 today," I said.

"I know who you are," he said gruffly, waving off the ID.

He hastily made the martini and shoved it toward me, spilling some of it across the countertop. Then he hurried off to the next customer.

"Happy birthday to me," I muttered.

"Happy birthday, kid," my bodyguard said.

I turned toward him as he sat beside me at the bar. I called him Bruce Lee, because he was half-Asian, liked martial arts movies, and had the same kind of lithe, muscle-dense body. He pretended like he hated the nickname, but I knew he secretly enjoyed it.

"You're not drinking?" I asked.

"Not when I work, no," Bruce Lee said.

"Order a drink so you can toast with me at least."

Without any more protest, he ordered a whiskey neat. He sat facing the bar, shoulders and arms relaxed, but I knew he was always aware of what was happening around us.

"A toast," he said when his drink arrived.

He lifted his glass and when I moved to lift my own it was as if all the exhaustion from the last few weeks flooded into my bones. I hadn't realized until that moment how tired I was. I was so sore from my work that it hurt to walk, and it seemed no matter how many Kegels I did and warm baths I took my body couldn't seem to keep up with the demand for the magic that everyone wanted. Even the shiny new dress I wore seemed like a weight tugging down on my neck.

"Here's to being fucking tired," I finally said.

"To fucking tired," Bruce Lee said, and we drank.

I'd barely gotten to taste my martini when a young woman came up to me, swinging her Chanel purse as she walked with her hips jutting out almost far enough to knock pictures off the walls.

"Can I take a picture with you?" she asked, fluttering her gold eyelash extensions.

"I—"

Before I could respond, she leaned in and snapped the picture and scurried off.

When I'd first hired Bruce Lee he'd tried to get people to stop taking unsolicited pictures of me. But now he just sat staring straight ahead without response, except that his shoulders raised a little in a way that reminded me of the raised hackles of an animal.

A young man came up to the bar beside me, his elbow

brushing against mine. He smelled of a thick mixture of Axe body spray and cedar cologne.

"Can I buy you a drink?" he asked.

I glanced over at his profile, with his smooth chin and Roman nose.

"Sure," I said. "I'll take a drink, but if you want to fuck I've got a six-month waiting list."

He blinked a few seconds, trying to process what I just said.

"Wait a minute," he said. "Holy shit, you're Beverly Sykes. I had no idea."

"Yeah, right. Everyone knows who I am."

"Beverly Sykes," he said with a sort of wistfulness, and then motioned toward Bruce Lee. "Is that your boyfriend?"

"A friend," I said. "We're celebrating my birthday."

"Happy birthday!" he said.

He raised his hand to the bartender. As he did so, a rolling wave of his smell assaulted my senses. I had to resist the urge to pinch my nose.

"A cake shot for me and the young woman right here!" he said.

The bartender threw down the shots with the same deliberate carelessness as he had thrown down my martini.

"Excuse me," I said. "Is there a problem?"

He turned toward me. He was young, maybe younger than Axe Body Spray standing beside me, but his eyes were shriveled like worn out leather shoes.

"No ma'am," he said, flicking his tongue at me like a snake. "It's just, I can't believe they call you a sex goddess. I've definitely seen better."

He headed toward the other side of the bar before I could respond.

"Ugh. What an asshole," said Axe.

"Don't worry. There's always someone who has a problem with me. Puritanical culture and all that."

I sighed and took the shot. When I tilted my head

back the sweet hazelnut seemed to spread down my throat with the added weight of the last three years. It'd been three years since Dr. Jones in Los Angeles had published his studies about me. Three years since I'd gotten my sex therapy license. Three years since the world had turned in to crowd my every step. Three years of bartenders with attitudes and my picture uploaded all across the Internet.

I tried my best to ignore the bartender's razor eyes as I finished my first martini and ordered another.

Then another. And another — until those fancy cocktails with their organic ingredients and special herbs turned into a muddle inside me. I couldn't remember the last time I'd been drunk.

"I have to go pee," I said and stood up.

I felt like all my sharp edges had been sanded away.

"Watch yourself," Bruce Lee said.

As if on cue, I tripped in my six-inch platforms. He caught me, and I pulled him into a little twirl.

"You know what," I said to Bruce Lee, "I think you're drunk too."

"It's my job to keep up with you, isn't it?"

We laughed, swirling with dizziness.

Come to think of it, I couldn't remember the last time I laughed.

* * *

My phone buzzed.

I thought I cleared my schedule for tonight but my assistant had placed a new appointment in ice-blue on my Google calendar. And I'd already missed a few calls.

"Fuck," I said. "I'm late for an appointment. We've got to go."

I called a cab and we headed to my office.

I heard soft music playing through the speakers inside as I

pressed my thumb to the bio lock. The door clicked open and I walked into the waiting room.

"Oh shit, thank God you're here," Melly, my assistant, said, rising from her desk.

Melly was a thin poodle of a woman, barely eighteen. Her curly hair hung around her eyes, giving her a harried look.

"I told you to clear my schedule," I said.

"You didn't get my message?" she said. "He was willing to pay 5 times the normal rate, and he didn't want to wait."

"Okay," I said. "We're talking about this later."

I took a step, stumbling a bit.

"I don't mean to be rude, Bev, but, are you drunk?"

"It's my birthday," I said, and walked into the main office.

At least the maid already changed the sheets on the bed, which lay on an elevated platform next to the stand of toys (also cleaned and sterilized), lubricants, and muscle relaxants. I kept the lighting blue to hide scars and imperfections, just like at the Aquamarine.

I set my purse down on the bureau, stumbling a little, and headed to the closet to change. I had to grab the door frame to keep from falling over.

I'd barely managed to shimmy into candy-colored lingerie when Melly rushed into the closet.

"He's here. Are you done yet?" she asked.

"Tell him to come in," I said, and she ducked back out.

I shoved my feet into pom-pom heels and peeked out into the office. The client walked through the door with his chest barreled out. He wore a brown woolen suit, and a thick layer of sweat ringed his neck. He breathed heavy as if he'd rushed the whole way here.

He'd brought a woman with him, and he held her by the wrist with two fingers, like she was a child. She had the glazed look of someone used to being dragged around. I'd seen that same look in prisons and mental hospitals.

I nodded to my bodyguard, and he went to wait in the front room.

"Hello," I said. "Did I book the both of you?"

"My wife," the man snapped. "Don't you remember the email I wrote you?"

I tried to smile, but his face, quivering like an angry dog's, made the muscles in my face slide downwards of their own volition.

"Sorry" I said. "Melly handles the emails."

I jumped up onto the platform and sat on the bed.

"Would you like to come here?" I asked, patting the sheets beside me.

"We've been in and out of therapy. Treatments. Hormone injections. Shock therapy. Everything. She needs serious help," the man said.

I didn't need a special gift to see that. He gripped the woman's wrist so tightly he left red marks.

"You both need help," I said, and exhaled, blowing a wisp of my hair out of my face. "I wasn't expecting a double booking, but that's fine."

The man's head turned nearly purple, and the woman's face froze in a nervous expression. Her nails were painted red, but she'd badly chewed the ends until they were ragged.

"I told you I'm not here for that," the man said.

"Yeah, okay. You just want your wife to be fixed, right?"

"Yes!" he said, as if admonishing a stupid dog.

Fuck. I was so tired. I thought if I closed my eyes for a few seconds too long I'd pass out for a week.

"Hello?" he said.

I sighed.

"Look, it's my birthday today. I'm very good at my job, but I'd rather be anywhere but here right now."

"Is that supposed to be my problem? If you think we're going to leave you a good yelp review after this kind of behavior, you're mistaken. My wife needs treatment! And she needs it now!"

"Oh, I get it now," I said.

"You get what?" the man said.

He lengthened his spine and squared his shoulders as if getting ready for a fight. In response, I sighed languorously and lay back on the bed. I wanted him to see just how much he didn't threaten me.

And anyway, I'd installed a button underneath each nightstand, and one on the bed railing, that'd alert my bodyguards and Melly in case anything went wrong.

"You're one of those people who thinks that after I fuck your wife, she's going to give you exactly what you want."

"Marty—" the woman began, but he quickly cut her off.

"What kind of business are you running here? This isn't very professional."

"I get called in by therapists and rich daddies and the police because they think I'll make troublemakers into good little model citizens. But I don't make obedient people. I make good people. And good people rarely fall in line in the way you think they will. Trust me, I learned that one really quickly."

"This is absolutely ridiculous. I was assured this was a professional, competent service."

"Let me tell you a story," I said suddenly. "A rich man wanted me to fuck his adult daughter. She was an artist, one of those Bohemian types, and she didn't want to run the family business. According to her father, that meant she was sick and needed to be cured.

"I really don't have time—"

"It's your life we're talking about. What else do you have time for?" I said.

I lifted my head up. It felt heavy, like something ensconced in amber.

"The moment I saw the man's daughter, I knew nothing was wrong with her. Well, not much more than any woman who has a father who thinks her existence is shameful. But we fucked anyway, because she was beautiful, and she had such a gorgeous smile. You know what happened after that?"

I didn't wait for a response.

"Her art took off. She became world-famous. Her smile got even more gorgeous," I said. "And she cut off contact with her father completely. Refused to speak to him anymore."

'I—"

"Look, just come here," I said, quietly interrupting him. "I can make everything okay. I promise you. Once we're finished, you'll see exactly what I'm talking about. Both of you."

The man puffed up his chest. He reminded me of a toad trying to make itself look big so a wolverine wouldn't eat it.

"There's nothing wrong with me," the man said.

"Do you want her to leave you?" I asked. "Because she will, once she becomes who she's supposed to be and sees that she's been kowtowing to a miserable, slick lowlife. And once she sees that she's been making herself sick because you've convinced her that she's sick, she'll leave you so fast there'll be a crater left behind where she used to sleep. You think I don't know? I've seen it dozens of times."

I laughed. It was a sick, heavy sound.

"Are you drunk?" he asked.

"It's my birthday," I said. "Now are we going to fuck or not?"

"This is completely outrageous."

He left, dragging his wife behind him. The front door slammed shut so loud the room quaked.

Bruce Lee and Melly both came into the office.

"What was that about?" Melly asked.

"They didn't get me a birthday card," I said.

I clapped my hands, and the lights went from a dim blue, back to white. I got up, and stumbled a bit, nearly falling off the platform.

"I'll take you home," said Bruce Lee.

I sat back down on the bed. I clapped my hands one more time, and the lights shut off.

"No," I said, sinking down into the sheets, already feeling too sleepy to move. "Don't bother."

* * *

The Beverly on the television didn't seem like me. She crossed the stage like a movie star. She's still got brightness in her eyes, ebullient skin, a body that's taut in all the right places.

Late at night I often searched YouTube for videos of myself. I found an old interview, my first one on national television. At first I didn't even recognize myself because that Beverly had eyes that hadn't seen the point beyond the horizon.

"She's one of a kind, folks, a real marvel. Some people say she's a goddess. Others say she's a gift from God himself. I say she's kind of like a sexy Joan of Arc, a real modern day warrior woman. We have here live on the show today. Beverley Sykes, a licensed sex therapist who can change people's lives with as little as 7 minutes in heaven. And as far as we know, she's the first person in history who's ever been granted such a power."

I was 20. I'd just moved to Manhattan and set up my practice. I wore a silver dress and had my hair done in curly waves. I remembered I couldn't sleep that night because I was so excited about being on national television.

The interviewer, a chuckling big man in a gray suit, asked me questions that seemed just the right demographically researched combination of sleaze and mystique.

"Everyone wants a piece of you, Miss Beverley. No doubt you're a very special young lady. But I've got to ask, are the rumors true?"

"Well, which rumors have you been listening to? Because there are quite a few."

The audience laughed. I laid back on the studio couch like I owned it. I wore six-inch heels like I was born in them.

"Can you really make me rich and beautiful just by sleeping with me?" he said.

"It doesn't quite work like that," I said.

He snapped his fingers in fake disappointment and the

audience laughed again. We'd already rehearsed this the day before.

"Well, that's all right, I am already quite a catch," he said.

Bev rolled her eyes.

"But tell me, how does it work?" he asked.

"Just think of me as a motivational coach of sorts," she said. "I can't give you anything you don't already have. I just unlock the potential inside you."

I scraped the bottom of my pint of red velvet ice cream. Absentmindedly, I'd eaten the whole thing again. My personal trainer told me I was getting too soft, but still, I reached for my cell to order some pizza like it was becoming muscle memory.

"Was there really a religion founded about you?" the man on the television asked.

"Well, kind of," television Bev said. "It's called the Church of the First Sacrament. The whole idea is that the way to achieve eternal happiness is through sexual union, so to speak."

"And what are the meetings like?" the host asked. "Sounds just like an excuse for a plain ole' orgy."

She shrugged. "I've never gone to one, but it sounds like it'd be a good time."

The young Beverly Sykes had quickly learned to be an excellent liar when cameras were involved.

"Patron's Pizza!" the voice on my phone chirruped. "How can I help you?"

"Yeah, hi," I said. "I'd like to place a delivery for a medium pepperoni with jalapeños. And some cheesy breadsticks."

The television host leaned in close as if we were sharing a conspiracy.

"Now Bev, you've got to tell me, do you ever get tired of, well, all the sex?"

"Never! I love sex!" Bev shouted.

Someone in the audience howled. Bev mouthed "Call me," and mimed a cellphone.

More laughter. I cringed.

"Would you like to make that a large? We're running a special so it's only 1.99," said the man from Patron's.

"Yeah, sure," I said. "Why the hell not."

I gave my address and credit card over the phone and turned back to my laptop. Television Bev leaned forward, her arm against the plush studio chair.

"Now, I want to be serious for a minute, George. If you've got a power like mine, using it is the only thing that makes sense," she said. "I want to help people. I want to change the world."

I paused the video and messaged T-Bone. His real name was Clarence, but it didn't quite fit his broad shoulders and beefy center, his body that seemed to sizzle as it walked.

U still coming over? Yep

I had to admit, that the stillness of my $5000/month apartment frightened me. I bought all the decorations myself —the burnished gold mirror, the lion mouth bookends, the vintage Tiffany lamps and the noisy crystal chandelier, but still, I didn't quite feel as if I belonged here.

While waiting for T-Bone, I turned to the news.

It became a compulsion of mine to watch the news late at night on my laptop, even though it was the same night after night — fire, rapes, beatings, bombings, police shootouts, with the same reporting from the same people who talk with scratches in their throats and sardonic quips like they have no faith in humanity left.

If I wanted to have sex with every adult in the U.S., which was about 125 million, and it took me around 7 minutes each time, that'd take me 875,000,000 minutes. I'm still really bad at math, but I didn't think I had that many minutes to spare. Still, I've had enough sex with criminals, bad boys, the mentally ill, trauma victims, that I thought I might see some sign that what I was doing mattered.

Instead, I just felt like we were getting closer to the apocalypse, night after night.

The doorbell rang. I thought it might be T-Bone, but it turned out to be the pizza delivery guy. He stood there with one of my security guards who'd escorted him to the door.

"Another late night, Bev?" the pizza guy asked, pulling the pizza out of the warmer.

"You didn't forget my breadsticks again, did you?" I asked.

"Definitely not," he said. "That's them on the top."

He glanced over at my security guard, who was standing stoic and pretending not to listen in on our conversation.

"I brought two pieces of chocolate cake," he said. "In case you know, you wanted company."

The pizza guy had dyed his hair since the last time I'd seen him — gone from smoke white to black. His skin and eyes were clearer. He no longer slouched when he walked. He stared at me underneath big baby eyelashes with an intensity that confused me at first.

Right. I'd forgotten we'd had sex one night after I'd ordered a medium pepperoni and told him he was too cute to leave without giving me a kiss.

"Oh. Oh! I'm sorry," I said. "I already have company tonight."

T-Bone appeared behind him as if summoned.

"Yeah, no problem," Pizza Guy said, fumbling to hand me my receipt.

I gave a nod to my bodyguard to let T-Bone pass. Pizza Guy disappeared.

"Was that a client?" T-Bone asked.

T-Bone carried a giant bag of groceries. A stalk of celery peeked out of the top. When he saw the pizza, his face fell.

"I wanted to cook something healthy for us," he said.

He'd lost some of his bad boy slump but he still had the lip ring and the ear gauges. He chewed on the lip ring then.

"Sorry," I said.

But I really wanted to say was *"Ugh, why did being good have to make you so boring?"*

T-Bone took up the entire doorway with his body like a

broken train. I found him on the subway a few months ago, busking with a 2-string guitar, somehow managing to make it sing like an infernal siren. He played the blues like he was hanging upside down off a cliff, played like it was the only thing that separated him from a chasm.

"How are you?" T-Bone asked, glancing at the cameras I kept around the apartment.

"I'm good. Sorry again, about dinner."

When I first met him, he didn't smile. His mouth used to be like a concrete cistern. It used to be only his eyes would light up, his mouth remained stern and concentrated. A smile still didn't seem to fit on his face.

"It's totally fine, I should have told you," he said. "I just thought, you know, we should be eating healthier."

He set the groceries down on my counter.

"Why do you keep looking at me like that?" I asked.

"Oh. Uh, it's just, you look good in sweatpants," he said.

"Err, thanks," I said. "I'm in lingerie all day, you know. The garter straps make my thighs red. I just want to feel comfy sometimes."

"I really like when you look natural."

I rolled my eyes. "Every guy says that."

We ate pizza on my white bed sheets and I perused the internet for more news. T-Bone ended up eating half of the pizza as he lay like an oil slick taking up half my bed.

He told me he'd been planning to kill himself that night I found him on the subway. He called me an angel that saved devils. He really had been playing on the edge of an abyss – I hadn't imagined it.

We watched a couple episodes of Daredevil while we polished off the breadsticks. About halfway through the third episode we began to slowly drift toward each other. Fuck, he still smelled good, like hot leather and wind and desert. I hadn't taken that away from him.

"Be gentle," I said. "I'm a little sore."

So we moved gentle, while Daredevil still played in the

background. We kept shifting to occasionally look at the laptop as he touched my hair and moved slowly in me. Soon I became bored and asked him to fuck me from behind.

"But I want to see your pretty face," he said.

I rolled my eyes again. He said such corny things now.

I missed the suicidal two-string guitar version of him. There must be some biological imperative inside of me to want the bad boys, boys who seemed like they lived in trees and caves, or crawled up out of the ocean, more scum and spore than a human being. My body always wanted to wrap around the dark fantasy they promised, the excitement of primal depth. Come on, let's create something new from something very, very old. Let's dance the dance that the molecules have been rearranging themselves to since the beginning of life.

Now I couldn't even seem to orgasm.

"Everything okay?" he asked while still inside me.

I couldn't orgasm because I'd just realized something about T-Bone.

He grabbed one of my vibrators out of the nightstand and I came when he used it on my clit, but it felt mechanical, because I knew it was expected of me.

Then I exploded. I shook and groaned, and the world tilted upside down, but I couldn't enjoy it because my mind was focused on a singular point. A singular, aching, infinitely important, and damning point.

T-Bone was in love with me.

Afterwards, we laid together and watched more television and I tried to keep the panic from swelling in my throat.

"That power you have," T-Bone asked me. "Do you think what you do to other people, you also do to yourself too?"

I sat up and gathered one of my silk pillows to my chest.

"What are you trying to say?" I asked.

He ran his hands through his hair.

"I was just curious."

"You think there's something wrong with me, don't you?" I asked.

I sank back down into bed and flung my arm over my eyes.

"No, baby," he said. "It's not like that."

"Don't call me that."

I rolled to my side, I found myself staring at the empty pizza box.

"Sorry. I'm stressed. I just have a lot of responsibility right now," I said. "Well, all the time."

"Have you ever thought of giving it up?"

"Giving what up?" I asked.

I knew what was coming because it'd happened with the last six men I'd brought home. Men that I found in their dark holes, and scum-ridden bars, and back alleyways. It happened every time I snuck away from my bodyguards and entertained romance with the alluring beasts that clacked and howled in the night with their bones bleached of love.

I made a strangled noise and buried my head in the pillow.

"Beverley," he said.

"No," I said.

"Beverly, I love you"

"No, you don't," I said, my voice muffled.

"What did you say?" he asked.

I lifted my head. I forced myself to turn toward him, to lift my body up in some semblance of dignity. I took a deep breath.

"I said, no you don't."

"How would you know?"

"You want me to quit my job, so we can be together, right?" I asked.

He said nothing. God, I didn't even want to look at him anymore.

"Beverly..."

"Would you quit saying my name like that?" I snapped. "It's fucking killing me."

I heard a ticking clock and for a moment imagined it to be a bomb.

"You don't want me," I said. "If you wanted me, you wouldn't ask me to do such a thing like quit the one thing that gives me purpose in my life."

"No, that's not—"

"Yes," I said, surprised at the ferocity in my voice. "It is. You want someone to love and it's not your fault that you think it's me because I'm the one who fixed you, right? When I found you in that subway you were broken and now you're not broken and you realize you don't want to spend your life alone, because time is precious and you're not going to live forever, and the only thing that truly matters is connections between people, right? You want someone to love, just not someone who fucks other men every day. That's just not who you are."

He stood up from the bed. "I guess it's not."

The silence that followed confirmed I was right.

"Just go," I said.

He opened his mouth to speak, but I interrupted him as I flung my hand toward his groceries.

"And be sure to take those with you. I'm sure they were expensive."

I managed to remain silent as he turned and gathered up the groceries, even though I felt like screaming.

I couldn't believe this was happening again.

I was supposed to be a goddess at the center of a temple, with fauns lounging around my painted toenails. I was supposed to be Kama Sutra 2.0., sex on tap forever, the center of a great colossal shift in human history.

I was supposed to be changing the world with skin-to-skin, weighty sighs, oh god, and silk sheets. Not standing here in this horrible mundanity of a moment, feeling bloated and dissatisfied, kicking another man out of my apartment because I knew I couldn't give him what he wanted.

Do you think what you do to other people, you also do to yourself?

When he left I doubled over in the pain I'd been holding in.

My bodyguard knocked on the door and asked me if everything was okay. I grunted something back, and he left me alone.

I laid on the bed for maybe half an hour, listening to the street noise below and the noise inside of me, its own gushing city of blood and magic. All the air seemed to rush out of me. I felt weightless, paper-thin like I was a floating consciousness inside a comic book.

Maybe T-Bone was right. Maybe whatever magic I gave to other people to fix their lives was somehow devoid inside me.

My gut churned. I grabbed my phone and send a text message to Pizza Guy.

Hey. You still want to eat that cake w/ me?

9

The businessman entered my office like a stiff billboard. He called me "Miss Sykes," and paid in cryptocurrency. I think he did something with computers, but almost everyone did something with computers these days.

"Is there somewhere I can undress?" he asked.

Maybe under different circumstances, I would've found his nice jaw and steely coldness attractive.

"Well, most people just undress in front of me," I said. "But we can get comfortable first."

He said nothing, just stood in front of me like a machine waiting for orders.

"You can undress over there," I said, nodding to the partition on the other side of the room. "There are some clean robes if you want one."

I scrolled through my twitter while I waited for him. I was nearing 4 million followers. People often @ me pictures of their great new lives, thanking me for the magnificent changes in them, when they weren't using my likeness for their ad campaigns for legalizing sex work (I was actually a sex surrogate, a bit of legal loophole) or deriding me for ruining society.

I scrolled through pictures I was mentioned in – travel

pictures to Iceland and Spain, pictures of weight loss, smiles that came easier, dinner with new friends.

One woman in fluorescent maternity clothes was hugging her red-cheeked toddler, and the text said:

"Thank you @theonlybeverly, now my husband can be the father he was always meant to be!"

Another tweet said, "Ayahuasca ceremonies, antidepressants, magic, and LSD couldn't solve my depression – but thanks to the @theonlybeverly, I'm living the life I always wanted!"

That morning I tweeted a picture of my rushed breakfast – a sparkly mimosa that I didn't have time to drink and the French toast and bacon that my personal trainer sent a text message to scold me about.

"Another lovely brunch! Need to fuel myself right for a hard day at work! #dream #brunchtime #livingright."

The businessman still hadn't come out, so I checked my Instagram as well. Yesterday I posted a picture of my office bed to show off the fresh eggshell-colored sheets. #readytowork!

Devil horns and eggplants littered the comments.

The businessman came out wearing one of my white robes, looking a little bit like a duckling with his big head and his skinny legs. I put the phone away.

"Do I just lay down?" he asked, glancing over at the bed on its raised platform.

"Whatever feels comfortable," I said.

He hesitated.

"What kind of music do you like?" I asked.

I turned on the purr and the charm, all in the eyes and the hips, and strode toward him. I'd had enough experience doing this that I could drip like honey as easily as turning on a water tap. But he didn't answer my question, and his shoulders tensed as I approached him.

"May I touch you?" I asked.

He nodded, so I took his arm and led him to the bed.

"Jenny, play playlist 1," I said to my smart system, and it began to play some non-intrusive ambient music.

He pulled off his robe. He still wore his undershirt underneath.

He couldn't get hard at first.

"I've got pills," I said, trying to keep my voice sultry. "You want some?"

"No," he said, sweating. "I'm on a raw diet."

I took a deep breath and then went down on him. I sucked on his cock, employing as much enthusiasm as I could muster, and he managed to get semi-hard.

When I came up I found him scrolling through his iPhone. He must've tucked it into one of the robe pockets.

When you first start to break, you don't even realize that's what's happening. The cracks form, little by little, webbing across your skin and heart, and when you finally realize what's going on the damage has already been done.

He didn't put his phone down even when I mounted him.

"We can put up some porn on the projector," I said. "I know I'm not everyone's type."

"No, I'm fine."

He didn't put the phone down.

I kept riding him, even though I was afraid his limp cock would slide right out of me. As that familiar pressure built inside me I tried to imagine I was floating on a cloud, in an airplane, on Mars. Anywhere but fucking a half-limp, bored businessman while he ignored me.

I exploded and our bodies rocked against each other. His face went pale and his eyes rolled up in his head and finally, he dropped his fucking iPhone.

After he left, I called Melly to cancel the rest of my appointments for the day.

"I'm not feeling well," I said.

"Oh, I'm sorry honey. Try melatonin and vitamin C," she said. "You should get lots of rest."

"No, I mean, this is more like a mental health thing."

"Oh," she said. "A shrimp cocktail and a pedicure, then? I can tell them to save your table at Tracy's?"

"No," I said. "That's fine. Thank you."

In the main office, one of my bodyguards waited at the door. He started to follow me as I was leaving.

"Don't bother," I said. "I'm just going to grab something out of the car."

"Are you sure?" he asked.

"Yep!" I said and bolted before he could get a word in.

I drove outside of the city in my new Lexus.

I rolled down the window because I wanted to feel alive and dangerous, but then I rolled it back up again when my hair blew in front of my eyes and kept getting stuck in my mouth.

I stopped at a greasy diner where the countertops were yellow with age and nicotine smoked the wallpapers. I stepped out onto the gravel, feeling conspicuous in my Louboutin shoes and Balenciaga bag and my Chanel jacket. I remembered being so excited when I was able to afford designer clothes, but looking at myself in the reflection of the diner's front, I realized I should've gone home and changed.

Oh well. Too late now.

I walked inside and ordered the breakfast special – eggs over medium, hash browns, sausage, and a stack of blueberry pancakes.

"And coffee. A lot of coffee," I said.

"Hungry, huh?" the waitress asked.

I lifted an eyebrow. She couldn't have been more than sixteen. She smelled of weed and Victoria's Secret perfume and had her bleached blonde hair tied back in a neat ponytail.

"I think I've seen you on Instagram," she said.

"Probably," I said.

"Beverly Sykes!" she said, smacking her forehead. "Wow. My dad talks about you all the time."

"Oh really?"

"Yeah," she said before walking off. "He thinks you're a fake."

I watched the news while waiting for my food. There's a possible impending war between the U.S. and North Korea, who may have been setting up secret bases in South America. The U.S. dollar was plummeting in value. Unemployment was rising.

"It's getting bad out there," the waitress said, returning with my coffee.

"It's always been bad," I said.

"Not this bad," she said. "Threats of atomic bombs every day. Polar ice caps melting. Tornadoes and volcanoes all over. And now we've got mutants walking the face of the earth."

"So I'm a mutant?"

"Well, you're not *normal*," she said, and walked off again.

I drank my coffee and flashed the busboy when he walked by. His face went red even though he quickly looked away and pretended he didn't notice.

He kept making different excuses to walk past me. Every time I caught him looking at me, I'd wink, and he'd stammer or glance away.

"So what are you doing all the way out here?" the waitress asked.

"Looking for love. Can you get me some more coffee?"

"You don't have love in L.A.?" she asked.

"It comes out on these little conveyor belts, like sushi," I said. "Prepackaged and prepaid."

"Yeah," she said, trying not to roll her eyes. "Okay."

"Coffee?" I said, pushing my cup toward her. "Also, you remind me of me you know."

She went to go get my coffee with a huff.

"I don't think you're looking for love," she said, almost accusatory.

"So what am I looking for?"

"I don't know," she said with a huff. "Figure it out yourself."

* * *

I slipped a note to the busboy to meet me behind the restaurant. He came to me in a way that reminded me of larvae squirming out of pupae.

"Who you are?" he asked. "I heard Jane talking, but—"

"You don't know who I am? Are you serious?" I asked.

He shrugged. "I don't really watch television. Are you an actress or something?"

"You mean, you just came out here because—"

"I'm curious. I want to know you," he said.

He took a step forward, and he sucked in air.

I ran my fingers along his chest. He shuddered at my touch.

"Okay," I said. "You can know me."

We fucked behind the dumpsters. The explosion inside of me came without warning. It rushed through us in huge milking waves, like the predatory gasp of the ocean. The busboy's eyes rolled back into his head as he came and he shuddered so hard I thought he might be having a seizure.

When he calmed down he leaned, pressing his chest covered in cold sweat against my shoulders.

"Wow," he said, breathing hard. "Really, wow. That felt so good. You're so gorgeous."

"Look at the stars, they're really beautiful out here," I said, but he only wanted to look at me.

"What's your Snapchat?" he asked after we dressed.

"I don't have one," I said, and headed for my car.

He called out to me, but I kept going. I climbed into my Lexus and his eyes bugged out at the sight of the car. I smiled, flushed. My last image of him was his face washed out and exhausted, a young phantom in headlight gleam.

In a few days, maybe even in a few hours, he'll begin to feel a great gushing change moving through his stomach.

Maybe he'll stop whatever he's doing with a sudden lurch as if he'd been shot.

He'll feel the blood welling up in him, but there'll be no wound. He'll look down afraid that he's falling apart, but all of his skin will remain intact.

And he'll hear something new, something he might have understood existed but never truly grasped until that moment — a symphony constructed from the rhythmic hum of everything in existence. He'd look back at his hands, and then at something in the distance, and realize they were connected. That he too, was part of that eternal, interlocking music.

Maybe, finally, he'll see the stars then.

PART 4

10

I was late for my therapy appointment. I'd worked overtime, again, and slept through two alarms. I had my driver pull me up to the front so I could rush inside. Dr. Angela held her office in what used to be an abandoned warehouse, and I had to walk underneath industrial fans through a long echoing hallway to get there.

This new therapist had come to me on a recommendation. I fired my last therapist after she told me I needed to quit my practice and treat my body with the respect deserving of a proper young woman. I should've done my research and found out she was hyper-religious before attending sessions. I'm sure she jumped at the chance to redeem Beverly Sykes, professional pervert.

Dr. Angela however, was like an angel that lost religion a long time ago.

Most therapists decorated their offices with seashells and serene pictures of beaches, with cerulean carpeting that was supposed to resemble still waters. She waited for me in an old upholstered red velvet chair that reminded me of a villain's throne. She'd papered over the steel walls with red and gold wallpaper and decorated with surrealist paintings from Dali, Kahlo, and Magritte.

Dr. Angela regarded me for a moment with the hyper-awareness of a predator when I burst into her office, panting and nearly bent over as I tried to catch my breath.

"Rough day already?" she asked, and nodded for me to sit on the gold-threaded couch opposite her.

I sat. I hadn't meant to just jump right into what was bothering me, but it spilled out anyway.

"I've gone numb," I told her "I'm 24 and I feel like an old lady. I can't feel anything down there anymore."

"I'm guessing you've already checked to see if it's a medical issue?"

I nodded.

"I'm in perfect health," I said. "Or well, I should be."

I glanced around the room, as I usually did when she lapsed into a prescribed silence. Her own photographs took up an entire wall. She liked to take portraits of people in various stages of distraction. Her "soul series," she called it. She said she placed it there to remind people that others are fully human, and that they too have moments of indecency, fear, and forgetfulness.

I liked her.

"I read this study recently," I said. "People who are promiscuous are generally unhappier than people who aren't. Crazy, right? I mean, not to religious nutbags, they think all sex is bad, but variety is the spice of life and all that. I mean, isn't it? I guess Susan Nordstrom who married her high school sweetheart, has a happier life than me."

"Correlation doesn't equal causation," Dr. Angela said.

"I know, I know."

"Don't do that," she said.

"Don't what?"

"Don't 'I know' me like that, like you can just dismiss the fact. If you're ever going to get to the truth, you can't just take what you want and throw out what you find inconvenient."

"God," I said. "It's a little annoying how right you are all the time."

"Hypersexuality is a symptom of many mental illnesses. But we know that's not the case with you. Your hypersexuality is a result of your unique condition."

"They call it Sykes Syndrome," I said. "All that means is they have no idea what the hell it is. What the hell I am."

"So you can't feel anything anymore," she said, steering the topic back.

When she leaned backward in repose she looked like an old-fashioned cigarette ad.

"Yes," I said. "Are you waiting for me to elaborate?"

"If you're numb but it's not a medical condition, that means you're disassociating," she said. "There's something you're avoiding."

I held my breath for a moment.

"Well, I know that I'm fucking bored," I said on the exhale. "Everything feels so clinical. I rented out a new office space — it's got a hot tub and a freaking yoga studio. I've got a whole wine cooler full of champagne. It's supposed to be fun, right? But it's not. Nobody is any fun. I'm just like a doctor performing a routine exam."

"What about your personal life?" she asked. "Do you find pleasure in that?"

"What personal life?" I asked, and laughed like an old toy winding down. "Boys don't want to have a girlfriend who's a glorified prostitute. Fuck, I can't even find anyone who just wants to have fun. If you sleep with me enough times you start wanting more for your life, I guess."

"You're catastrophizing again, we've talked about this. Plenty of people have trouble finding a partner, or a boyfriend," she said. "And there are plenty of sex workers who've been able to find love."

"I'm Beverly Sykes, and that means everything is different for me."

She waved her hand.

"That's just your ego talking," she said.

"My ego?" I said, trying not to sound like I was offended.

"Lots of people come in here thinking they're a special kind of horrible," she said, and she glanced at the wall of photographs. "But we're all people, and none of us are doomed to fail at being human, as much as none of us are fated to succeed. Maybe dating is more difficult for you because you're Beverly Sykes, but that doesn't mean it's impossible."

I sighed and sunk down further into my chair.

"Would you stop putting things into perspective for me?" I said.

I felt the people in those photographs watching me. Was it possible to feel the heat of an eye long ago recorded and no longer present?

"You could always quit, you know," she said.

I knew she was testing my reaction, but I still felt an involuntary wave of nausea.

"I can't quit. The world needs me. I have a purpose. How many people can say that?"

"Don't take offense to this, Beverly, but you don't strike me as the martyr type."

"What do I strike you as then?"

"As someone who was raised to be strong," she said. "Someone who doesn't take shit from anyone. To rely on no-one but yourself, and especially to not rely on kindness from others. You either give or you take, but you expect nothing back because you need to take care of yourself."

"This is the job I wanted," I said, fully realizing I sounded like I was trying to convince both of us.

"Yet you are here with me, and you say you can feel nothing. People who enjoy their jobs don't disassociate from them."

"I just want it to be exciting again," I said. "No, I want it to actually mean something. I mean, I'm not good at anything else. I just..."

I sighed.

"I guess I don't know what the hell I want anymore."

Time was up.

* * *

Bruce Lee escorted me out of the building. When I got back to the office, Melly told me I had an appointment in ten minutes.

"Fuck, I thought I at least had another hour. Who is it again?"

"Ray McGontmory. He works in finance."

"Of course he does," I said.

I went into the bathroom and popped a benzo.

In the mirror my face was red as if I'd been crying.

I pressed my fingers to my eyes and felt the bags underneath. Fuck, I shouldn't have eye wrinkles. I'm only 24.

Time moved so fast I'm being dragged behind it.

I pulled my shirt up and pressed my fingers to my stomach.

I went lower and unbuttoned my jeans.

With a sharp intake of breath, I pushed my fingers into my pants.

I slid a finger into my cunt. I might as well have passed my finger through a portal in space-time, for all I felt. When I rubbed my clit it was like touching a clone of myself who stood alone on a dead world.

Melly sent me a text message. I jumped at the noise.

He's here.

I undressed quickly, grabbed some lingerie, and headed to work in the next room.

You could always quit, you know.

Ray stood in the middle of the room fiddling with his apple watch.

"Would you like some chardonnay?" I asked. "I was thinking maybe we could soak in the hot tub for a bit."

"Oh, sorry," he said, not looking up. "I've got another appointment in an hour."

"Yeah," I said, heading toward the bed. "That's what I thought."

While Ray the finance man was on top of me I fantasized about working in an office. I'd wear a cream colored blouse and a gray pencil skirt and have my long blonde hair up in a top knot. I'd even wear glasses although I didn't need them. I'd make coffee and answer phones like Melly. Maybe I'd even have a boyfriend with meaty hands and emotional scars, who'd get into fights at the bars and not come home until 4 in the morning. He'd want to pick a fight with me until he saw I laid his work clothes out next to mine for the next morning. He'd melt into my sweetness, and we'd have sex until the sun came up.

And most importantly he'd never tell me things like, "Have you ever thought of giving it all up?" or "Sorry, I have an appointment in an hour."

"Earth to Miss Sykes," said the man on top of me, jolting me out of my fantasy. "Where'd you go?"

I tried to think of something funny to say, but for once nothing came to mind.

11

Every week, I headed into the local clinic to get an STD check. I sat on my phone playing Angry Birds as the nurse took my blood and went into the back room.

"Hey Norma, kids doing okay?" I said when she came back, and stood up to leave.

"Hold on," she said. "Don't leave just yet."

I glanced up from my phone for the first time since I'd entered the clinic that day.

"Your test results came back with something," she said. "You have chlamydia."

"Are you fucking kidding me?" I said, and groaned. "You're kidding me, right?"

Norma's face, almost gray, like a reflection of the blood suddenly rushing out of my heart, held no punchline.

"Chlamydia is very treatable," she said. "You'll need to take antibiotics and abstain from sex for a week."

"No way! I'm already behind schedule!" I said. "I've been trying to cut my sessions in half just to fit everyone in! And why did I have to find out about this right before my radio interview! It's live, you know!"

I pressed my face into my arm, clutching my Hermes bag to my stomach. The world seemed to lurch underneath me.

"This can't be happening," I said. "I screen everyone beforehand."

"Even if there's just a few hours between the screening, it's possible they became exposed between then and the time they saw you again," she said. "And some STDs can have a dormancy period. Short of jailing people between tests, there's no foolproof solution."

"What if it was HPV?" I asked. "Or fucking AIDS. What if they'd given me goddamn AIDS? I'm Beverly Fucking Sykes! I'm not supposed to get STDs!"

I leaned so far to one side that a tube of YSL lipstick fell out of my bag.

"Miss Sykes, try to put things in perspective. This isn't the end of the world. Not yet anyway."

"Sorry," I said. "Sorry. I'm ranting."

I scooped the lipstick off the floor and rushed out to pay my bill.

I ran out of the office with sweat beading on my forehead. When I breathed it seemed like little daggers insinuated themselves into my lungs.

* * *

I called my mother as Bruce Lee drove me home. I curled up in a ball in the back seat of my car.

"Bev?" she answered after a few rings.

"I'm sorry, I don't know who else to talk to."

I sucked in air and swallowed the sob.

"What's going on?" she asked.

"All I wanted was to help people," I said. "And I get treated like trash. To them I'm just another slut."

"Bev, have you been drinking?"

"No!" I said. "Just listen to me, okay?"

I couldn't stop the tears.

"You haven't had a good day today, have you, baby?" she said.

I balled my hands into fists, trying to force the tears back. But of course, that only made it worse.

"They don't fucking deserve me," I whispered.

"What happened?" my mom asked. "You're not in some kind of legal trouble, are you?"

"No, mom," I said.

"Then what is it?" she asked.

I felt like if I tried to sit up straight, my spine might pop out the top of my back and my eyes might slide down my blouse.

"I have chlamydia," I whispered.

"Oh honey," she said.

"This week it's chlamydia. What if next week it's something worse? Do you know how many times people have tried to kill me? Kidnap me? I haven't, because I lost count!"

I pulled myself up into a seated position.

"Are you still there, Mom?"

"I'm here," she said.

"What should I do?" I asked. "Because I can't keep doing this."

"You mean you actually want my opinion?" my mom said. "What do you want to do, Bev?"

I took a deep breath, and forced myself to slow down my panicked heaving.

"Not this," I said. "I feel like I'm just bleeding my life away every day. Am I really helping the world that way? I want to do something real. Something important."

"Then you know what you have to do."

"No. I really don't."

"It's your life," she said. "You have to make it happen."

I swallowed.

"Yeah. I guess."

"You know."

We'd just pulled up to the front of my apartment complex. I checked my face in my compact, raw and red.

"Get what you need, baby," she said. "It's the only way."

"I've got to go. I've got an interview. We're pulling up now."

"K7 101 right?" she said. "I'll be listening online."

"I love you, Mom," I said, my voice weak, like there wasn't enough air behind it.

"I love you," she said, and I couldn't remember the last time we'd spoken those words to each other.

But they'd been hanging in the air between us that whole time, waiting for the wind to pick them up.

* * *

I wiped away the excess mascara with some makeup wipes in my purse, and forced myself to stop crying. The tears would only make me ugly. I couldn't find my lipstick in my purse, it must've fallen out again, but I reapplied powder to my cheeks just as my driver rolled up to the studio.

A silver glitter bomb slammed against the tinted window. I jumped at the sudden noise, and powder flew everywhere.

"Beverly! Beverly Sykes!"

Fans stood outside on the sidewalk chanting my name and photographers snapped pictures as I stepped out of the car. I probably looked like a partially-reconstructed trainwreck, but still men and women alike waved signs that said SEX GODDESS and SEX B-B-B-BOMB and LOVE ME ROUGHLY. Fourteen-year-old girls stood on tiptoes with bubbly eyes and nude lip gloss and screamed. Fourteen-year-old boys made their best sexy pouts and jostled each other trying to get a better look.

So young, I thought, but I'd barely been older than them the first time I had sex.

Bruce Lee gave the keys to a valet and guided me through the crowd.

"Oh, thank God you're here," said the receptionist.

She ushered me into the recording studio right away.

A tech sat me down and showed me how the mic worked.

"Are you okay? You look a little pale," said a breathless intern in a cocoa dress.

"I'm great," I said, rubbing one eye.

"We're on in two minutes."

The tinkling intro music played and a headache formed in the back of my skull.

"And we'd like to welcome to our show a very special guess. Beverly Sykes!"

I leaned into the microphone.

"I am so happy to be here!" I said, and cleared my throat.

I didn't recognize that voice. When had I developed that fake voice? When had I lost myself underneath the mountain of daily bullshit? I started living the image I constructed until it seemed to be living instead of me. It wasn't really me who posted on Instagram and created sponsored videos about skinny teas and made pretty pleas to donate to sexual abuse victims.

I'd abandoned myself. The real Beverly was somewhere back in that diner I went to three years ago, eating overcooked eggs and asking for more coffee.

"Miss Sykes?" the announcer said, and I realized I hadn't heard anything he'd been saying.

"I'm sorry," I said. "What did you say? It's been a very hectic morning."

"Oh, do tell?"

"I, well, I'd rather not," I said.

The intern frowned on the other side of the glass.

"Well, Miss Sykes, like I was saying, what does a typical day look like for you?" the host asked, trying to bring back interest with his booming voice.

I wake up dragging my bruised body behind me like a carcass and fuck people I hate while I try not to scream, who then repay the favor by ignoring my rules and giving me STDs. Thanks, bitch, here's your gift.

"Oh, you know, I don't really have a typical day. I lead such a crazy life. Who knows what's in store for me when I wake up?"

It sounded like something a cartoon character would say. Or something printed on the back of a cereal box. The host waited for me to elaborate and a pregnant pause ensued. I sucked in air and tried to think.

"I mean, I never know who's going to show up in my office!" I said. "It could be a celebrity, or a politician, a philosopher. I meet so many interesting people!"

I laughed heavy. The intern seemed to be looking around for emergency exits.

"For those of you just tuning in, we're talking to Beverly Sykes. Yes, THE Beverly Sykes, and let me tell you, folks, she is just as lovely in person if not more so."

The host's frown seemed to spread from his forehead to his neck.

"So tell me, Beverly, what kind of challenges have you faced in your career?"

"Well, there's always lots of crazy fucking people," I said, and then, "Shit, I can't cuss on the radio, can I?"

"We'll bleep it out, don't worry," the intern said.

"Any cool stories?" the radio show host asked. "We're all just dying to know what it's like to be Beverly Sykes."

"That's confidential. I can't talk about my clients. Didn't my people go over that with you before the show?"

Silence.

Silence like a wound gaping open and then being sewn back.

The host's expression changed to something between embarrassment and chagrin. The oil slick on his big forehead seemed to ripple.

"What about when you were sixteen?" he asked.

"What about when I was sixteen?"

"Well, ah, we did some digging and found that—"

"You found what?" I interrupted.

"Your math teacher in high school, Mr. Ainsworth. He died shortly after coming into contact with you."

It took me several seconds before I could reply.

"I haven't made that a secret," I said, my voice coming out scratchy and worn. "He assaulted me. Did you bring me on the show just to ask me about him?"

"Did you use your gift on him, Beverley?"

My insides pulsed with the memory of my math teacher. It was an old feeling, or so I thought, but in that moment it was scratching and heaving and alive.

"Mr. Ainsworth had no history of violence or depression before he came into contact with you," said the presenter. "And yet he killed himself with a pair of scissors. A rather violent way to go out, isn't it?"

"They found child pornography on his computer after that night!" I said. "His wife found out and was going to divorce him. If you're trying to say that he was some kind of saint, you really fucking suck at doing your homework. Oh, sorry, I swore again."

I leaned back in my chair and took a deep sip of my coffee.

"Hey, can I get some sugar?" I asked the intern with as much violence as I could muster.

She jumped and scurried off.

The host continued.

"People think you're a savior, that you dole out miracles — simple as taking a pill. But it's a bit more complicated than that. Wouldn't you say, even dangerous?"

I forced myself to unclench my jaw and place my hands on the table. I wouldn't let that asshole see how angry I was. I wouldn't give him the satisfaction.

"I can't be held accountable for what people choose to do with what I give them," I said.

"But knowingly imparting a dangerous—"

"Look, let me be clear. I want to make the world a better

place," I said. "The world is a better place without pedophiles and rapists like Mr. Ainsworth. I knew that, and after he raped me, he *raped* me by the way, I had no choice in the matter, he knew it too. If you think making the world a better place is all rainbows and butterflies, that real change doesn't fucking hurt, then you're just naive. Where is my sugar?"

"Miss Beverly—"

I dropped the microphone and rushed outside. My bodyguard followed after me.

"Send a text to get the car, please," I said.

The sunlight hit me like a fist. I put my hand over my eyes to shield them.

Outside the crowd was silent. The fourteen-year-old boys went slack-jawed. The teenage girls huddled together, gaping.

A woman in a beige suit stepped forward. She had her hair in such a tight top-knot, I was surprised her face hadn't torn at the bottom.

"Miss Sykes, on behalf of the New Prestige Foundation, I'd like to give you a recommendation list."

She tried to thrust the list into my arms, but I shoved it back into her hands with such force that she stumbled backwards.

"I don't give a fuck about your lists!" I shouted. Several people dropped their signs and gifts. Their faces slid down into contorted, angry masks. A bald, middle-aged man with an "I heart Beverly" t-shirt raised his fist and screamed my name like a curse.

My car pulled around and I rushed toward it.

Someone tried to grab the car door. Bruce Lee pushed them back, positioning his body between them and me.

"Get in!" he shouted, and when I did he slammed the door shut. I locked the door behind me. People spilled out on the street. A young woman with dreadlocks and a navy jacket jumped onto the hood before we could drive away. Others crowded in front of the car, a soda can slammed against the window, followed by half of a fast-food burger. I flinched. The ketchup looked a lot like blood.

Bruce Lee ran around to the other side and dove into the front seat. He had to kick away a young man who was waving his arms like a helicopter, and then forced the door closed. He locked it afterward.

He honked the horn, but that made even more people spill out.

"I'm calling for backup. Sit tight, Miss Sykes."

They began to rock the car.

I tried to maintain my composure and hold back the tears, even as I felt my blood might bubble up and spillover, as if I might be left dried and hollowed out, nothing but a husk with an expensive balayage.

"So," I said, clearing my throat. "While we're waiting, you remember when you mentioned to me you had a few 'special connections' from back in your secret service days? People that worked on global scale, underground kind of government stuff."

A brief pause, as the woman on the hood leaned in and screamed, shoving her middle finger against the glass.

"Yes," he said. "I do remember that."

"I'd like that number," I said. "If you don't mind."

A shirtless man walked out of a nearby gas station, holding an old boom-box over his head and blaring some kind of 80s metal and screaming something incomprehensible at my car. The people around us continued to rock the car, screaming.

Someone shoved their head into my window with such force that the glass cracked. A little bit of their hair embedded into the crack.

I sighed.

"God, I hope I don't have to go waste another day in court over this," I said.

Bruce Lee gave me the number. I called and they picked up on the first ring.

The voice that answered was genial and smooth and bright, like sugar in good coffee. After the experience at the radio, it startled me.

"Miss Beverly Sykes."

"Yes, that's me," I said. "How did you—?"

"We've been expecting a call from you for a while," came the voice on the other side, not losing any of its brightness.

A police car pulled up behind us. Two officers jumped out and cleared the people off the sidewalk, giving Bruce Lee just enough space to begin maneuvering out of the parked space near the sidewalk.

I swallowed.

"I want to help you change the world," I said.

A pause.

"Are you to calling to arrange a meeting?" he asked. "We don't like to conduct business over an insecure line."

A man holding a torn "SEX B-B-B-BOMB" sign threw himself in front of the car. Bruce Lee slammed on the brakes. The car squealed and I lurched forward. I had to press my hand against the seat to keep from being thrown.

"Is everything all right over there?"

"Yes!" I said, and then cleared my throat. "Yes. I'd like to meet."

"Excellent!" he said.

The police grabbed the man and pulled him out of the way. Bruce Lee gunned the car and we raced out into the street.

I lay down in the backseat, phone still cradled to my ear as the man on the phone discussed the details of our meeting. I felt hot as if with fever as we drove away, but I was shivering all over. With fear. With anticipation. With the hope that maybe tomorrow wouldn't end like this.

12

I headed inside of Moxy's lounge a little earlier than planned. A cool breath of air blew my hair back as I entered. The bartender sat underneath neon white light, his fingers the color of strobes as he cleaned a glass.

"Your table's ready upstairs," the bartender said to me, "Your guest is waiting."

So he'd come early too.

I ascended the marble steps into the soft blue light. He sat waiting at my table, his arms folded, a pomegranate mojito in front of him.

"This is for you," he said by way of greeting.

The pomegranate mojito was my favorite drink at Moxy's.

But I knew it wasn't just a nice gesture. He'd bought it for me to show me that he'd been doing his research. Watching me.

My anxiety surged. I forced myself to walk forward and sit down, but it felt like an iron bar had suddenly been implanted itself into my back.

I knew a dangerous man when I saw one. He reminded me of a snake bent through broken machinery.

"Beverly Sykes," he said. "I'm glad you reached out.

We've been watching you for quite a while and we think you have great potential."

I couldn't tell if he was the same man I'd spoken to over the phone, but he had the same smooth and bright tone to his voice.

He nudged the drink toward me.

Not sure what exactly to say. "I'm looking to expand my business. To make more of an impact," I said. "Why should I work with you?"

He smiled. "An excellent question and right to the point. Although I believe over the phone you used the words 'change the world,' which have quite a different meaning." He took his glasses off and revealed his powdery blue eyes. Maybe it was supposed to make me less intimidated to be able to see his eyes, but it only made my gut tighten. "I've looked into your past. You are an intelligent young woman, despite your terrible academic records. You're business savvy. Witty. Many young women who discovered they had such a gift as yours would not have the foresight to see the potential and create an empire. And yet—"

"And yet." I repeated.

"We had always thought it was a shame, that you were not used more intelligently," he said.

"How should I be, *used*, as you put it, then?"

"Look, nobody else can tell you how to use your gift, and you're a headstrong woman. I can tell just by looking at you. But if you really want to change the world, you've got to have a strategy. You need to target the people that really have the power."

I stared down into my pomegranate mojito. It looked like the bright, cheery blood of a fairy.

"Have you watched the news lately?" he asked.

"I wish I could stop," I said.

"So you know the whole world is tearing itself apart?"

"Tensions in the middle east and Asia. Shadow governments in South America, civil war. Rumors of terrorists coming to U.S. soil. The works."

He tilted his head just slightly to the side.

"What?" I said. "I read when I'm not fucking."

"I know you want to fix some of that," he said. "And we do too."

I took a sip of my mojito. The nerves strained in my mouth and neck.

"It'd probably help me sleep at night."

"I know you went to some lengths to contact us. You're lucky that many of the employees of the security firm you hired have past ties with us. We're very difficult to get a meeting with. But then again, you are a very special woman."

"And yet I still don't know what you do, not exactly," I said.

"I work for an organization that technically, doesn't exist," he said. "We have locations all over the world. Our thumbprints are all across the global network."

"Organized crime?" I said. "Or like the Illuminati? I'm not interested in furthering some—"

"No. Neither," he said. "We have contracts with several governments. We provide services that are outside their usual jurisdiction. For the common good, so to speak. We contract out specialists, among several of our other services. Specialists like you, for instance."

"Who do you want me to sleep with?" I asked.

I forced myself to take a sip of the mojito, like this was all routine to me.

He leaned back and regarded me. He seemed to be keeping a pressurized cold back with every word he spoke, and when he breathed it was almost as if ice curled underneath his nose.

"You really are like they say," he said.

"Like what?" I asked. "What do they say about me?"

Instead of answering me, he continued.

"There is a very dangerous man currently living in an

undisclosed location in Guatemala," he said. "A terrorist. We can't eliminate him directly, because he's got ties to the government and it would cause too many problems. But we can—"

He paused, waiting for me to fill in the gap.

"You think I can change his mind about his occupation," I said.

"Yes. If he no longer has the affinity to cause trouble for us, then he ceases to be a problem."

"There's a chance it might not work, you know," I said. "I can't control what my gift does. It depends on the person."

"We know," he said. "We're willing to take the risk."

"And why would I risk it?" I asked. "You said he was dangerous. You're dangerous. I don't even know if I can trust a single word you say. How can I?"

He raised an eyebrow. There were mountains underneath it.

"You can't. But to answer your question. Why would you risk it? It doesn't really matter to you if you are appreciated, does it?" he said. "Or that you're famous. Or that you have a fancy apartment and fine things. What matters is that what you do feels real. That it feels right. Am I right?"

Breathe in. Breathe out. I felt like I could fit the whole world inside.

"Yeah," I whispered. "You're right."

"This would be something right. Something important," he said. "You would change the world, like you told us you so desired. Do you still want to change the world?"

"Yes," I said. "Of course."

"But that's not the real question, is it? We're not even having the real conversation."

"What's the real question, then?"

He leaned forward across the table, and the air seemed to cool around him. He glanced briefly at my neck, and then lower, inspecting my body, before slowly returning to my eyes. I caught a whiff of his cologne, the musky scent of him as if chilled against his skin. For the briefest moment, something long dormant in me fluttered.

"I told you, we've been watching you for quite a while. We know more about you than you can imagine. I know why you are so tired all the time," he said. "I know why you have a soreness that goes beyond the physical. I know why you're so bored that you feel like a fire's gone out that cannot be reignited."

Then he asked me:

"Would you like to feel something again?"

13

The knock on the door came exactly at 4 A.M. Right on schedule.

I'd been awake waiting up for them, unable to sleep, my blood feeling flush with new electricity. I opened the door and found two burly Hispanic men in dark sunglasses waiting for me. They took up the width of the hallway like two silent, well-oiled machines.

"Are you ready, ma'am?" they asked me.

"Yep."

I headed for the door with my overnight bag.

"Sorry ma'am," one of them said, holding out his hand. "We have to hold that for you."

"Seriously?" I asked, and trying to be funny, I said, "I need my silk pajamas when I sleep."

Neither of them met my eyes or laughed. "There won't be time to sleep, and it's primarily for your safety."

I handed over the bag and with the both of them on either side of me, we headed out into the parking lot.

A black Hummer pulled up. The three of us climbed into the back. "Sorry again, ma'am," the same man said again. "We're going to have to blindfold you. For your—"

"Yeah," I said. "For my safety."

They blindfolded me, and I leaned back in the seat, trying to relax. They didn't speak the entire ride. About an hour later, we were on a private plane and I sat shoulder-to-shoulder wedged between them as the engine droned. Again, we sat in crushing silence that seemed to lay over me in thick, oppressive folds.

"So," I said. "Seen any good movies lately?"

They said nothing.

"I don't really go to the theatre anymore," I said. "I don't really have the time."

"We can't talk to you unless absolutely necessary, ma'am. Those are the orders."

"Can we listen to music at least?"

No response.

"I'm really just going to have to sit here and do nothing?"

Again, no response. I sighed and sank down into my seat.

I didn't know how much time passed, but the minutes became glued together with excruciating boredom. The hours passed without sleep, or even a sip of water.

Finally, we landed. They escorted me off the plane with a grumbling stomach and full bladder.

Wherever we were, it was hot. The muggy heat quickly lay thick in my lungs.

"Christ," I said. "Can I take the blindfold off at least? It's so goddamn hot, I feel like I'm going to suffocate."

"Not yet," they said.

"Let me use the restroom at least. I'm going to explode."

They took me to the restroom and escorted me into one of the stalls. I took the blindfold off and wiped the sweat streaming from my eye sockets. I only saw the gray concrete and the dirty toilet. There were no windows, and I didn't want to chance taking a peek through the cracks in the stall. I peed, placed the blindfold back on, and went back out.

They led me back outside to a waiting car and guided my head so I wouldn't hit it against the sides as I ducked into the back. There was no air conditioning, and my legs quickly became glued to the leather seats with sweat.

"Can you at least tell me how long this is going to take?" I asked.

Of course, they didn't.

* * *

When I was finally allowed to take the blindfold off I found myself in the lobby of an abandoned hotel. The hotel might have once been elegant, but its color had been rubbed out with time. The carpet was stained with a gray-green and mold grew along the ceiling. Outside, it was nearing dusk, and purple light pushed through palm tree leaves swaying next to a drained pool.

I rubbed my eyes as we headed toward the elevators.

"I need to warn you, you are about to meet a very dangerous man," one of the men told me. "None of your usual jokes."

"How is he dangerous?" I asked.

We got onto the elevator.

"When you meet him, do not speak to him unless spoken to. Address him by sir. He speaks English very well, so you shouldn't have a problem communicating with him. Show no signs of disrespect. It might be best if you do not look at him."

"And what's so important about him?"

"That's classified," one of the men said. "You've already been told that. You are on a need to know basis. And all you need to know is you are here to fuck him."

We went up in the elevator.

The boredom of the last few hours whirred away, to be replaced with a thick, pulsing anticipation.

I wondered what I would find when the doors opened. I imagined a silhouette at the end of a hallway, its gaunt shoulders and smooth faceless head.

Its arms opened wide for me.

One of the men leaned in so close to me that his mustache tickled my cheek.

"He can smell fear," he said, his voice stripped of its robotic politeness.

I said nothing. I wanted to appear like what he said didn't phase me, but I had to admit when he said that my heartbeat seemed to push itself into my head.

And maybe I was just weak from low blood sugar but the world underneath me felt like wet cardboard. Like one step and I'd fall through.

"He may not be receptive to what you have to offer, depending on his mood," the other man told me. "If he seems hostile, I'd advise you to leave immediately. We'll be waiting for you in the lobby."

"You're not coming with me?" I asked.

The elevator opened on its destination floor, and they ushered me out into the hallway. The elevator doors closed. They were gone.

If I didn't think too much about the smell or look at the cockroaches flitting back into the darkness beneath the windowsills, I could imagine I was eighteen again, walking through a sunny resort in Mexico back when I still liked the way men moved without any clothes on, when I still liked the taste of my expensive perfume on someone else's knuckles.

Or maybe I should imagine I was on that vacation in the Bahamas I took a few years ago, on a cruise ship that circled lazily around the island as I gorged myself on cheesecake and Mai Tais and sex for five days straight. I fucked my way through the cabins until Friday night, when the cruise liner parked and I went down to the beach with a fair-headed party boy, flexing that muscle inside of me until we were rolling together in the twilight sands.

I wondered if it'd have been different, if I knew back then I'd never quite feel the same way again. I reached the one open door at the end of the hallway, and swallowed a bundle of nerves in my throat before entering.

* * *

The man stood looking out the window, his hands behind his back. I could tell by the stiffness of his posture that he'd been waiting for me. He had a laptop on the desk beside him. The screensaver was a woman in a sarong standing on a beach underneath a dipped-red sunset, and that red light flickered against his shoulders.

"Hello, Mr..." and that's when I realized they'd never given me his name. "I'm—"

"I know who you are," he said, cutting me off. He turned to me, dark-haired and unshaven, with the kind of eyes that sucked all the heat out of a room. The secret muscle inside of me pulsed with such a ferocity, I grabbed my stomach.

"Is something wrong?" he asked.

I shook my head.

"Undress," he said.

My insides spasmed again.

"Who are you?" I asked.

"Do as I say," he said, in that casual way people do who are used to being obeyed.

His gaze seemed to penetrate my skin, and pain radiated through my entire body.

"You are the girl with the magic cunt, are you not?" he said, his words sharp.

I nodded.

"Undress," he repeated. "And then come here."

Another violent spasm traveled from my chest to my groin.

The way he said *come here* reminded me of Mr. Ainsworth. It had a mercury coldness to it. A coldness that could only come from years of honing sociopathy like a skill. My first instinct was to freeze. Suddenly I was sixteen years old again, with my shoulders trying to hide my heart and my hair in my eyes the only weapon I possessed. I could see a phantom moon sliding in front of me, as it did that night across the window's iron bars.

No. I had to keep going. I couldn't freeze.

I slid out of my skirt, trying to ignore it, trying to imagine Mai Tais on the beach.

I unbuttoned my blouse. He kept his eyes on me the whole time, examining every trace of my skin as it became exposed.

I felt just like that. Exposed.

I took a hesitant step forward. And then another, but still kept my distance from him.

"You are just a small-town girl," he said. "You are what little boys imagine when they think of the American dream, just a petite blonde sip of creamer. It's hard to imagine what you're carrying inside of you. The power that you possess."

"Yet here I am," I said.

"Yes, here you are," he said. "Tell me, what does your husband think of you being here?"

"I don't have a husband," I said.

"Of course you don't."

He moved toward me like a subterranean animal. I commanded every muscle in my body to hold still, to not scream and run.

"Go to my desk," he said. "Bend over."

"You first," I said before I could stop myself.

* * *

He was on me faster than a light switch shutting off.

I thought he was going to hit me, but instead he laid his hand on my collarbone with an almost gentleness. I tried to control my breathing as he pressed his thumb against my throat.

"They brought another girl here earlier," he said. "They told me that she was magic. She was nothing like you, and the power of her sex had been greatly exaggerated. I was offended by her appallingly mediocre presence, her audacity to exist in the same space as me."

He cradled my face as he spoke.

"So I gouged her eyes out," he said.

"You're just trying to scare me," I said, my voice strained.

"Am I?" he said.

It took every ounce of strength in me to not flinch when he pressed his fingers against my cheeks, the tips against my bottom lashes.

"We'll take it slow," he said. "Would you like to kiss me?"

His lips hovered over mine, but I didn't move. With him this close to me, I felt light-headed. There was nothing remarkable about his body, and he was, in fact, a little overweight, but raw power came off his skin in waves, like he could break my bones or fold my body in half with his mind.

"Do I frighten you?" he asked.

"No," I said.

He lifted my body without any noticeable strain and shoved me against the wall. The wall quaked, and my teeth vibrated.

"Ask for forgiveness," he said.

"What?" I said, my voice faint.

"Ask for my forgiveness, for lying to me."

"I'm sorry," I whispered.

He released me from the wall and my knees buckled. I found myself actually clinging to him to keep from falling.

"Now tell me again," he said. "Are you afraid?"

"Yes."

His lips once more came close to mine.

"Say it," he whispered. "Just so I know you understood."

I sucked in air and my lips quivered.

"I am afraid."

As I said it I found myself parting my lips, angling my body toward his.

We kissed. The kiss ignited me from the roots of my hair to the bottom of my toes. It was a kiss that engulfed my entire body and bore down on me so hard I could do nothing but cling to it. It was a kiss that demanded everything in me. It was a kiss that would've grabbed my soul and squeezed, wrung it out until there was nothing left but a spasm in its place.

* * *

I'd never been in love but I always imagined it would feel like this. We moved toward the bed. He lowered me down on the sheets, knelt and kissed my ankles and thighs. Everywhere his lips touched me it was like he was eating light, sucking up the heat stuck to my skin. Being touched by him was like being pushed into the underworld. His hands slid up my thighs. I grabbed the sheets underneath me and squeezed as if to orient myself, back into the physical world, so that I wouldn't be lost in his touches. I wondered what horrible things he'd done. How many people he killed. He gripped my shoulder in one hand with a murderous and cold pressure.

"Do you feel this?" he asked.

I realized he'd slid a finger inside of me.

I shook my head.

"Not surprising," he said, as his finger worked inside of me. "I had suspected that might be the case."

He slid another finger into me.

"Would you like to know why?" he asked. "Why you can feel nothing?"

I knew I couldn't lie. Not again.

"Yes," I said, my voice crumbling.

"It is because you have no passion in your life," he said. "A girl like you has been run ragged by the desires of others, and you have forgotten your own. The girl with the magic cunt has no magic left inside of her."

He pulled my legs up over his shoulders.

"I can give you your passion back," he said. "Would you like that?"

Maybe it was the way he said the word passion, like a river polishing a stone. Maybe it was the way his unflinching stare seemed to focus the world down into a tunnel between our faces. Maybe it was the adrenaline surge, focusing me on this pivotal point as if for the first time in a long time I was actually and truly present in that moment.

But I found myself nodding. Yes.

Yes, *please*.

He smirked.

He pressed his mouth against my vagina and flicked his tongue across my clit.

* * *

I began to feel again.

It returned to me slowly, like ice melting into water over my skin. And the more it melted, the more I felt until I became soaked in it, caught in the grip of it, seized by sudden, overwhelming sensation.

Fuck, it'd been so long since I felt anything at all.

I don't know what it was about him that was different – many of my lovers had gone down on me in the last few months, but I was more bored than anything else.

Pleasure like a long languorous wave rolled over me. His tongue worked slowly at first, then faster, until it was humming and heavy. And all the while he went down on me he had his thumbs pressed into my inner thighs, making small circles as if to remind me that I was caught in his grip. He wouldn't let me forget for a moment that I was his prisoner.

I came hard and gasping.

Then his cock was inside of me.

I found myself reaching up to kiss him. My thighs parted, and my hands grabbed his shoulders to pull him in deeper.

"How did you do that?" I asked, breathless.

"I told you," he said. "I know who you are."

That's what I'd been missing.

That's what I'd been missing since Spider on the rocks, since the days of house parties and teenage summers lost in a kind of motionless bliss. What I'd lost through all the years of trying to make the world better by being crushed underneath rich boys with languorous sweat and fat fingers. Every time his cock pushed into me, I felt ripples of pleasure bending throughout my being.

But as he moved in me I became aware of a new sensation. Not the pressure of an orgasm, or the pressure of my explosion building in me.

Something else.

Something cold and spoiled.

I realized then, why he understood my body and my gift.

If the magic inside me was small and golden and hot, his was like a dead hand floating underneath a sheet of black ice. And he's building pressure inside of him like I'm building pressure. That's what my insides had been trying to warn me about, why they'd clenched at the sight of him.

I tried to pull away but he pinned my arms above my head. I struggled fiercely underneath him, but he held me casually with one hand with an enormous and easy strength, as if it meant nothing.

"I have always wondered," he said, his voice surprisingly even, "What it would be like for someone like me, to love someone like you."

He continued to thrust inside of me as he spoke.

"You wouldn't believe how difficult it was to get a hold of you," he said. "It took me this long because I was convinced you were a fake. But well, indeed, you are very real."

"You mean you brought me here for this?" I asked. "They told me—"

"That you could help fix the world?" he said. "Yes, I made sure that they'd mention that to you. I knew you were a bleeding heart, searching for purpose."

For every psychopath, sociopath, convict, mentally-ill, drug-addicted person I'd been exposed to, I'd only ever met one other person who was truly evil, someone I could not fix.

"Like I said and I'll say once more," he said. "I know who you are."

Mr. Ainsworth became the rot that only merely dusted the other people's souls. The only way to escape his own darkness was to stab himself to death with a pair of scissors.

But this man inside of me was worse.

"Would you like for me to love you?" he asked.

I spit on his cheek. He laughed.

"After I'm finished loving you," he said. "You'll never be able to love again."

I hated the way his touch brought waves of pleasure, building pressure, even as whatever dark thing inside of him insinuated itself into me, like a snake worming its way into a new nest. It wanted to get into my heart. It grew bigger, and longer, as it spiraled into me, pulsing to such a size that soon I knew it'd tear me apart.

"I want you to get off," I whispered.

"I intend to," he said.

I tried to move my arms and buck my hips, but it was useless. I couldn't fight him like that.

I closed my eyes.

I focused all of myself down into that muscle inside of me.

I became so used to it being there, being a part of me, that I rarely flexed it anymore. I'd been spoiled by its gift, even some days resenting its presence. But I needed it now.

I knew if this man's energy, like black milk, got too far inside of me I would be gone.

I would be replaced by a kind of creature that had my name and wore my body, but it wouldn't be me. Not anymore. The girl who once walked down that high school hallway wearing Forever 21 crop tops and a new breath of exhilaration would be an echo of another life. Even the tired girl, bent out of shape, who thought she might crumble with each step, would be gone as well.

Maybe I'd become like him, a cold and savage misogynist fuck who gouged people's eyes out and feasted on my own self-importance. Or a petty parasite cashing checks from desperate men who thought they needed me. Or maybe a lunatic unable to claw my way out of the paranoiac chambers of my head, sitting forever in the black shit that'd become my new mind.

It'd feel like there were scissors slicing through the thin skin of my wrists as I sat in a steely classroom trapped in moonlight forever.

That's what it'd feel like to have magic leave you.

He pressed deeper into me. His heartbeat dripped on top of me. With that inner magic I tried to pry him away from my bones. He wound further into me. Sweat broke out all over my body. He was stronger than me, and we both knew it. It'd been too long, I'd become withered and weak with the lack of passion inside of me, and now I'd pay the price.

The tendrils of blackness, gushing up through me like rotten air, hovered inside my body. An animal over its kill. He was taunting me with his power, watching me struggle, waiting to take me.

"Do you remember what it felt like the first time?" he asked, taunting me. "Would you like to imagine that I am your first lover?"

It wasn't Spider I remembered, but that feeling. 2 A.M. star shine.

Breathe in. Air feels cool. Breathe out. Air is cooler. That night my chest felt like a cavern and I could fit the whole world inside.

I sucked in air.

I actually felt the hoary frost of that air nearly a decade ago, as it came winding through time.

I held my breath, and the coolness spread through my lungs.

I exploded.

The pleasure was overwhelming, like having an orgasm

that could rearrange DNA. Like the landscape of me was ruptured permanently, so that no old landmark would be recognizable ever again. I couldn't feel my hands. I couldn't feel my face. All I felt was the buzzing hum of the new sun that I'd become. I was a new being composed of light, and my consciousness floated above the scattered molecules. His face emerged from the light. I slowly sank back down into my body.

He whispered something.

"What did you say?" I asked.

His face turned white. His lips parted.

"Don't," he said.

"Don't?"

"Don't *stop*."

I rolled on top of him. I grabbed one of his arms and pinned it above his head. I slammed my whole body down on his cock. With his free hand, he clung to me like someone falling.

I flexed the thing inside me again. I obliterated every piece of him that tried to invade me. I was strong. I never realized how strong. My warmth was back. My feeling was back. The sensation of glittering magic that'd been scraped out of me by years of banal duty sex was back.

I pushed my light into him, dissolving the rottenness from his bones until he was born anew.

* * *

I got up to leave after I was finished with him.

He said with a new kind of weakness, "Watch the sun go down with me."

I wanted to laugh but when I glanced over at him his dark face had sunken down, and his mouth was parted like a child's. He held out his arm for me to snuggle up against him.

I felt worn out and gleaming, like a bowl full of gold slowly emptied.

I came close and cuddled him, my knee in between his legs, my arm across his chest. He squeezed my shoulder and we lay together with our breathing synchronized.

He looked at me with eyes extinguished of their frozen darkness and said, "You are one of the prettiest girls I've ever seen."

As if I hadn't been taken here, blindfolded, to have sex with him across the ocean so that he could take my gift away. As if he hadn't just tried to rape me and erase everything inside of me.

The shadows lengthened over the bed as we lay together. I calmed listening to his breathing.

"Would you like something to drink?" he asked me after a while. "Rum?"

"Yeah," I said, surprised how calm I sounded. "That sounds nice."

The hotel was quiet, and in the parking lot below there were no cars. We could've been on the precipice of the world, for how quiet it was.

He poured us rum from a bottle on his bureau. He handed me the crystal-cut glass and sat behind me. He drew his knees up and pulled me into him. I drank the rum as he played with my blonde hair. My eyelids felt heavy. I could've fallen asleep in his arms.

The sun went down. As red painted the sky he kissed my neck, my cheek. I felt his erection stirring against me, and thought maybe he'd try to have sex with me again.

But instead, he got up and moved toward the desk with a silent calm.

My stomach sank into my groin.

"Hey. Wait," I said.

He stopped and turned to look back at me for a moment.

"Can I ask you something?" I asked, my voice cracking as I said it.

He nodded, and a bright flush like a jewel seemed to shoot up my throat.

"Are you afraid?" I asked.

Maybe for the first time in his life pinpoints of light entered his eyes like cracks in a dense webbing of darkness.

"Say it," I said. "Just so I know you understand."

He opened the drawer of his desk. I tensed.

"You have a bright future ahead of you," he said. "Remember who you are, and you'll never go numb again."

I held my breath and my hand shook, spilling rum across my lap.

"And you're right, I am afraid," he said, "but less so now."

He grabbed a gun from the drawer and put it to his head.

My blood roared so loud I didn't even hear the shot.

* * *

The agents found me lying facedown on the bed. Everything hurt. I felt foreign to myself. I wanted to throw up, but there was nothing in my stomach. My bones seemed to have sharpened against my insides, and I thought they might puncture my organs. Even nighttime itself felt like a razorblade against my thighs. I knew that I'd never leave that room with my whole self intact, but in that moment I didn't even know how to move away from the broken pieces of myself.

I knew where he lay dead. Even though I wouldn't look over at him his body seemed to be denser than the earth's gravity, pulling my mind into the center of the room.

I heard his whispers echoing through the room long after he pulled the trigger. Like he'd blown his ghost out onto the walls.

"Excellent work, Miss Sykes. Having you on the team will be a great asset."

I sat up on my elbows with my arms shaking. One of them grabbed my clothes off the floor and threw them to me.

"I'm never doing this again," I said.

I dressed. The clothes on my body felt too heavy. Being in a body felt too heavy.

The other draped a sheet over the dead man and carried him out of the room.

"As you wish. The rest of the money will be deposited in your account tomorrow, like we agreed. But if you change your mind—"

"No," I said, with all the gravel in me. "No. I won't. Get me out of here."

I wanted to scream, but I didn't think there was even enough air in the room left to breathe. I huddled inside of me, and flinched when the agent turned to look me in the eyes.

"Not to worry. We'll be returning to L.A. shortly," he said.

"No. Not L.A., I want to go somewhere else. Somewhere I don't have to interact with people. I should probably lay low for a while."

He nodded. "Okay. We'll take you somewhere safe."

"Somewhere cold," I said. "Somewhere cold as hell. I don't want to see any more damn sunsets."

He just nodded brusquely at my strange request. Maybe he even understood.

The other agent came back, brushing his hands against his pants. The three of us headed toward the elevator. I could barely walk straight. At one point I slipped, and one of them had to catch me by the arm so I wouldn't fall. That's when I realized I'd left my shoes back in the room.

I definitely wasn't going to go back and get them.

"Are you all right?"

"I just watched a man kill himself," I said. "Again."

We headed into the elevator. The molecules inside me seemed to be being burning up, because every time I took a breath they seemed to swirl and singe me.

I didn't know why I kept finding new ways to hurt.

New ways that I couldn't seem to contain the pain.

Was this what growing up felt like? What taking control of your life felt like? Old tragedies in shiny packaging, gifted to each of us again and again?

When we reached the lobby, one of them brought out a blindfold.

"Put that on me, and I'll bite you," I said.

To my surprise, they put it away without comment, and let me into the plane.

It turned out they didn't need the blindfold. I couldn't see anything by the time we lifted off. The tears were my blind haze.

PART 5

14

I found myself sitting on a freezing toilet, staring down at a pregnancy test. The last log in the furnace downstairs had died an hour ago and I could almost see frost forming on the walls.

I never really realized how long two minutes could be, how many shades and variations of thoughts and emotions I could transition through, until that moment I sat waiting for the results to appear.

I felt like I could have run from the tip of the earth into the sun in those two minutes.

My bare feet were cold against the tiles. It was snowing outside, and I couldn't see anything outside the window except the blinding whiteness of Alaska. The brightness of it stung my eyes every time I looked out the window.

I cupped the pregnancy stick in my hands. My eyes hurt, and I realized I hadn't even blinked for god knows how long.

I rubbed my cold feet together.

The nausea had been so bad that I hadn't put on pants before lurching to the bathroom to throw up. It'd come on about a month after I'd been in Alaska.

When I closed my eyes I saw his body facedown on the floor.

And I saw his eyes like dragon spit as he plunged his fingers into me. His eyelashes fluttered against my cheek like corrosive acid and his whisper thrummed through my inner ear.

He was always both alive and dead inside me.

I rubbed at my teeth with my tongue. I still tasted his lips, and it wouldn't go away no matter how much I scrubbed.

And you liked it.

I threw away what little clothing I had. I bought used clothes from Goodwill and chopped off my hair. I didn't need Balenciaga bags and Fenty sneakers and YSL makeup and expensive lace pajamas.

I needed to look in the mirror and see a version of myself who never spread her legs wide to let evil inside.

But every time I did I saw his fingers on my throat.

I covered the mirror with a quilt to keep from seeing the bruises.

But the entire earth had become a mirror to reflect back the things I didn't want to see.

When I switched channels on the television, a woman appeared with mascara running down her face. Her lips were bright red, and a bruise lay brushed over her eye with sloppy makeup.

"You liked it!" she screamed.

I lunged for the remote and shut the TV off.

At that moment, my phone rang. I answered without glancing at the number.

"Beverly Sykes? This is a representative of The President of the United States. We'd like to—"

It took everything in me not to scream.

I hung up.

My phone buzzed again. I grabbed it and threw it out in the hallway.

I assumed it was the government. They'd been wanting

me to meet with The President for weeks, but I hadn't responded.

It should've been the highlight of my career that the President of the United States wanted to meet with me. Two months ago, I would've thrown a party to rival New York's New Year's Eve, but the thought of having sex again made me go numb from feet to fists.

So I ignored the calls, and the emails, and the messages as they kept coming.

Two minutes had passed. I shoved my fist in my mouth, something I hadn't done since I was a child.

The symbol appeared on the pregnancy stick.

You already know what happened.

I went out into the hallway. I leaned against the wall and closed my eyes. I felt like I was standing on a tight-rope made of frozen crystals, and the ice was extending upward through my toes.

I dropped the pregnancy stick and it landed face-up on the carpet. The little plus sign might as well have a big neon emblazoned sign.

I touched my stomach but I couldn't feel anything except how much my teeth ached.

Do you have his eyes? I asked the baby, that a few seconds ago I didn't know existed.

Do you have his smooth voice and his dragon confidence and his poison blood?

* * *

I needed to think.

I needed to think without panic scraping its black teeth against my brain.

Without feeling like my ghost was slipping out my lungs with every breath.

I went back out into the woods. The cold seeped through my coat, and the snow looked like charcoal in the dusk. I blew air out my cheeks and headed further into the dense trees.

I forced myself to breathe even with the icicles forming on my lungs.

My phone rang and rang in my coat pocket.

But as I walked, I filtered out all the noise and the stillness expanded around me.

His phantom stood behind me. It was always right behind me, no matter where or how far I walked. Every spot was a cold spot then, but he was colder.

His shadow rattled like a snake.

It's mine, you know.

I could feel his breath like nitroglycerin on the back of my neck, and his phantom fingernails scraping against my back.

I shook my head, freed my hair, forcing his illusion to move backwards.

No, I thought suddenly.

It's mine, came the ferocious hiss inside of me.

Then he was gone.

The stillness was ground into a powder, became loneliness, and I wished I didn't have to be out here, exchanging angry whispers with ghosts.

I sat underneath the trees, on a fallen branch. The wetness sank into my pants.

I wanted someone to hold me, just once, since all of this had begun.

To cradle my face and wipe away the tears brought to my face by monsters in human skin.

To tell me it was okay.

I wanted *my mommy.*

I pulled my phone out of my pocket and went to her contact info. I stared at the words "MOM" for several minutes before I inhaled like taking a plunge into deep ice water.

And then I called her.

Just like always, she answered on the second ring.

"Bev?" she said.

When she spoke, her voice crackled over our weak connection.

"Mom?"

"Oh Bev! Thank god you're alive."

"Mom," I said, rocking back and forth a little against the tree. "Mommy."

I clung to her voice.

"Where are you? Turn on the news, Bev," she said.

"What's going on?" I asked.

"It's horrible. You have to see for yourself."

The crackling grew louder. Whatever had just happened didn't seem like it could possibly be as big as what I saw on the pregnancy test.

I didn't hear anything except her panicked breathing, distorted by the connection.

"Mom, I'm pregnant," I said.

No response. The hair on my arms raised up.

I pulled the cellphone from my ear and saw that the call had been dropped.

* * *

I stumble back home and turned on the television.

At first all I saw was smoke.

It seemed to fill the room. I became sucked into it. I seemed to breathe it.

I fell to my knees and didn't realize it until I found myself hugging the television, drawn into the image.

My nausea disappeared into the static sea in front of me.

The scrolling marquee at the bottom of the television said: Bombing in Manhattan. Hundreds Suspected Dead.

They played footage on repeat. People stumbled onto the pavement, bloodied and crying. A firefighter dragged a young girl out of rubble. A young couple, their foreheads bleeding, stumbled together across the street.

A woman wailed off-camera like she'd never be able to put the pieces of herself back together.

The sky filled with fire.

The camera angled upward, showing the neighborhood now reduced to rubble and ash.

I recognized that neighborhood. That apartment building.

That was my apartment building.

I found myself grabbing my stomach, as if trying to avert the eyes of the child I now knew was inside me.

A reporter spoke with a shaky voice. She kept running her hands through her hair, as if trying to clear away invisible debris.

"We're still trying to gather information about the bombing that happened a few minutes ago in Manhattan. The number of dead is as of yet unknown, but suspected to be at least in the hundreds. We'll be here as more information comes to light."

The President appeared on the television with gray skin like a sick reptile. He clutched the podium like he needed it to stay upright. He opened his mouth to speak, and for a moment, couldn't. Then he cleared his throat.

"In light of this tragedy—"

I switched channels, trying to see if I could catch any more footage of my neighborhood.

I came across mugshots of several people displayed on the screen.

I recognized one of them. I had to clap my hands over my mouth to keep from moaning.

"We're currently investigating several suspects in the bombing—"

That face.

That face had breathed its poison into my lips.

That tongue had been inside me.

I thought the earth might try to squeeze my own body out of my ears. And for several seconds, I couldn't move at all with the pressure.

I forced myself to reach up and turn off the television
I headed toward the mirror I'd thrown the quilt over.

Ever since I tried to disappear, the world kept showing me
new ways that I couldn't hide.

I pulled the quilt down.

My reflection stared back at me as if we didn't recognize
each other. My eyes were upset mirrors. My splotchy red
nerves had broken out across the bridge of my nose like fire
ants.

I couldn't look away anymore. I wouldn't let myself.

I had known people in that building on that block.
Clients. People who'd worked for me. Even friends. They'd
died because of me.

I had holed up here in the dark Alaskan winter, letting the
cold pinch me as punishment because I didn't want to do the
work to fix what I'd done.

I pulled my sweater up and turned to the side to examine
my body in the mirror. I couldn't see any indication that I was
pregnant. Not yet.

I pinched my stomach, then pooched it out, imagining
what it'd look like when I was swollen.

Then I grabbed my cell-phone and made a call.

They picked up on the first ring.

"Beverly Sykes? Have you considered our offer?"

When I spoke, it sounded more like me than anything else
I'd said in the last few months. I'd gotten used to slinking
around like a whisper. And as I spoke I forced myself to stare
at myself in the mirror, at the belly that'd soon be squirming,
and I found the legs underneath my words.

"I need protection." I said. "I'm ready to work with The
President."

15

The Secret Service escorted me through a network of badly lit underground tunnels. I didn't know where we were, not exactly, we'd gotten onto a private plane and disembarked on a private runway, then driven out beyond the edges of a nowhere town. Then we'd taken an industrial elevator down into a sort of underground living quarters.

At least they had the courtesy to not blindfold me, but I didn't know how much more walking I could take. My feet were swollen and the baby had decided that day it wanted to be a tap-dancer on the inside of my uterus.

"How much longer?" I asked at one point, but they didn't answer me.

Finally, they led me to a room at the end of a hall of identical doors. The President stood in the center of the small room waiting for me, his hands at his sides.

He must've dropped 20 pounds since I last saw him on the television. I expected him to rustle like paper when he moved. He seemed not just haggard, but hollowed out, like someone had scooped out all his organs and left only the skin.

"Miss Beverly Sykes," he said. "I wish we'd been able to meet sooner. But you've been quite a high-profile target."

I took off my trench-coat. I was visibly pregnant underneath in my too-tight tank top and sweatpants, which were the only pants that seemed to fit me these days.

"Yeah. I just wish people didn't have to get caught in the crossfire," I said.

"Luckily we've been able to track down most of these terrorists. Now I think with your help, we can do all we can to mobilize the recovery effort."

I glanced around the plain white room. I fantasized about fucking presidents and kings, but never in a windowless, undecorated space like this. Never on a bed with such simple cotton sheets next to a little oak nightstand that looked like it came from Ikea.

I wondered if there was lube in the nightstand drawer, at least.

He nodded to the security and they left.

"They'll be just right outside the door. If at any point you feel uncomfortable—"

He began to sweat. He was much smaller in person, and I realized he was going prematurely bald.

It was easy to forget that the leader of the free world could have sad eyes like everyone else.

He looked at me in that way I'd seen a thousand times before. And it was a look that said *rescue me* and it was a look that said love me and it was a look that said *make me believe in the power of existence with the curve of your naked spine.*

I imagined him trying to explain to the First Lady what he was doing that day. And her response, "Yes, honey, I know that you have a responsibility to millions of people to be the best leader you can be, but do you really have to have sex with that fucking whore?"

I began taking my clothes off.

He stared at my bare breasts and bit his lip and I realized I was going to have to talk to him to ease him into this.

I started with some small talk. "I know what's wrong with you."

"What?"

"Ever since you were a child you dreamed of being president, right? You worked all your life to get here because you knew you had the capacity to change the world. And you did. You change the world. But then—"

"But then what?" he asked.

"No matter how much you changed the world, you felt the same."

He said nothing, and I knew that meant I was right. I took one of the folding chairs propped up against the wall and sat down. He did the same. We sat there for several minutes without speaking. Like most of my clients who came to me, he was expecting me to make the first move.

"Why did you come to me?" he finally asked.

The baby kicked and I put my hand on my stomach.

Nobody ever told me how difficult it would be to carry around a second heartbeat. Once in high-school, we had to carry around sacks of flour to simulate taking care of a baby, and we were graded on how much flour was left at the end of the week. I tripped and fell off my skateboard, scattering flour everywhere, and got a D—. Janna got so sick of the assignment that she baked cupcakes out of hers and showed up to class with them.

It was nothing like this feeling now, starting in my throat and working its way down into my uterus, a warm feeling like standing in the heat of an oven but somehow, that oven was in an empty dark field.

"Are you doing this for your baby?" he asked.

"That's one part," I said.

"And the other parts?"

I stretched out and laid one of my legs on his lap. I kneaded the muscle of his thigh with my toes.

I thought it'd be physically painful to touch another person again, and I admit that I felt a hesitant twinge as I stretched my leg out. But the moment I made contact with his skin, my heart sped up with excitement.

Yes. I had to admit, I missed this.

"Then for what?"

"You're quite handsome," I said. "You've got a certain something — you know? I bet it makes women go crazy."

I withdrew my foot and climbed into his lap, the bulge of my stomach between us, and I kissed him. He tried to return the kiss but he was hesitant, and there was no energy in it.

"I'm making you nervous," I said.

"No, I—"

"I want to tell you something."

I brushed my lips against his earlobe.

"I dropped that bomb on my apartment."

"Don't be ridiculous," he said. "Insurgents dropped the bomb. We already know that."

"I fucked a terrorist because I wanted to fix the world," I said. "And I did. He was a terrible man, and I made sure he wouldn't hurt anyone ever again. But because I did that, even more people had to die. I didn't think about the possible unintended consequences of what I did. Not even for a second."

I wasn't sure how I expected him to react, but I definitely wasn't expecting what came next.

"So what? Are you going to blame yourself? If we took responsibility for every flutter of a butterfly wings, we'd all be damned," he said. "Is that why you decided to do this? Come to me? Because you felt guilty?"

"No," I said. "Because the world doesn't stop moving if I stop trying. Maybe someone else could stop, but I can't. I have to keep trying to fix this."

"I think I have some idea what that feels like," The President said, and for a moment he was a thousand years old, dust accumulating in the space behind his eyes.

"I thought it was the Beverly Sykes Show, 24/7," I said. "But it isn't. There are more lives at stake than I ever imagined."

I paused.

"Oh! I almost forgot. Thanks for reminding me. I want something."

I got off his lap and went back to the pile of clothes I'd left on the floor. I withdrew a folded piece of paper from the pocket of my sweatpants.

I walked back to him and gave him a list. He unfolded it.

"What is this?" he asked.

"Everyone in your cabinet," I said. "that I think would benefit from my services."

"I can't authorize that," he said.

"I think you can be very persuasive. Even more persuasive when we're finished here. But that's not all I want."

"What else?" he asked.

"I want you to put me on retainer, for as long as your presidency lasts," I said. "I have an amazing power, you know, not to brag. I sometimes forget how amazing but I haven't been using it in the best way. I want to maximize my potential. "

"Why?" he asked.

"Do you really have to ask me why? Aren't you trying to do the same thing?" I said. "New York was in smoking ruins. Every time you turn on the television something else is going to hell. I think we can change that."

I touched my stomach. They said pregnant woman glowed. For a brief moment, I felt it. I was like an animal who'd scratched away at the dirty skin until it touched pearl underneath.

"Because I still want to try to save the world," I said. "Starting with this. And after this, no more goddamn fluff piece radio interviews, no more special edition perfumes or sponsorships. I'm not a fucking celebrity. I should've demanded that I be treated with the respect that I deserve."

"What are you, then?" he asked.

I stirred in his lap, grinding my hips against his. I felt his erection underneath me.

"I'm a goddess," I said.

I laughed. I actually laughed. It came so easy and free like it'd been maturing inside of me for months, while in Alaska I scratched my legs on the floor and threw up in a cold bathroom. Everything in my body harmonized and focused down on this moment.

I wouldn't be surprised if sparks flew off my fingers when I touched him.

"You have no idea how good it'll feel to excise all that shit from your brain once we're finished. But if you don't agree to my terms, then you'll leave here the same as you've always been. Do you want to spend the rest of your life wondering what it'd be like to be brand new? As far as I know, I'm the only one who can do what I do."

His erection swelled.

"You're right, Miss Sykes," he said.

"I'm going to need it in writing," I said.

I moved out of his lap. The President cleared his throat and pulled a phone out of his pocket. A few seconds later one of the secret service men came in.

"We need to draw up a new contract," he said to the guard. "A few revisions are needed."

A lawyer came in and for the next half hour we worked up drawing the contract while I sat naked (daring anyone to say anything about it). When the contract was signed and The President and I shook hands in front of the lawyer, everyone tried not to look at the way my breasts bounced.

"Congratulations," he said.

"No," I said. "I should congratulate you."

The lawyer whisked away the files and the secret service disappeared with him. Then once more, we were alone, staring at each other like we were waiting for another explosion to go off. I wondered briefly how many meetings he had to cancel to be here with me.

The President began to undress. I found out he was actually quite toned underneath, despite his huge weight loss. I'd expected him to be wrinkled and deflated, but there was still youth in him.

Instead of throwing his pants and shirt on the floor he actually got up to fold them over the back of one of the chairs.

He sat back down on the bed and seemed to relax for the first time since I'd entered the room.

"Okay," he said. "Does this excite you?"

"Does what?"

"Fucking the president."

He blushed a little when he said the word fucking, and his husky timbre faltered on the word just enough for me to notice. I giggled and climbed onto the bed beside him. His erection began to stir again. The way he looked at me made me feel sinuous even in my pregnant body.

"I never imagined it quite like this," I said.

He leaned up on his elbows.

"How did you imagine it?"

"Oh, you know, I'd be the leader of my own country, but it'd be in a space station. I'd be on a levitating throne above the planets. You'd come to me riding a space tiger."

"Space tigers?" The President said.

I burst out giggling again.

"What?" he asked, actually smiling a little.

"Here I am, telling The President of the United States about my absurd sex fantasies," I said.

I stretched out on the bed and imagined that the sunset splayed across those white sheets. I imagined being dressed in snow white wolf furs and diamonds, shedding them as I moved.

This was what it felt like to be myself again.

To shed the worn skin I'd worn for years because I thought I had to fuck bored people who didn't appreciate my gift. I fucked people who didn't really want to get better, but who thought having sex with me was just another way to exercise their power and influence, just another way to show off their status.

My real self didn't need to appear on magazines and radio

shows, and obey the whims of the public that thought they owned the ways I should help them.

To focus on the singular want, and discard the rest.

"Let's make it fun," I said. "I know the whole world's at stake, but we should make it fun for once."

He kissed my breasts, one after the other.

"What were you saying about the space tiger?"

My skin felt like a nuclear reaction strained through a fine white mesh.

"Yeah, okay, so you're riding on a space tiger and – wait a minute. Is there lube in that drawer over there?" I asked.

"I don't think so."

"Yeah, okay. Nevermind then."

I straddled him. My huge pregnant belly pushed against his hips.

I hadn't had sex since that night with the terrorist. I thought maybe I'd become too damaged to do it anymore, that I'd flinch or freeze and be unable to go through with it.

Or worse, I'd be so numb and hollow inside that I'd become like a cavern without an echo.

But I gasped when he pushed his cock inside me. I found pleasure driving into me, and when his fingers found my ass and he squeezed, ripples of sensation passed through my entire body.

I hadn't lost that feeling.

I bent to his fingers, arched my back, felt my body winding itself to an ancient rhythm.

The baby kicked again.

All the chains inside my nerves unlocked and I let him in.

My magic built inside my stomach, small and timid at first, like a glowing coal struggling not to grow cold in the dark.

But it became stronger.

It grew hotter, and bigger.

"You're really something else," he said.

"I haven't even gotten started," I said.

He kept his eyes on me the entire time, looked up at me with something almost like adoration, but also something like fear.

Reverence. That was the word.

The President of the United States, naked and underneath my pregnant body, hands on my ass, his cock inside of me, leader of the free world, thought I was a goddess too.

I felt the explosion building.

I felt myself coming closer.

I felt the rubbing heavy grinding blinding pressure of a celestial flood ready to burst through both of us.

16

I slid down into the hot tub holding my pregnant belly with champagne froth on my lips and warm bubbles in my hair. Across from me sat the Vice President, and in the corner on a royal blue divan, his wife lay in a bathrobe sipping Grenache.

Steam fogged up against the night glass of the suite, and I felt encased in a transparent rocket. We were nearly fifty stories up, in the Vice President's favorite honeymoon suite, and the night seemed to be spinning around us.

The baby kicked, as if awoken by the warmth of the tub.

"You're close, aren't you?" said the Vice President's wife. "You look about ready to pop."

"She's rattling my teeth," I said.

"Yeah, I remember my first," she said.

My phone buzzed on the edge of the tub. I leaned over and checked it. It was a message from my mom, showing me a few bassinets to look at.

The one with safety bars looks good. Oh, and have you bought a stroller yet?

Another buzz. A notification on my calendar for another baby class tomorrow. Shortly before my next doctor's exam and another meeting with The President.

Time still moved at the same pace, but I seemed to need more and more of it.

I glanced up. The Vice President was on his phone.

"I have a few rules," I said.

"What are they?" he asked, without glancing up.

He reminded me of The President's dark twin, if he had siblings. Smaller, with glassy eyes and a deeper voice, and hands he never quite knew what to do.

"Whatever I say they are," I said. "And the first one is to get off your damn phone."

"But you—" he said, gesturing at the phone in my hand.

"Yeah," I said. "But that's me."

"Okay," he said, putting the phone away. "Sorry."

His wife in the corner smirked.

I moved toward him across the giant hot tub, through the jets, feeling like a mermaid with the ocean churning underneath me. It was as if I could hear the second heartbeat swelling in my ears.

I held my arms out to him. Come. Come with me into the sea. I've got a glass window in my hair and the earth underneath my feet.

I'd forgotten that sex could be the channel between reality and mythology. That it could turn anything into a story.

"Are you sure this is okay?" he asked. "With—"

He placed his hands on my swollen belly.

"Yes," I said. "The doctor said it's fine. With any luck, this'll help speed things along."

He took me in his arms, and seemed to find a new strength in his fidgeting hands when he pinned me against the side of the tub.

"What's going to happen to me?" he asked.

"Do you ever look into the mirror and wonder how you can see all the mistakes etched in your eyes, and you wonder how nobody else can?"

He glanced over at his wife. She hadn't moved.

"That's going to go away," I said. "And one day you'll look

into the eyes of your reflection and forget that you ever saw something you felt you couldn't live with."

He didn't need much more pressing. He drove his cock into me and after I exploded we crawled out of the tub like shipwreck survivors. I collapsed against the bed, still wet and naked.

I didn't have time to enjoy my post-sex endorphins, because my phone rang with its special ringtone.

"Can you hand that to me?" I asked.

The Vice President gave me my phone.

"Are you finished? I'd like you to come into the office," The President asked when I answered.

"Don't we have an appointment tomorrow?" I asked.

"This can't wait," he said. "I've been up all night thinking about this new Environmental bill and I'd really like your feedback. And I thought we could go over a revised schedule for you. I have new—"

"Okay, okay," I said. "I'm coming."

I hung up.

"Duty calls?" asked the wife.

"Work never ends," I said. "I've got to go."

I reached for my clothes and started dressing.

That's when my water broke.

It felt like a weird popping sensation. I stopped what I was doing and stared down at my round belly.

"Uh-oh," said the wife, smiling underneath her curled ringlet hair. "Is that what I think it is?"

"I don't know," I said. "Maybe?"

It wasn't like in the movies, where a fire-hose amount of water spewed out from between my legs. It was more like a little trickle, so subtle it could've been almost mistaken for accidentally peeing myself.

Then I felt a strong contraction.

"Yeah," I said. "I should go to the hospital."

"I'll get your car to come around," the Vice President said, and he dressed and ran outside.

His wife tossed down the rest of her Grenache.

"I'll walk you out," she said, taking my arm, her body trailing a smell like acid and rose perfume.

I felt suddenly dizzy, and was glad she was there to guide me around the walls.

"Remember, the first is always the hardest," she said.

I walked down the hallway unaware of my surroundings. My head became a tunnel I was crawling through.

My security caught up with me in the lobby, and she handed me over. We went outside, and the cool breeze was a relief against the heat burning against my skin.

When my car pulled up, the Vice President, face flushed, ran toward the door and opened it for me. I climbed inside feeling like a wet balloon.

"I think it's working!" he called out as we drove off.

* * *

On our way to the hospital, I called my mom.

"It's coming," I said. "Are you going to be here? I need you here."

"Yes, I already said I would be," she said.

"Just get to the airport like we talked about," I said. "I have a private jet waiting for you."

I glanced down at my belly. When the car moved, it rumbled, and I imagined my stomach splitting like a fertile egg.

"Mom. I'm scared."

I'd be worried if you weren't scared."

"Just say something reassuring," I said. "Please."

"The baby's right on time," she said. "All of your check ups were normal. You're healthy. The baby's going to be healthy. Everything's going to be fine. Just like we've talked about."

I felt like I had to breathe deep or the air would evaporate out of my skin.

"But what if something happens?" I asked. "What if...what if I lose my gift? What if I can't help people anymore? I mean, it could happen, right? It's not like there's much research on the subject."

"Just keep breathing," my Mom said. "In and out."

"I just want you here," I said. "And I want everything to be okay."

"I will be," she said. "And it will be."

"But what if it's not?" I said.

I felt like a small child wanting to be cradled, as if the baby inside me had made me give birth to a younger version of myself.

"What if I can't do this? What if I'm a terrible mom? Oh my god, what if she has my gift too? How am I supposed to explain to a child what I do for a living?"

"Beverly," she said. "Just think. When your father left us, we had nothing. I was scared to death what it'd do to you. I thought maybe the reason you were having so much sex was because you didn't have a father figure."

I groaned.

"Then you nearly gave me a heart attack when I first saw you on the cover of Times, but—"

"Mom," I said. "What's your point?"

"The point is," she said. "You turned out fine. Everything's going to be fine."

Another contraction came. I braced myself.

"Are we there yet?" I called out to my driver.

"Almost, Miss Sykes," he said. "Just try to hold the baby in."

"Beverly. Repeat after me," my mom said. "Everything's going to be okay."

"Everything's going to be okay," I said forcing the words out through my teeth.

Even though I didn't quite believe it, my body began to relax.

"The baby is going to be fine," she said. "And we're going

to be fine. You'll have me. You can come back home and you don't have to do this alone."

Tears welled in my eyes.

"Are you sure?" I said. "I know my old apartment is rubble, but I can stay in Washington and hire nannies and—"

"Come home," she said.

"So we can be a family again?" I said, and my voice cracked.

"We always were, baby," she said.

* * *

We pulled into the hospital parking lot and I said goodbye to my mom. I'd had my baby bag packed for the last few weeks and waiting in the car. My security guard grabbed it as we headed inside. We went straight to the labor and delivery wing, past the waiting room that became a slobbering hush as I passed through.

Inside the room I shed my clothes and put on the delivery gown. Just as I was finished the midwife hurried in. She was younger, with green hair done up in ringlets and a beaming smile that usually got hammered out of people by age 22.

"Ooh, Miss Sykes, you're about to be a proud mommy!" she said as I lay down on the hospital bed.

Another contraction came. They were coming stronger, and with more frequency. I found myself clenching my fists and grinding my teeth.

After it was over, I peered up at the midwife, who was drumming one fingernail with chipped black nail polish against the hospital bed's steel railing.

"Did you just graduate from college?" I asked.

"Yep! Six months ago!" she said. "How are you feeling?"

"Like I'm about to have a baby."

"Don't you worry, I know what I'm doing," she said.

She checked my vitals and felt my stomach.

"Yep, she's dropped," she said. "Excellent. Now let's see how much you've opened up."

She lifted up my robe and inserted two fingers into my vagina, pushing up into my cervix.

"It's about 5 centimeters," she said. "You've still got a ways to go."

"How much longer?" I said.

The midwife pulled her hand out of my vagina.

"A few hours," she said.

I suddenly felt nauseated enough to throw up. I wanted my mother to be there. Right then, in the room with me. It'd been so long since I'd felt the need to have her with me, but now I felt like a lonely island, huge and floating inside of myself.

"I've got security posted at all the exits," my bodyguard said when he entered the room. "I'm sure word will get out that you're here, but we're prepared for it. Do you need anything else?"

Yet another contraction hit me. I felt like a heart attached to an earthquake.

"Can you just reach in and get this baby out of me?" I asked.

The midwife laughed, a cheery bright sound.

"This is the hardest part," she said. "Just wait. Try to relax."

* * *

Night came before I was ready to deliver. I tried to relax and watch bad reality television on the tablet I'd brought in my overnight bag, but I found myself watching the skyline. Whenever a plane passed by I wondered if my mom was on it. The midwife periodically came back to check on me, practically skipping into the room when she did so.

"Please tell me we're almost there," I said.

She kept saying, "Not yet! Just hold on."

I kept checking my phone to see if my mom had sent me a message.

"Ten centimeters," said the midwife, and then finally, "You're ready."

I thought I wanted a natural birth, because it sounded so decadently spiritual to me at that time, like I would give birth being surrounded by maidens in white while I wore a halo, in perfect makeup, no sweat, with birds chirruping the name of my child from the tops of swaying treetops.

But then the real pain started. When I pushed it felt like I was going to be ripped from my vagina all the way to my asshole.

"Yeah, I'm going to need that epidural now," I said.

The nurses gave me the epidural, and also a catheter so I didn't have to get up and pee. Glamorous, I know.

I checked my phone once more. I couldn't remember the last time I'd felt so anxious.

Just landed. OMW. said the text.

I held onto that message like a lifeline.

A few minutes later, my mom showed up in a whirlwind, bringing with her motes of light from the hallway, her hair falling out of her top-bun heavy with hairspray, the smell of her stress-cigarettes still in her hair.

She seemed to be alight as she walked through the door and strode toward me. The fluorescent lights became her aura that pulsed with a heavenly message, and her skin beamed like golden highlighter.

I heard her shining, blocking out the noise of everything around me.

It was probably just the drugs, but still, it was beautiful.

I held my hand out through the bursting of light. She took it without a word.

Then I pushed.

And I pushed.

And I pushed.

And through the sweat and the glint I held onto her hand to keep me from getting lost.

And my stomach was a rolling tide as well as an earthquake, and my body was an ocean of nerves, and my hair stuck to my face with sweat, and in between pushes I thought about how nothing after this moment would ever be the same, and that all of my life had been converging for this, and also how badly I needed a shower. The doctor was speaking to me, but his voice was like a distant pinprick of light.

The pain receded with the epidural, but I still felt the pressure and a burning sensation ringing my vagina.

"Just a few more pushes," I heard my mother say through the rumbling apocalypse that was currently my body.

I felt I might be stuck there forever, unable to get the baby out of me.

But then I pushed again, and then there was a great relief of pressure.

"Her head's out," said the doctor. "Stop pushing for a moment."

"Is she okay?" I asked. "Is she alive?"

"She's going to be fine. It's okay," my mom said.

Her hand on my forehead felt like ice.

Without speaking, they suctioned the mucus from the baby's face.

I could've driven across the United States on the distance that stretched in the silence of that moment in which nobody spoke.

"Okay, one more push," the doctor said, holding her head, as if I hadn't spoken at all.

She came out all the way, and began to cry. I wanted to sob with relief as the tension evaporated inside me.

The contractions didn't stop though.

"Don't tell me it's twins," I said.

"No, the placenta," the doctor said as she held the baby.

"Oh," I said, my voice hazy.

"This is it, baby," my mom said. "This is the last thing and then it's over."

The placenta came out, and they waited until the umbil-ical cord stopped pulsing to cut it.

My mom began to cry. It was the first time I could ever remember her crying.

When I held the baby I looked down at her all soft and pink and raw, with her eyes squinting nearly shut, and although I didn't sob, I wanted to. Fresh tears sprung up from my eyes.

"Congratulations! A healthy baby girl!" said the midwife. "That wasn't so bad, was it?"

When I laughed it hurt.

When my mom glanced at me, and back at the baby, I felt something snap into my being, like a piece had been missing.

I hadn't known how badly I'd wanted this moment. Me, my mother, and the baby. I'd been so worried I'd miss the father the baby never had, miss the accoutrements of an ordi-nary life, miss the normal feelings of wholeness that a birth should've brought.

But I didn't feel empty.

My skin was singing.

"We're a family," I said, my throat full of a new pain.

A good pain.

"Yes," my mom said. "We are."

When I glanced at my mother's face, streaming with tears, it became a mirror.

I looked back at my child.

Her face seemed to expand to fill my entire vision, my entire brain, every molecule of attention. And I was less me, and more her.

People say that everything changes once you have a child.

What they don't say is that it's like you pushed out a piece of your soul, and now instead of staying safe inside of you it's walking around in a new and tender skin.

* * *

That night in the hospital I dreamed that I was on a boat, rolling my baby in a stroller across the sunny deck.

My terrorist baby daddy lay on a white-canopied bed, arms crossed, his eye sockets empty. He held a teddy bear in one hand and a gold balloon in the other. Storks circled around the bed with lace trim in their giant beaks.

"Congratulations! I wish I could've been there," he said.

I rolled the baby's stroller to the foot of the bed. A stork swooped in with a bouquet of lilies in its mouth, and dropped them into Jo's lap. She giggled.

"I hope you won't be making these dream visits a regular occurrence," I said.

"You're going to have to get used to seeing me," he said. "Seeing my face inside of hers."

"We don't even know if it's your baby."

"But you do, Bev," he said, his voice soft.

A city appeared on the horizon line, its skyscrapers streaked with gold, the valleys beyond like diamonds. The boat sailed toward it.

"Aren't you worried that she's going to turn out like me?" he asked.

I looked down at the baby in her stroller.

"To be honest, I've been worried about a bunch of other shit instead," I said.

She held her arms out for me to pick her up. I bent down and pulled her up, and when I came up out of the stroller I found that the city had been leveled, fire burning where the glass and streets used to be, ash rushing toward the sky, our boat rushing faster and faster into a gray night tinged with smoke.

"You think this is the end?" he asked. "That you've got this all figured out?

"You're only twenty-four. You've barely started to discover all the ways things can go wrong."

He released the golden balloon. It floated into the air and popped, showering golden pieces down onto the deck.

It began to rain fire all around us.

"That's okay," I said. "I'll make it okay."

"What if she turns out bad?"

"She won't."

"How do you know that?"

I looked into her eyes. They were like two kaleidoscopes full of fiery beads.

"Because I tried to save even a worthless person like you."

* * *

I awoke to screams and shouts outside the window. To flashbulbs, and the clicking of cameras. The lights spattered across the walls and the hospital bed, reminding me of glow paint.

I glanced over at my newborn baby, who was swaddled and wide awake in the crib next to my bed. She remained silent except for an occasional gurgle.

The moonlight spilled into her crib and became her crown. We lay suspended together in a spell of light, and the noise outside the window receded into a low background hum.

My mom came back into the room with a cup of coffee and a Snickers bar. A security guard followed here. The volume outside surged again.

"What happened?" I asked.

"Someone leaked your location. Your security thinks the press might've followed me from the airport. We're going to get you moved into a new room," she said. "So you and the baby can rest."

I tried to get up from the bed.

"Don't," she said. "I'm sure you're exhausted."

"It's okay," I said. "They just want to see the baby."

"Bev. No. You need your rest."

"And after I rest, then what am I going to do? Hide from the world for the rest of my life?" I asked. "They're not going to go away. Mr. Anderson, can you grab that wheelchair?"

He did, and eased me into it.

Mom sighed and set down her coffee.

"Well, I'm not letting you go out there alone."

When the baby began to cry, Mom took her and then placed her into my arms.

Warmth radiated through my entire being when we came into contact. An unknown tension inside me folded and dissolved. I rocked her as my mom wheeled me out into the hallway. All of the nurses stopped and turned to stare, eyes like busted lights. A few took out their cellphones and began to film and take photos, ignoring privacy regulations.

"Get ready," my mom said.

She wheeled me into the waiting room.

As the double doors flew open the camera flashes and the bright lights dazzled me. At first I couldn't see anything except a bright light pressing into my eyes. Instinctively I pressed the swaddled Jo closer to me.

"Beverly!"

"Beverly Sykes!"

When my vision adjusted the crowd appeared multi-eyed behind cameras. My pain medication was still wearing off, so their bright clothes and hair swirling in the heavy light seemed like one enormous, stitched-together being. They took up the entire space of the waiting room, painting the white walls with their attention, covering the wide swathe of the tiled floor. A little girl with wide cheeks waved from the shoulders of her father. A teenage girl snapped pics while standing on a waiting room chair, her iPhone held over the crowd like a submarine's telescope.

Several of them carried banners and signs, painted with tiny feet or cartoonish babies or storks carrying bundles.

Hello Baby Sykes!

Welcome to Planet Earth!

One had painted a globe of the Earth, with a pink party hat.

Welcome Home Baby!

The nurses and security pushed them back as I sat in the wheelchair in my exhausted glow.

"No touching the baby!" a nurse shouted. "She's too young!"

In response, the crowd actually relented and stopped surging forward.

"Beverly! Beverly! Look over here!" shouted a woman.

I looked up, my neck heavy, my whole body seeming to swing detached from my head. More cameras snapped.

"What's her name?" someone asked.

A tired smile years in the making spread across my face.

"Jo," I said, wiping at my tears with the back of her hands. "Let's call her Jo."

"Short for Joann?" My mom asked me.

"No," I said. "Just Jo."

Welcome home.

I looked down at baby Jo, and at the crowd, and felt my mother's hand on my shoulder. My feet had never quite touched the ground before. Not like this. I'd never been able to grab onto a singular moment, a singular space, and feel like I belonged there.

But now I was here. This was it. My bones were for once, settling down in my skin. And for once I felt ready for a new beginning. For once, I felt,

Welcome home.

17

I went home to spend my maternity leave back in my childhood bedroom. The President still called me almost every night since I'd left the hospital.

Sometimes he wanted to talk about work, but mostly he wanted to talk about the new thing he saw behind his eyes.

"Last night I dreamed of a golden utopia on top of a mountain of ice," he said. "The people that lived on the mountain used machines to pump the smog out of the sky, and turned it into crystal."

His voice was wistful, like he still had half of his body inside the dream.

"I never thought I'd dream again," he said. "Not like I used to."

I pressed a hand against one of my sore breasts.

"That happens a lot," I said, trying not to let the exhaustion creep into my voice. "Your body is telling your mind it's okay to believe again."

I glance over at Jo sleeping in her crib. Maybe after this call I'd be able to get some sleep. I felt warm at the edges, like I was dissolving into fuzziness.

The President cleared his throat.

"Anyway, I wanted to see if you could go over some more of the details of this energy bill. I'm thinking that by the year 2040 we should roll out new efficiency standards for all cars produced in the states. Previously the House and the Senate would never go for it, but I think with your new input—"

I yawned. "Don't you have tons of advisors for this sort of thing?"

"Why do you keep asking me that?" he asked. "Miss Sykes, your opinion matters to me."

I tried not to tip over. The whole room seemed like it was sliding.

"I've been doing some research when I can. There are a few key members in the Senate that are going to be the biggest deciders in blocking the bill. Maybe I can take care of that."

The list of influential people I needed to fuck was growing by the day.

"We have a long road ahead of us," he said. "To the new Utopia."

After I got off the phone, Jo began to wail. I'd already began to differentiate her cries, and knew this one meant she was hungry.

I lifted Jo up out of the crib. At this point, my blood was probably more caffeine than hemoglobin. I pulled my shirt down and she clamped down on a sore nipple. I winced.

I heard my mom doing her late-night rummaging in the kitchen.

"I think my nipples are going to fall off!" I shouted to my mom.

"That sounds about right!" she called back.

I sat down on the edge of the bed as she nursed. The old springs groaned underneath my weight. Travis, my mom's new husband, poked his head into the room.

"Need anything from the store?" he asked.

"Sleep and a hot shower, do they sell those there?" I asked.

"I'll check," he said, and ducked back out.

"And some gum! Spearmint!" I called out.

I hummed a nursery rhyme to Jo on autopilot as she fed. I thought of Washington as I did. I grew more restless by the day about all the unfinished work I had.

Do you know how long it takes before you can have sex after pregnancy?

A whole four to six weeks. Just to make sure everything healed up, the cervix closed up, the bleeding stopped, and there weren't tears in the skin.

Most days I felt like I couldn't go four to six hours without sex.

I should've been enjoying this time with my baby. But as I sat in a replica of my teenage life – underneath posters of Fallout Boy and Paramore and crescent moon string lights that mom never bothered to take down after I first left home – all I could think about was I needed to be saving the world.

I needed to *fucking* save the world.

I rubbed my thighs together, imagining fingers in my mouth and cocks thrust inside me. I wanted to go back to my silk sheets, lube, and vibrators. I hadn't been this horny since I was fourteen years old, masturbating on top of the washing machine.

Jo gurgled, and when she was finished breastfeeding, I rocked her.

I logged into my fake Facebook profile that I used to message my old friends and checked our group chat in Messenger. I hadn't talked to Heather or Janna since I'd been back in town, but I'd barely had time to brush my teeth.

I sent a message as Jo began to fall asleep against my arm.

About to lose my mind. Send memes?

No response.

* * *

At least Jo didn't cry much. Mom told me I'd been much more fussy as a child.

Oftentimes she stared at me from the crib with eyes that reminded me of a queen inside a child's body.

I put her back in the crib and fell asleep with my head pressed into the slatted sides, the glowing cloud mobile above her head making its soft, repetitive music.

I had nightmares of losing Jo in shopping malls and in the centers of giant beds.

I dreamed that I lost her during bath time, as if she'd disintegrated into the water. I dreamed that a crowd of fans waited outside my house and when I walked through them with Jo in my arms, they grabbed her and she disappeared into their center.

I awoke with a start to a stranger climbing through my window.

I thought it was a remaining figment of a dream, up until the point my security guard grabbed her by the hair and pulled her back.

They both fell to the ground.

"It's okay! I know her!" came a voice. A woman's voice.

I bolted upright and ran toward the window, to see my security pressing a woman with dark hair into the pavement, her arm twisted behind her.

She struggled under the weight of my security guard's armlock and lifted her head just enough so that I could see her face in the streetlight.

"Janna?" I asked, then waved at my security. "Stop. I know her. It's okay."

My security released her and offered a hand to get up. She brushed him off and stood up with a huff.

I glanced over at the clock. It was a little after 1 A.M., and the house was hushed. Jo was still asleep.

"I'm guessing you got my Facebook message?" I asked.

"Why didn't you tell me you were back in town?" she asked.

"Why didn't you just send me a reply instead of trying to climb through my window?"

"Ugh. Can't I just come in?"

I sighed. "Come around the front. Just be quiet."

Janna pretty much looked the same as I remembered her – dark and boisterous, with hair big enough to be an insect net. She wore cat-eye sunglasses, even though it was night, a pleather jacket, and worn-out combat boots. When we hugged I felt the imprint of a flask in her jacket.

"Fuck, I missed you so much, big shot," she said. "And oh my god, look at baby Beverly! So freaking cute. Don't tell me the Daddy skipped out on you?"

"Shhh," I said. "I told you to keep your voice down."

She looked at me with a grin that brought back a rush of familiar memories. I could practically taste the Jell-O shots on my tongue.

"Want to go to a party?"

"Are you nuts? I have a newborn baby."

"So? She's sleeping," Janna said. "And I bet you've got breast milk you pumped in the fridge. If she cries, your mom can wake up and feed her."

"Yeah, but—"

"Yeah, but," Janna said, teasingly.

"I can't."

"Come on. I haven't seen you in forever. Don't be boring. Just come out for an hour. We'll be back before she even wakes up."

I glanced back over at Jo, who looked so angelic, suspended in sleep. The lights from the mobile seemed to make her glow, as if she was suffused with an ethereal radiance. She probably wouldn't even wake up before I got back.

"You said you were 'losing your mind.'" she said. "I've got the remedy."

"Okay, but just for an hour. And then we're right back here."

I opened my closet. I didn't own anything that was party-ready anymore, just a bunch of maternity clothes and over-sized sweaters.

"God, I really am turning boring," I said, and grabbed a big sweater, leggings, and my coat. "I'll change in the car."

I was actually sneaking out of my parent's house with my own security guard, in a Bentley, to go party in small town Michigan. I should have reveled in the absurdity more.

I made the mistake of checking my reflection in my compact.

"My hair's a mess," I said. "I can't believe I'm doing this."

"Here," Janna said, handing me a lipstick. "If everyone's looking at your lips, nobody's going to notice your hair."

She then pulled a pair of heels out of her purse, black with stiletto heels to rival the height of the shoes I wore in my stripper days.

"There's no way," I said.

"Come on, we're the same size," she said. "It'll make you feel sexy."

"Patrick," I called out to the front seat to my security, "What do you think?"

"I love a woman in heels," he said.

I took the heels from Janna. "Fine."

I kicked off the dirty sneakers that Jo had thrown up on more than once and put on the heels. Luckily they still fit even with my swollen feet. And even without my usual pedicure I did have to admit, they made me feel sexier.

"So why are we going to this party anyway?"

"Trying to find you a boyfriend."

"Yeah, right," I said. "Hey, my boobs are leaking, I'm ten pounds overweight, and I just shoved a baby through my vagina. Marry me."

"Oh please, you're still hot," Janna said. "And you're like, world-famous now, right? That gives you a lot of extra points."

"Don't forget I'm also rich," I said.

"Yeah, rub it in. If I had a magic pussy I'd be rich too."

I regarded Janna.

"Hey, you always talked about getting out of this town the first chance you got," I said. "What the hell happened?"

"Ugh, I fell in love."

"You said that wasn't going to happen either."

"I say a lot of things, Bev," she said. "You know that."

* * *

The party was at a house near the edge of town, standing by itself at the edge of a road with cars parked all the way up and down the driveway. My security guard parked, and we climbed out together.

I kept checking my phone for the time. Only 50 minutes to go.

"Everyone's in the back," Janna said, and we headed around the house. This far out of town, people didn't bother with fences.

I tried to image what I looked like, walking into that backyard in stiletto heels, my hair a nest, bright red lipstick on an unwashed face, wearing mom clothes and owning a butt big enough to cause a lunar eclipse. Most everyone was either floating in the pool with beers or sitting in the jacuzzi. Janna ran up to a man with a body like an oak and jumped full force into his arms.

I'd probably been to a thousand parties and usually, I'd be scoping out the hottest boy, trying to figure out how I could take him home that night. Instead, I found myself sidling up to the food table so I could munch on a cupcake and try not to worry about Jo.

Thankfully, nobody seemed to recognize me at first, which I attributed to the darkness and the mess that my body had become over the last few months. I stared off into the distance as I ate. At the edge of the property a small river ran, full after a recent rain, like a silver ribbon in the full moon.

"You look a little lost," said someone to my left.

I finished my cupcake and tossed the wrapper in the garbage can.

"I was just imagining what it'd be like to float down that river on a raft and disappear into a beam of moonlight forever."

He laughed, and that made me actually turn to look at him.

Most of the men in this town had bodies like beer bottles, with whiskey-bloated faces. He looked like a full-bodied sip of wine. He had a sharp chin, and smart eyes, and clothes that actually looked tailored.

"You're not from around here, are you?" I asked.

"Is it that easy to figure out?" he said. "I'm visiting my cousin for a few weeks. Her mom's sick."

He held a cupcake in his hands. "At least the food isn't terrible."

"So, what brings you here?" he asked.

"I was just about to leave."

"So soon? But I haven't even gotten a chance to work my charm on you."

"I'm sure you're oozing with charm," I said. "But I don't think now is a great time."

"You and me together," he said. "Seems like a great time to me."

I couldn't help it, I smiled. And he latched onto that smile like a weak joint suddenly exposed.

He nodded toward my security, who was definitely not blending in. He held a beer he hadn't taken a single sip from and tried to get away from a blonde woman in a bikini and cowboy boots who was urging him to take a shot with her.

"He's with you, right?" he asked. "Just in case someone around here gets a little too handsy with the superstar?"

"I doubt most people here even recognize me. I don't really have a sex goddess glow at the moment," I said.

He stepped closer toward me. I felt heady in his proximity, like I'd just downed a glass of warm rum. It'd been weeks since I'd had sex, and that unbidden desire, even with the whack job that was my hormones and sleep deprivation, rushed to the surface of my skin, making it flush.

"There's nothing sexier than a woman living the way she wants," he said.

"That's a nice line," I said. "I'll have to remember that."

"I never thought I'd meet someone so famous out here in Michigan. I thought you'd be different. But you might not just be the blonde barbie that you try so hard to appear to as."

"Now you're just negging me," I said, but I was still smiling.

"No neg, I swear," he said. "Just being honest."

He unwrapped the cupcake and held it out for me to take a bite. The saliva in my mouth began to flow.

"I just had a baby," I said. "I can't be doing this."

"And yet, here you are," he said. "I imagine your baby is well looked after."

"My mother, but—"

"Come on," he interrupted. "I see it in your eyes. You really, really want this cupcake."

The thought of Jo receded with the sound of the river and his close presence. When he leaned closer, it tumbled to the bottom of my mind into the silt and darkness.

"Can I tell you something?" he asked, the cupcake nearly squished between my breasts.

"I'm sure you will regardless of what I say," I said.

His breathy whisper was like a silk string tightening itself against my spine.

"I want to press my tongue so far and deep inside you that I leave marks on the inside of your ribcage."

I glanced over at Janna. She was busy talking to her man.

I took his hand in both of mine, with a deliberate slowness, caressing the individual fingers.

I pulled his hands to my mouth, and took a huge bite out of the top of the cupcake.

I should've known I wasn't just going to come to a party, eat a few snacks, and leave.

Please, I'm Beverly Sykes.

He nodded once again at my security.

"When he's not looking, let's sneak away."

"Sneak away? What are you, sixteen?" I asked.

"What are you," he asked, "dead?"

Little pinpricks of warmth studded the inside of my skin. The sensation reminded me that I was very much still alive, and up until that moment my pussy had been so dry that if I rubbed my legs together it might've burned. Now I was wet, practically streaming, an oasis on fire.

"Let's go to the river," he said. "Behind the trees, where they can't see us."

The woman in the cowboy boots grabbed my security guard by the arm and dragged him toward the shots. That was my chance.

"Let's go," I said.

I headed toward the river, toward the puffy-limbed trees, trying not to giggle, and he followed after me. After I got behind the pool and out of the line of sight of the partygoers, I broke out into a run.

I was a great runner in heels, even in the wet grass.

As we neared the tree line my blood pumped as if seared with fire.

Maybe if having to take care of a newborn and being confined back in my old childhood home hadn't made my brain so mushy, I wouldn't have ignored the blaring warning signs leading up to that point. But I wasn't thinking of how far away I was from safety, how coolly he delivered each line as if he'd rehearsed it, how he seemed to insinuate himself into my presence like a too-convenient ghost.

I was, as you might say, only thinking with my clitoris.

"Come here," I said, holding my arms out.

He grabbed me and twirled me into his arms. He lay me down into the earth, into the wet leaves and the dirt.

I reached up for a kiss as he loomed over me, but my body suddenly went numb. My expression seemed to slide off my face. My outstretched arms thudded back into the dirt.

"Something's wrong," I said.

At first I thought I might be having a stroke, or a seizure, but then his smile faded into a thin line, and the spark went out from his eyes.

"Did you put something in my drink?" I asked.

But I hadn't drank anything. I wracked my mind, as it seemed to dissolve into itself, trying to figure out what it could've been. And then I realized.

The cupcake.

He'd been holding it when he walked up to me. I hadn't seen him take it from the table, and he'd actually never bit into it himself.

"Fuck," I said, my words slurring. "Really?"

I glanced toward the party, which now seemed so far-away, like firefly's body worth of light, and getting dimmer by the second.

He smirked.

"And they told me you were smart."

Then he hit me over the head. Hard.

As I was losing consciousness, he picked up my limp body and threw me over his shoulder. I was past struggling at that point.

The sound of the river surged. I imagined Jo sitting in her crib in the dark, waiting up alone for her mother, quiet, unblinking, eyes full of the glowing mobile, as water poured over me.

The image got fuzzier and fuzzier until it faded into the hiss and the stream.

* * *

I awoke in the backseat of a car with my hands duct-taped together, my head pounding with a red violence, as we zoomed down a dark road.

When I moved my head, I felt a sharp pain. My entire body ached. It hurt to breathe, like my lungs were cracked on the inside with dried mud. I felt that numb, tingling feeling like I'd been pumped with anesthesia at the dentist.

"What the hell?" I said, or at least, tried to say. The words slurred.

Then it all came back to me.

I glanced down. There were dead leaves crumbled in my sweater, and dried mud caked on Janna's heels. The heat was cranked up in the car, and sweat trickled down my thighs, and pooled underneath my breasts.

I caught his reflection in the mirror, and seeing that cold-set stare as he focused on the road, I wondered how I didn't see any of this coming.

I was *so* fucking stupid.

"Do not tell me you just kidnapped me."

"Okay," he said.

The clock on the dash read 4:50 and it was still night out. I didn't know whether we'd been driving for a few hours, or for an entire day. He sped down some unrecognizable country road, flying over the bumps. The only light came from the headlights in front of us.

"You fucker," I said.

I struggled with the duct tape on my hands, even though I knew it wasn't any use. I searched around the back of the car for something, anything, but it was empty. I tried the doors, but they were locked.

"I don't just get to have a normal night, do I?" I asked.

"Are you just now figuring that out?"

He hadn't bothered to strap me into a seatbelt, so every time he took a sharp turn I slid across the seat.

Maybe it was just an effect of the drugs wearing off making me loopy, and the dark road with its lack of light, but in the mirror his face seemed to have unraveled. His eyes drooped, and his mouth spread, and his face seemed to have stretched into a worn out, angry mask.

"Are you going to kill me? Sell me off to slavery? What?" I asked.

"Maybe you can tell me something useful," he said. "And I'll see what I can do to make things easier for you. I know you've had conversations with The President late at night. "

I groaned.

"You should've just fucked me," I said.

We took another sharp turn. My body jerked to the side and my cheek hit the glass.

"We could've had a good time," I said, "and you wouldn't be in such an enormous amount of shit. Because if you think you're going to get away—"

"You're not my type," he said abruptly.

"What?" I said.

He paused for a moment, as if chewing on the words.

"I prefer thinner women."

"Oh, fuck you!" I said.

I thought of Mom waking up to Jo's cries, and discovering my car gone. I thought of Jo saying her first words, those first hesitant steps, first day in Kindergarten, first kiss.

And always, there would be a cold spot behind her where her mother used to be. All because Mommy decided she was too horny to stay in the light and keep it in her pants.

Fuck. I really was an idiot.

I needed to figure some way out of this.

"People would kill each other to get five minutes with me, and you're just going to pass up my gift?"

"I don't need it."

"You're fucking insane."

"Stop talking. You're giving me a headache," he said.

"Tell me right now what you're going to do with me," I said. "I have a right to know."

I glanced out of the car once more to try to to see any

recognizable landmark, but my vision was still blurry and I couldn't read any of the signs. We seemed to be approaching a town of some sorts. The distant lights looked like floating star stickers.

"I don't like you, Miss Beverly Sykes," he said.

"I think you've made that pretty clear."

"You're a symbol of everything that's wrong in America."

"Really, me?" I said, trying to sound nonchalant despite the sludge in my head, "That's a big pair of shoes to fill."

"You're a spoiled, entitled, rich, bratty little cunt who had a gift fall into her lap. Instead of using it for good, you decided you want to play at being a little bitch queen in a little palace. And everyone's fallen for your act."

"Is this a joke?"

"You're a symbol of freedom for feminists and degenerates. They think you're a god-sent gift when you're nothing but a fucking whore looking to be worshipped for spreading her legs. Honestly, I wouldn't be surprised if you're a sign of the fucking apocalypse."

"Oh my god, you're serious, aren't you?" I said.

A new kind of warmth pulsed through my blood. Fiery and golden, like the burning sensation that filled my stomach on the day my daughter was born.

"You're going to regret all of this," I said.

"I doubt that," he said.

"You think that what I can do is overhyped, that it couldn't possibly be as good at it is. Don't you?"

I leaned forward in the seat and pressed my chin against the backseat. The drug seemed to be wearing off, and I could talk more easily.

"But it *is* that good," I said. "It's so fucking good that it's transcendent, you might say. You'd be the glow that gurus spent years trying to spot on mountaintops."

"Oh, quit your bullshit," he said.

His hands on the steering wheel tightened. In the mirror, I caught him grinding his teeth.

"For the rest of your life, you're going to have to wonder if I'm telling the truth," I said. "You'll wake up in the middle of the night, over and over, and feel a twinge, wondering what could've been, and unable to even comprehend its shape."

He took another sharp turn, throwing me down into the seat, my legs higher than my head. In just the right position so my feet were aligned with the back of his neck.

The image of Jo, with her wispy hair and sleeping face, became fixed in my mind.

This was my moment, and I doubted I'd get another.

I took a deep breath and held it.

I kicked at the back of his head, and my stiletto heel slammed into the back of his neck.

His head slammed forward, and he jerked the steering wheel.

"The fu "

Before he could finish the words, I pulled my heel back and struck him again.

The car skidded off the road, striking the bumpy ground as I tried to brace myself. My head slammed into the seat in front of me. We broke through a fence and the splinters flew past the windows.

He slumped forward unconscious. The car squealed to a stop as the field ruptured underneath the tires.

I kicked him a few more times, just to make sure he wouldn't wake up.

I climbed into the front seat and kicked open the passenger door. I stumbled out into a field, the night quiet except for the sound of the car, the engine still on, the hood crumpled, the smoke pouring out.

I cut the duct-tape off against barbed wire and then climbed over a fence into the road. My feet lurched underneath me as if they belonged to someone else. My headache tilted the world on its side.

I kicked off the heels and ran barefoot down the road, toward what seemed to be the direction of town.

* * *

Imagine this like a movie scene:

The protagonist (me, of course) stumbles home while dawn kicks up under her feet like the gleam of her triumph. Picture her small silhouette with smoke curling out of the top of her head as she walks up the sidewalk toward the front porch. She reaches for the door with sunlight sparkling against her bruised wrists. She opens the door in slow motion to the sound of swelling orchestral music. Holding her breath with an exhausted, exhilarating pause, she heads into the kitchen.

Then:

Record scratch. Our beloved protagonist is thrust back into her body, and her movie debut is promptly cancelled.

Because in the kitchen sat my mom with Jo, my mom's husband and stepdaughter, the local police, and my entire security team.

They all turned to stare at me.

My body ached like I was leaking out of it. My breasts felt like they were going to pop. I was barefoot and bleeding all over the tiles, my clothes dusty and torn, my bones like cornmeal ground up into my blood.

They'd been eating pumpkin pancakes that I'm sure my stepdad cooked. The warm scent grew teeth and clamp down on my stomach. I was starving.

My mom fed Jo some of the breast milk I'd pumped.

"Miss Sykes," said one of the police officers, standing up abruptly to rattle the chair. "What happened? Are you hurt?"

I rushed over to Jo, who didn't seem too disturbed by my absence, by the burnt reek that rushed from my clothes. I reached out to touch her, until I saw the ashy grime on my fingers. I pulled my hand back.

"I missed you so much," I said. "Your momma is a goddamn idiot."

One of my security guards cleared his throat.

"Miss Sykes?" he asked. "What happened?"

"Oh. I got kidnapped. A truck driver gave me a ride home."

"We should take you to the hospital," said one of the police officers. "Or at least, down to the police station, to take a statement."

"I just want to be alone with my daughter," I said. "I'm fine."

She worked at sucking down the milk, her big eyelashes batting like she was angling for a camera.

"She's fine," my mom said. "Although you knocked about five years off my life."

I coughed up a chunk of phlegm in my hands, and then wiped it away.

"No offense, but you look like a hot mess," said Tracy, my mom's stepdaughter.

She leaned against the counter in yoga pants and a white sweater, nursing a cup of coffee.

"At least I'm still hot," I said.

Nobody laughed.

"Uhm. Are there any pancakes left?" I asked. "I'm really hungry."

Mom glanced at Jo, and then me, and then back at her husband. She seemed to be deciding whether or not to become hysterical.

"Yeah," she finally said. "On the counter."

I lurched over to the counter, grabbed a plate, and mechanically began to fill it. I didn't even bother to use a spatula or fork, just grabbed the pancakes with my hands. I stood over the sink and began shoving them into my mouth in fistfuls.

"Honey," my mom said. "Beverly."

I glanced over at her, at the security, at the police, with my mouth stuffed full of pancakes.

"This is the last time, okay?" she said. "Promise me this is the last time something like this will happen."

I swallowed, and glanced around at the room full of people, before I settled once more on Jo's face.

She gurgled, and something inside my body, deep at the center of me, shifted.

I wiped my sticky hands on a nearby towel. I walked toward them with steps so heavy I was surprised I didn't leave scorch marks behind. I picked up Jo and cradled her to my chest. Her softness seeming to push back my throbbing headache and sore throat.

I held my hand out for my mom. She took it. Then we were both standing, hugging Jo from both sides, forming a temple with our foreheads pressed together. My mother's Coco Mademoiselle perfume intermingled with the sweet new baby smell, like cotton and summer jasmine and freshly made cookies all rolled into one.

If only I could carry the geometry of our bodies like this forever I think it would cast out every bad memory I ever had.

"I thought I'd never see you two again," I said, a quaver in my voice.

Tears seemed to spring to my eyes more easily these days. My doctor said it was all those post-baby hormones, making my system go crazy. But when I looked back at my mother's face, she was crying too.

Enveloped in my family like that, it didn't even bother me that all those people in the kitchen were watching us break down.

"You understand now, don't you?" my mother asked. "How things are different?"

"Yes," I whispered.

"You can't go back to how it used to be," she said.

"I don't want to go back," I said. "I want my family."

My mom squeezed my hand. Jo cooed. I knew she couldn't know what was going on, but I heard it as her agreeing with me.

"We want you too," she said. "So promise me."

I closed my eyes for a moment and breathed in that new

smell. And in the years that followed, I knew that every time I thought of taking some stupid risk, it would come back to linger in my mind, to remind me of the new world I'd created and didn't want to destroy.

"I promise," I said. "Always."

PART 6

18

I got out of my Bentley and strode into Jo's private school escorted by my security. One of the dads stopped in the roundabout to stare at me, so I blew him a kiss. He blushed and looked away.

I just turned thirty years old, but I still needed my cheap thrills sometimes.

My security waited out in the hallway as I headed into the main office where Jo's teacher and the principal waited for me.

Their spines shot up like they were in the presence of royalty.

"Mrs. Sykes, welcome," said the principal. "Please have a seat."

"Miss Sykes," I corrected as I sat down.

Jo sat in the corner with her big dark hair and her deep-set eyes focused on the notebook in front of her. She was scribbling something.

"Hey Mommy," she said without looking up.

I took a pack of Wintergreen out of my purse.

"Gum?" I asked.

"Oh, no thank you," said the principal, but the teacher reached out and took a piece.

I glanced back over at Jo, who was still absorbed in her drawing.

"I loved your TED talk," the teacher blurted out and shoved the gum into her mouth.

Silence.

"So, what's the deal?" I asked when nobody said anything.

The principal and the teacher glanced at each other.

"Your daughter, well, she's been providing services to the other children. In exchange for candy."

Services was spoken like spitting out an insect.

"What kind of services?" I asked, as if daring them to speak.

The teacher clenched her knees together. The principal scratched the back of her hand, but other than that, she was doing a good job of keeping composed. Maybe her hairstyle was twenty years out of fashion, and she wore a gaudy string of pearls like a parody of a grandma, but I shouldn't hold that against her.

Still, nobody answered me.

"If you're going to make me take time out of my busy schedule to come here, the least you can do is be straight with me," I said. "This is supposed to be one of the best schools in L.A. I'd expect a little more professionalism."

"She's been kissing the other children, in exchange for candy."

I sat back, waiting for them to continue. They didn't.

"That's it?" I asked. "Kissing? Well, if Jo wants to be an entrepreneur I don't see the problem. I mean, I try to get her to eat healthy when we're at home, but maybe I've been a little too strict with it."

"Bartering and selling goods on campus are forbidden for children."

"Oh, well, Jo, you shouldn't do that then. Will you do it anymore?"

I glanced over at her, and she shook her head as she continued to draw, as if the adults around her were playing a game she had to indulge them in.

"Good. See? Are we done here?"

"Well, you see," said the principal. "It's a bit more serious than that."

The teacher began to speak, hurriedly and with little hiccups between the words.

"We think that, uh, this happened perhaps because of your influence. And we'd like to encourage you to foster a more, ah, child-friendly environment and image. Some of the other parents have expressed their concern."

I clenched my hands together and my knuckles turned white. I forced myself to smile, but the scaly flicker of my eyes seemed to frighten her into silence, and she stuttered a few more times before closing her mouth.

"Jo, sweetie, can you leave the room, please? Just hang out in the hallway for a few minutes with Mr. Stewart? The grownups need to talk," I said.

She rolled her eyes in a way that seemed familiar.

"Is this going to take long? I have gymnastics class today," she said.

"No. It won't take long."

She sighed and closed her notebook with a dramatic flourish. We all waited until she left and closed the door behind her.

"So you think I'm a bad influence on my child," I said.

I leaned back and forced myself to keep calm. It was a little trick I learned a long time ago – I'd focus on each individual muscle and force it to relax. First the forehead, then the eyebrows, and so forth.

Again, neither of them spoke.

"It's not like I'm turning tricks in front of her, or telling her that she needs to get a sugar daddy. Jo doesn't even know what sex is. What bad influence could I possibly have?"

"Well, the other kids, they talk," the teacher said. "And it's made some of the other parents very upset. When they found out about the kissing thing, you can imagine how that went over."

The principal shot her a murderous glance.

"Excuse me," I said, "but did you know that for three years I was on retainer to The President of the United States? While being a single parent, I might add. And since then unemployment rates have been the lowest they've been in fifty years. The economy's improved. The middle class has expanded. Two wars were stopped. There's a new health insurance plan to cover all Americans, and in fifty years we'll have made harmful energy obsolete. Now, of course, I don't want to take all the credit for that, but I think that's a little more important than whether or not some kiddos are gossiping about me or if Jo kissed a few kindergarteners."

"Mrs. Sykes—"

"Miss Sykes."

"We don't mean to demean your accomplishments, but we think it'd be best if Jo found a school elsewhere more befitting to her personality and talents."

"You're kidding me," I said. "You're kicking her out of the school? Because some people don't like that Beverly Sykes is her mother?"

"I'm sorry. We think that's what's best for the students, and the parents."

I stood.

"Well, thank you," I said, with as much ice in my tone as I could. "You'll be hearing from my lawyer, but I really have to go. Jo hates being late for gymnastics."

I forced myself to turn, to keep from going red, as I went out into the hallway.

"Am I in trouble, Mom?" she asked when she saw my face.

A wolf sat inside her eyes. She sometimes seemed much older than she really was, and in moments like these she reminded me of a dark-haired ice-princess or an elegant cannibal.

"No," I said. "But I think we're going to have to find a new school."

She jumped to her feet and squared off at me, her hands thrust on her hips.

"Mom! I have friends here!"

"I know, I did everything I could. But sometimes, well, there are just things that are outside of our control."

Did my mom ever do that, try to incorporate some life lesson into everything like that'd make what just happened okay?

I briefly remembered a car ride we took together years ago.

Bev, are you having sex?

* * *

We headed to Jo's gymnastics class and I went to the gym across the street. For an hour my trainer yelled me into various pretzel shapes. Afterward, Jo came out of the gymnastics studio bouncing in her pink leotard with her hair drawn up and met me on the street corner where I stood with my red face, trying to match her enthusiasm.

"Good work today, kiddo?" I asked.

"Yep! I'm learning how to do a double flip."

"You know what I'm thinking? I'm thinking ice cream."

She studied me for a moment, skeptical.

"Is this because of the school thing?" she asked.

Maybe she had the same powers I did, to focus and get a sense of a person's inner working. I hadn't figured out that power until I was much older, but Jo often seemed much smarter than me.

"Yeah, you got me, it's because of the school thing," I said. "I just thought we both could use a break today."

"Okay," she said, reluctantly, as if she was doing me a favor. "But I want a banana split."

"Deal."

We headed over to Baskin Robbins around the corner.

She got her banana split with a double chocolate scoop and rainbow sprinkles. I got a scoop of chocolate, and we sat opposite each other for several minutes without speaking.

"Mom," she asked. "Am I evil?"

"Why would you ask that?" I said, the spoon hovering in front of my face.

"The kids at school, they say my mommy's a well—"

She spelled out the word.

"S-L-U-T. And my dad's a terrorist."

"Well," I said, swallowing. "Your spelling is improving. That's good."

I had to set the spoon down to keep it from shaking in my hands.

"Is my daddy really a terrorist?" she asked.

"You don't have a daddy, baby," I said. "You had a father. There's a difference."

"Is he dead?" she asked.

I sat back for a moment and closed my eyes.

Even after all those years, sometimes I could still feel his slick poison inside me, like our bodies were still wrapped around each other.

"You said you wouldn't lie anymore," she said.

"I did say that, didn't I?"

"Mom!" she said. "Nobody likes a liar."

I sighed. "Yes, baby. Your father is dead. He died before you were born."

She shrugged, as if this information didn't bother her, but I knew her well enough to see otherwise. She always drew up inside herself, cloistering her feelings as if she could dispel them with inner pressure.

"So these same people who say these terrible things to

you, are they the same people who want you to kiss them?" I asked.

"Well, yeah."

"You're not evil, they just want what you have, and they feel bad about it. Don't worry about it. We'll get this all sorted out."

We finished our ice cream and headed back to the car.

"But maybe don't go around kissing boys anymore. You're a little too young for that. I'll start giving you an allowance for candy or whatever you want – would that help?"

She acted like she was thinking about it.

"How much allowance?"

"How about thirty a week?" I asked, having no idea what the going rate for kindergartener allowances was these days.

"Deal," she said.

We headed back home. We parked behind my other car, the new Tesla model that had been a gift from Mr. Musk (although he had insisted I call him Elon). He'd revamped the engine and made the design more efficient shortly after our time together.

I helped Jo out of the car. She made her way around the white picket fence toward the canary yellow garage door. The dentist's wife on our left was outside watering her lawn. On the right, a YouTube-famous yoga instructor was practicing on her balcony wearing a pink band tied around her forehead and high-waisted Lululemon pants.

She waved at me coming up out of warrior pose.

I waved back. As I did I caught the neighbor's college-age son peering out at me through the window.

I'd seen him outside pulling weeds without a shirt, like a brawny piece of sunshine. I'd been resisting the urge to seduce him for weeks, although I risked flashing him once, even though it seemed like everything I did ended up on the Internet these days.

"Mom!" Jo called out for me, snapping me out of my reverie. "What are you doing?"

"I'm just wondering if we should repaint the fence," I said.

"Pink?" she said.

"You'd make everything pink if I gave you the chance."

She rolled her eyes, as if I hadn't figured out life yet. "So? Why not?"

Once Jo was settled at her desk, watching a YouTube video of a kinder egg opening on her tablet, I began to get ready to go out.

"Mommy has a date tonight!" Jo said.

"Why do you say that?"

"You look fancy," she said. "And you never wear that fur coat!"

"Yeah, you can say Mommy's got a date. I've got you a babysitter. A new one. Try not to ruin her, okay? Be nice."

* * *

I arrived at Maurice's Italian restaurant.

They took my fur coat and the hostess led me to my private table out on the heated balcony, where all of L.A. lay out in front of me like an oil painting, swirling black and light in panoramic.

It was the best view in the city.

The representative, Mrs. Mallory, already waited for me. She was a dark haired woman with cat-eye glasses and a sharp suit. Every time I saw her she looked like she came pressed from a magazine about a Teddy Girls revival.

"Miss Sykes. I ordered us some Pinot," she said.

"Make that Chianti for me, please," I said to the waitress.

I sat down and lit a cigarette. I didn't bother to ask her if she minded, because I didn't care. It was my private balcony, and I had special privileges to smoke, so I was going to.

"Tell me why you're here, first thing," I said. "This is my one night a week I have to myself, and I'd really like the opportunity to enjoy my dinner."

"We want you back," she said. "The newly elected president is highly interested in having you work for him."

"I bet he is," I said.

I leaned back in my chair and took a drag of my cigarette. I forced myself to only have one a day, and sometimes it seemed to be the only time I actually really breathed.

"The president you served under had one of the most productive and successful presidencies in the history of our country."

"I was on top," I said.

"Excuse me?"

"You said I served under him," I said. "I— nevermind."

I stared out once more at the city. I'd come to appreciate the lights of skyscrapers and the buzz of neon because it meant people were still alive. I felt like I'd been waiting with knuckles tense for the last few years, either for something to happen to my daughter, or for another bomb to drop. Or both.

"My daughter got kicked out of school today," I said abruptly.

"I'm sorry to hear that. Can I ask why?"

"I think it's because I'm not there for her," I said. "Not enough, anyway. I made a promise a long time ago, that I'd be there for my child. I had to have my mother watch her while I was in Washington, and it's not like my schedule has let up. But in between three years in Washington and my currently very busy schedule, I don't know if I've fulfilled that promise."

"Do you know how many mothers and daughters you've helped? How many people's lives have been saved by your work?" Mrs. Mallory said.

The waitress brought out my Chianti and a plate of bruschetta. Then the chef, Mr. Maurice himself, came out to greet us and said he'd create something we'd love before rushing back into the kitchen.

I ate a piece of bruschetta, but I couldn't really enjoy it. Which was a damn shame, because Mr. Maurice was the best in the city.

"You have enough money to afford nannies," she said. "The best private instructors. The best care in the world for your daughter. It's so strange that you live in that quaint little house, when you could afford your own island."

"Your perception is skewed. I wouldn't call any house in the Pacific Palisades quaint. Do you have kids?" I asked.

"You're going to say I can't possibly understand because I don't have children?"

"No," I said. "I think you don't understand because you're a robot. When's the last time you got laid? Hell, when's the last time you actually enjoyed your wine, or looked at a sunset?"

"That's not the point," she said.

"Of course it is."

Our meals were served a few minutes later.

"This is risotto with capers and espresso-infused stock," said the waitress. "And that's veal wrapped with prosciutto and sage, marinated in wine."

"Shit, I don't deserve this," I said, and the waitress laughed and walked off.

The chef came by after we'd both taken a couple of bites.

"It's divine," I said. "Mr. Maurice, I'd say you've definitely outdone yourself."

"It is worth it to see that look on your face," he said.

Mrs. Mallory leaned forward she reminded me of dynamite set in the bottom of a building, something ready to go off.

"The world needs you, Miss Sykes," she said. "I don't mean to sound dramatic, but a tide is rising. You've done some great work, but the world isn't going to freeze in place. It never does. We need you. We're potentially looking at another New York disaster, or something even bigger."

I tried not to blink, because I knew ash and smoke and a bubbling section of New York waited underneath my eyelids.

"Please don't talk anymore. I'd like to enjoy my dinner in peace."

"Just tell me you'll think about it," I said.

"Okay," I said. "I'll think about it."

* * *

I headed back home around midnight. I found the babysitter on the couch, eating Cheetos and watching Keeping Up with the Kardashians in a Snuggie.

"How was she?" I asked.

The babysitter tried to surreptitiously wipe Cheeto dust off on her clothes.

"Oh, she was an angel."

"It's okay," I said. "You don't have to lie. I know she can be difficult. I won't pay you any less."

"I'm serious. She just sat on the floor and watched her videos. Didn't really talk at all."

I felt my stomach sink. That was not a good sign.

"Thanks," I said.

I paid her and she left.

When I caught my reflection in the mirror it was like my eyes were trying to sink down into my cheeks. I was really tired. The kind of tiredness that I'd be paying for with botox before I was thirty-two, I was sure, but I tried to catch up on some work on my laptop anyway. My client list was full for the next three years, and I had several public appearances coming up. Maybe I could find some way to rearrange everything so I could make more time for Jo and I wouldn't have to keep working ten to twelve hour days.

Mrs. Mallory's words echoed in my head.

We're looking at another New York disaster.

Jo came into the office, wearing her satin pink nightgown, bows in her hair.

"You should be asleep," I said.

"Well I'm not," she said, matter-of-factly, and thrust a book out in front of me.

It was her favorite, *Moe the Dinosaur Gets a Job.*

"Read to me?" she asked.

I glanced at my laptop, then back at Jo, and blew air out of my cheeks.

"Sure," I said, shutting the laptop down. "Come here."

She snuggled up close to me and I opened the book to the first page. Moe, a kind of brontosaurus, was drawn in his stone house, wearing a top hat.

MOE THE DINOSAUR WANTED A NEW TELE-VISION... the first line read.

I lay the book down.

"What would you think about moving to Washington?" I asked.

She grabbed her heels and pressed her face down against her toes.

"I don't want to live with grandma again," she said.

"No, sweetie," I said. "You wouldn't. It'd be the both of us."

"Why can't we go to Disney World like you promised?"

"We will. I've just been busy," I said.

She flopped onto her belly and cuddled the pillow into her stomach like she was trying to melt into it.

"Would you be happier if I was home more?" I asked. "Do you feel like we don't spend enough time together?"

She groaned and lifted her head up. Her eyes seemed to bear an ancient burden.

"Mom," she said. "Just read."

19

Tickets for *Restart Your Life With Beverly Sykes!* had been sold out for months. I'd been flown all over the country to do the talks, but this would be my first one back in L.A. I rode up to the theater, greeted by posters of my face all over. My face was glammed up in a halo of light, hair blown out, clouds behind me like I was standing on the wing of a plane.

Backstage, the makeup artist had the news running on her laptop. The newly elected president was standing up at a podium in a blue suit that matched his eyes.

I wondered what it'd be like to slip him out of that blue suit and kiss the purple skin underneath his eyes. He wasn't as attractive as the last president I'd slept with, but he definitely wasn't bad looking. I wondered if he had to take male enhancement pills, or went soft whenever he tried to put on a condom. I wondered if his wife, who was a criminal lawyer, would want to watch, or whether she'd rather not know at all. I tried to imagine her with her dark curly hair, eyes like premeditated murder, taking off her gray business suit. I imagined she'd have pink underwear underneath.

Maybe she even had a hidden tattoo, of a clover or a cartoon canary.

"You seem distracted," said the makeup artist backstage, thrusting me back into reality.

She was trying to apply fake eyelashes, but I kept blinking.

"Sorry," I said. "I'm just thinking about the talk."

"Uh-huh," she said, unconvinced.

"Well, okay. Do you ever think about how life is a constant negotiation of priorities and circumstance? Like, no matter what you do, you're going to have to fight for happiness until you die?"

"Hold still or I'm going to glue your eyes open," she said.

The producer leered over my shoulder like a bird of prey.

"We're on in fifteen. Are you ready, Bev?" she said.

"I think I might be sick or something."

"Not funny," she said. "If you're going to be sick, at least wait after the show."

People always think fame is power. But the thing about becoming famous is that you have even more people to answer to.

"Wait until after the show at least," and then before I could reply she was gone.

I headed to the stage, tugging on my starched blue blouse (they wanted me to dress conservative, like I didn't take my clothes off for a living), waiting for my cue. When it came on, I crossed the blue-lit stage with the clicking of my heels ringing a headache up into the top of my spine.

I stood in the center of the stage and waited until the cheers died down. I'd given this talk so many times, that the words came without me even having to think.

"My name is Beverly Sykes," I said. "And I have a special power. I heal people with sex."

I looked out across the crowd, and thought of Jo sitting alone on the couch, wilting like an unlit flower. I thought of her growing up on that couch alone, snapping into her bones, flushing into the shape of a woman, while I was out here doing this talk, over and over again.

"From a very young age I didn't understand the power that I possessed. I was just a bored, small town girl who wanted to be a grownup, to get on with her life, to take owner-ship of her own body. And well, my solution to that was to have sex. A lot."

Usually, that line elicited laughter. But something in my delivery made it sound stoic, stern even. The crowd remained silent.

I swallowed.

"I figured out that what I did, changed people. In a good way. They stopped being depressed, left unhappy relation-ships, got better jobs, cut their hair so their eyes could really see out into the world again. And I soon realized it was more than just a coincidence."

I resisted the urge to press my hand against my stomach because I felt something dragon-like pressing back.

It'd been a while since I felt that sensation.

"It wasn't until a man raped me and killed himself in front of me, that I realized just how real my gift was. I decided from that point on, that I'd do everything I could to help people. To change the world."

Then, I said something that wasn't in the script.

"But once you change the world, what then? You discover you've been so focused on fixing everything around you, that your own life is—"

I paused, and reached for the glass of water on a stool nearby to try to get the lump out of my throat. The crowd seemed to lean forward in an expectant, awkward hush.

"Your own life is a ruin, and you have to start over from the beginning. Happiness that used to come so easily is a dream so distant that you cease to dream it at all. Ah, sorry."

I coughed. The producer mouthed "what the fuck" from the side of the stage, and waved her arms trying to get my attention.

I took another sip of water. As I did so, I turned back to the audience and caught a familiar face in the front row.

It was as if a spotlight had been thrust upon him, resonating with a light so bright it was making vibrations. That face seemed to make time flow backwards back to a moment near a creek on the rocks, make the water flow up out of my throat, and I struggled to swallow.

He sat there clutching hands with his wife, who was slim and dark-haired like a Degas ballerina. He was of course older than I remembered, eyes weighted down with fifteen years, a dark suit I thought he'd never be caught dead in, but it was unmistakably him.

Spider.

Whatever was left of my speech crashed around my ankles.

And when I blinked, I saw Badger sitting somewhere out in the audience. And Gene Conroy. Joe. Tara. Furby. And T-Bone. And Nessa. Ariel. Lily. Lindsey. All of the men from the strip-club and those that came after from The Church of The First Sacrament. That boy behind the diner. The bored businessmen, rich and sad daddy's girls, angry criminals, catatonic mental patients. The President. The Vice-President. Even that nameless terrorist, my baby's father, with an eyeless face and coffin breath, radiating black sparks like antimatter.

So, how's our little baby doing? I imagined him saying, exhaling smoke.

I cleared my throat and set the glass of water down.

"Listen. It's easy to lose your way. Easier than anyone might think. And as the years pass by your free will is constantly chipped at and whittled away. You make little compromises to your happiness, because you think other people matter more than you, that you owe it to the world.

"But it's become very clear, that every second I'm standing here talking to you is a second wasted that I could have used to be close to my daughter."

Spider was smiling, and the dam inside my chest broke.

"There's a good chance that my daughter might turn out to have my gift. I need to be with her right now, loving her, teaching her, experiencing with her. Not out here doing shows and telling you things that you already know. And I know you paid a lot of damn money for this show to try to change your lives, but this isn't where the real change happens. It's outside this theater. It's in the arms of the world. It's in those chaotic, crazy, big pits of our lives."

I found myself waving my arms, as if shooing away the audience.

"So let's go live. We have the rest of our lives."

I caught one more glance at Spider.

Spider, my first.

Spider, the bad boy who I ate from the inside, curled up into and changed forever, without even understanding how much he'd change me.

Spider on the rocks who'd let me drink his Four Loko and for a moment made me feel like maybe all of my life could be a candy-coated dream of slippery sex and skin.

We could've been hurtling off the planet at that moment, the sky cooled with meteoric ash, and still I'd smile at him.

"I've got to go," I said suddenly.

I pulled the microphone off my blouse and dropped it, then hurried off the stage. Everyone stood up to applaud. The noise followed me like a storm.

"What the hell was that?" the producer asked, trying to block my exit. "People paid money for this."

"Can't you hear them? It sounds like it went over well," I said.

"You're an insane bitch," she said, as I moved around her. "I knew I shouldn't have worked with you."

"Nice meeting you too," I said, and I didn't break stride as I headed for the exit.

Security waited out in the parking lot with my car. I found myself climbing into the back seat of the car, giggling and flushed. Giddy.

"Let's go home," I said, barely able to get the words out.

He raised an eyebrow at me.

"You're early. What's going on?" he asked, but he began to pull out of the parking lot.

"I just need to get home," I said.

* * *

When I got home, I rushed inside like I might burst if I didn't get inside in time. I found Jo and her babysitter out in the backyard. Jo had bottles with various bugs in them set out in the grass, and seemed to be writing notes about them in a spiral bound notebook.

"Mom, you're early," she said. Again, without looking up.

"Hey honey," I said. "Pack your things, okay? Before Mommy realizes what she just did was terrifying and changes her mind."

"Where are we going?"

"I think we should take a vacation," I said. "You're in between schools and well, it's been awhile since we've had some quality time together. I have all the money in the world and a beautiful daughter. So, let's celebrate."

She perked up. "Disney World?"

"Disney World," I said. "And Six Flags and Legoland and SeaWorld. Then we can go to Hawaii just for the hell of it. Then I think we'll travel the world for a bit. India, Paris, Tokyo. All the places I wanted to take you that I thought I didn't have time for. And anywhere else you want to go. We can hire private tutors along the way, so you don't get behind in schooling."

She stared at me with her wolf eyes.

"What happened to you?" she asked.

"Mommy was lost for a little while," I said. "But now she's not."

"What about work?" she asked. "Your clients?"

I tried to ignore the fact that my six year old knew the word *clients*.

"There'll be plenty of time for work," I said. "Don't worry about that."

Jo undid the bottles and released the insects. Then she jumped up and ran into her room to pack. I paid the babysitter, and when I was alone I called up Mellie.

"The phone's been ringing off the hook," she said. "What happened at that speech?"

The voice that came out of me seemed unfamiliar, heavy in its timbre, like if I spoke too loud I might accidentally fell a forest.

"I'm going to need you to book me a flight," I said. "And postpone my appointments for the near future."

"Are you serious?" she said. "What happened?"

"Uh, midlife crisis?" I said.

"Bev! Come on! You're only thirty!"

"I just need a break, is all."

A pause.

"Well, I have been telling you that you need a vacation," she finally said. "People aren't going to be happy, though."

"I'll be," I said.

Then I hung up. The next person I called was my mother.

"Come with me on a vacation."

"Well, I do have some free time this summer," she said.

"No," I said. "I mean now."

"Now? But—"

"We never had a vacation when I was a child," I said. "We always talked about going to Disney World, remember? Let's do it now. You, me, and Jo."

My mom laughed.

"Did something happen, Bev?"

"Yeah," I said. "I had one of those, what do you call them? They're bright and shiny and come when you least expect them to. Makes your whole head want to pop off with the noise?"

"An epiphany?"

"A revelation," I said. "That we need a vacation. As a family."

"Okay, okay," she said. "I'll come with."

"I love you, Mom," I said. "See you in Florida tonight."

I packed as fast as I could, before I might change my mind and back out of it. My insides buzzed. My throat felt like it might float away. Years ago I'd told The President of the United States that I was a goddess, but now I got a thrill just from taking control of my life again.

Jo lugged her suitcase outside and my security helped her get it into the trunk. Then I came outside, and before my body could catch up with my mind, we were pulling out of the driveway heading toward the airport.

On the way, I called Mrs. Mallory. I got routed to her assistant.

"Hey, this is Miss Sykes. I'm sorry I can't be there in person but please tell Mrs. Mallory that I'll have to decline the job," I said. "I know the fate of the world is in my hands and all, but maybe you can take it from me for a few months? And please keep me in mind, I may be around for future opportunities. Try not to destroy the planet while I'm gone. Thanks."

Before the assistant could respond, I hung up. As I did so a new surge of energy bolted through me, as if I'd been shot by the sun. I glanced over at Jo in the backseat, wearing her pink jacket with the fur trim collar. She had her tablet in her hands, but she was bouncing up and down so much that there was no way she'd be able to focus on the image.

The L.A. landscape we passed was brilliant in the midday light. I heard the blood in my ears and the breath in my body. The buzz inside of me turned into a sizzle. I thought I might fry my pants if I pressed my thumbs against the seams.

Everything seemed to call out to me, inviting me to experience it. Almost as if I could hear my name in between the spaces of the palm trees we passed, in between the gray crevasses of buildings, as if the hum and the vibration of existence was finally touching me again with its palms up, its fingers digging into the skin.

In the last six years, it'd never gotten so bad that I'd lost all feeling, but I hadn't realized until that moment how easy it was to mute the volume on my own body.

"Mommy," Jo said.

"Yes baby?"

"Is this another ice cream day?"

"It's going to be ice cream day every day for a while, baby," I said.

We headed into the airport, and an hour later, with a brief stop at an ice cream shop inside, we were on a plane to Florida. Jo hadn't stopped bouncing the entire time we waited for the plane, not even when she spilled dark chocolate mint ice cream into her lap, but once the flight took off she quickly passed out against one of my arms.

I leaned over Jo and opened the window, trying as best as I could not to jostle her. It was nearing dark and the dusk splayed across my lap. L.A. shrank against the skyline.

A tide is rising.

What she hadn't mentioned was that a tide was always rising somewhere.

I caught the eye of the man across the aisle. He was in a business suit, but he had tattoos of lunar phases across his knuckles, and wooden gauges in his ears. He was slim, and dark-eyed, and looked like he'd know how to use his hands.

He raised an eyebrow at me and smiled. That was all it took for me to imagine him naked. My entire body flushed.

I really did need this vacation.

Soon I'd be sitting near a pool somewhere, sipping a Mai Tai, while Jo ate gelato and then found the highest point to jump off into the waters.

I saw my daughter's dark hair intermingling with the ocean and the sky.

I saw us swimming in the dark, Jo's body like a pearl. We'd

stay out there until our skin was pruned and our hearts resembled coral reefs.

The flight attendant came by and asked the man if he'd like any refreshments.

"I'll have what she's having," he said.

"I'm having wine," I said. "A Cab. But only because they don't have Chianti."

After the flight attendant left he leaned over toward me in the aisle and raised his glass.

"To a beautiful woman," he said. "Want to tell me your name?"

I knew the look of hands that ached to wrap around my hips, and I found myself squeezing my thighs together. I was already imagining what it'd be like to explode inside of him, make my body his rocket, rearrange his insides.

Some things never changed.

"Beverly," I said. "Beverly Sykes."

And when I took that first sip of wine, I felt I could've swallowed an ocean's worth.

Breathe in. Air feels cool. Breathe out. Air is cooler. That night my chest felt like a cavern and I could fit the whole world inside.

EPILOGUE

The first time I saw him across the room, I knew I had to make him mine. His dark neck underneath the glass belonged to my fingers. It ached to be restrained. His touch would be cool, like the liquid that lingered on the top of marble long after the rain stopped dancing. My skin would flush to be so close to his, that maple body colored so deep it was almost black, his sharp waist like a jagged star.

"Let me see that one," I told Mom, and the clerk took the violin out for me to hold.

"This was made in Germany," he said.

He showed me how to hold it.

"It's quite an unusual one, isn't it? Most violins are meant to mimic female voices, but this one has a male resonance."

When I touched the strings everything in that little music store suddenly took on greater significance. Even the way that light pushed itself through the storefront windows. It danced on the particle board displays so intensely that I thought it might be trying to speak.

I didn't know each breath could hum like music inside me.

And I didn't know the first thing about playing the violin, but I saw myself in a great concert hall in the sky, a rainbow piercing my throat, the dark wood cradled against my neck. His warm voice emanated in my arms even though I had yet to play a single note.

People liked to talk to me about destiny. I was Beverly Syke's daughter, after all. The daughter of God's miracle, a broken-off piece of sunshine, Lilith's sinful mommy MILFy redeemed. I should've been grateful that the whole world looked at my developing hips and tiny breasts in summer camisoles, and slavered to spread my legs apart. It was my destiny to have my cherry popped like an abscess. Spine bent back to please damaged eyes. To sit on top of the planet, dress torn, thighs sore, and fuck the war and the death away.

Thank you, Mother. Thank you, Jesus. I never wanted a real job, anyway. Like I never wanted to save it for someone special. From the moment I was born doctors sifted through my blood searching for a miracle. Reporters showed up at my school and snuck into the cafeteria to ask if I'd lost my virginity yet. Panels of experts argued for five hours on Livestream about the possibility I'd inherited my mother's power. Saudi princes, presidents, and billionaires offered to pay my mother a king's ransom for the privilege of spending a night alone with her underage daughter.

Maybe I had my mother's power. Maybe I didn't. If so, was my gift just to be used by whoever wanted me? There was another word for that, and it wasn't destiny.

* * *

My first violin instructor was once a world-renowned concert violinist from Russia named Mischa. He was only thirty-four, but with his salt and pepper hair and a scar on his lip, the cold tundra seemed to have aged him. He seemed glass-proof, both freshly preserved and ancient. He'd been gifted a Stradivarius by an anonymous donor during the days he played in the Moscow Chamber Orchestra, and had even appeared on the TwoSetViolin Youtube channel to play the violin backward.

Beverly convinced him to give me private lessons. I guess there were a few perks to having a famous mother.

The first time we met, Mischa strode through the doors of our house, right past Beverly, where I sat in the dining room with my violin. Normally people couldn't take their eyes off my mother, but she might as well have not even existed.

"Show me your hands," he said to me.

I held out my hands. He regarded them for a moment, and then just nodded toward my violin case.

When I tried to play my violin in front of him, I thought I'd made a mistake. The bow fit clumsily in my hands. I didn't know where to hold my fingers. It ached against my chin. I was somehow both too big and too small at the same time, with fumbling elbows and swollen wrists and lips that now fit on my face like bolted balloons on my teeth.

"I can't do this," I said.

I moved to put the violin away.

"Be quiet," Mischa said, and I froze.

He took hold of the violin and placed it back underneath my chin.

Mischa showed me where to hold my fingers. He taught me a simple chord. I could barely produce a sound. And what sound I could produce was not the warm, exultant voice I imagined   like the sound of an angel with tousled hair and a Ralph Lauren jacket, whipping down an empty highway that curved through the night like a meteor. It was scratchy. Rough. It couldn't even be described as music.

* * *

The day I got my first period, I skipped school and ran away.

I threw my phone into my locker before I ditched. I'd convinced Mom to get rid of my security guards years ago, but she wouldn't budge on getting rid of the tracking device on my phone. I pulled my hoodie over my face and hoped nobody would recognize me when I boarded a bus a few blocks from the school building, carrying nothing but my violin case, and headed into the city.

I didn't know where I was going. I just knew I needed to get away. The quiet, soft spasms didn't hurt that bad, and I didn't bleed as much as I thought I would.

But getting my period meant that soon people would be digging my tampons out of trash cans, taking creep-shots of me in swimsuits, or undressing in front of windows. They'd be dissecting the curves of my breasts as they grew inside my baggy t-shirts. There were already several websites counting down to the second I turned 18. No matter how many times mom's lawyers went after them, more still cropped up.

Sometimes when I was having a particularly bad day I'd circumvent the blockers Mom installed on my laptop and look up the fan art, deep-fakes, animations, and memes people had created about me.

This was what the world saw of me. Joanna Sykes. Daughter of the saintly prostitute. Bitch in training. Anime eyes and giant tits dragged along the floor. Bent over sucking cock with a giant tribal tramp-stamp, too-big hands, veins in my thighs. Legs spread open and a light beaming out of my pussy. Sometimes they'd even artificially age my face and attach it to a porn star. I fucked a lot of brothers and step-fathers, stuck inside washing machines, or needing help with my homework. Sometimes I'd be inside of a dungeon, locked inside some kind of terrifying BDSM contraption, while a faceless man spanked me with a metal-studded paddle or shoved dildos inside of me.

I curled up in the back of the bus, my cheek pressed to the cool front of my violin case, and I told myself I was too strong to cry.

Everyone said that mother changed the world, but trash still blew across the streets of Los Angeles, festering with glittering rot, and when I stumbled out of the bus into the cool sunlight, a homeless person with plastic bags wrapped around his hands threw up on the sidewalk in front of me. For a block afterward all I could smell was stomach acid and each breath I drew sucked a little more light from the air.

Two men in suits stood at the end of the street. I stopped. With their boots and hawkish intensity, they looked just like mom's security.

They hadn't seen me yet. I took several paces back and crawled through a tear in a chain link fence. I had to pull hard to get my violin case to fit in after me. I headed across the street to a small park and slid underneath a tree. Like a lot of things in L.A., it only looked impressive from far away. I was surrounded by cigarette butts and crushed beer tops. Even the birds seemed to have flown away to better places.

I took my violin out of its case and began to play.

In between lessons with Mischa I practiced for hours. I practiced until my fingers ached, and my body cramped as I tried to contort myself around the instrument. Whenever I set the violin down my hands started to crave their shape. I practiced chords at my desk in class, in the backs of cars, while I was at dinner. The arrangement of clouds and the stucco on ceilings started to look like sheet music.

Every time I wanted to give up I imagined my violin's voice, his real voice, emerging out of the scratchy sounds. I heard his polished timbre, a language older than love. I dreamed of it when I went to bed, smelling of rosin.

Eventually, after months of practice, that voice began to emerge. Like the sound of a beloved in the next room, speaking quietly through the wall.

A woman holding a baby, her overgrown blonde hair in a topknot, came by. She dropped a few crumpled bills in my violin case.

"Hey!" I called out. "I don't want this!"

But she was already gone.

It took me a while to realize that my Mom was watching me. She looked a little silly standing in the grass wearing her

Louboutin's and Prada jacket. She wore a full face of makeup that was meant for nighttime and low blue light, so it appeared mawkish and dry in the sun.

"You sound good," she said. "I didn't expect you to stick with it."

I had a plan for all the things I was going to say to Mom the next time I saw her, but I didn't expect her to say that.

"It happened, didn't it?" she asked, crouching down next to me.

The most infuriating thing about Mom was that I couldn't hide a damn thing from her.

I set my violin and bow back in its case.

"I don't want this life," I said. "I didn't ask for any of this."

She smirked a little. "You sound just like a teenager."

"Well, guess what, Mom?" I said.

She laughed, and despite myself, I actually laughed a little too. She knelt beside me and reached out for my face. I turned away.

"Don't embarrass me," I said.

"Then stop crying."

"And do what?"

"Figure out what you want," Mom said. "So you can stop running away, and run toward something instead."

"Thanks. That's genius," I said sarcastically.

"It doesn't take a genius to figure that out," she said.

I hated the way her smirk mirrored mine, the way the front pieces of her hair got wavy in the heat just like mine. For the rest of my life, I'd have to hear how much I looked like my mother. Every man I ever met would have to resist the urge to lick his lips, let his eyes eat my collarbone, and whisper "save me."

"Let's go, I have a car waiting for us," my mom said, and held out her hand.

"I'm not going," I said and grabbed the crumpled bills in the case, "Look. I've already made some money. I'll just drop out of school and become a panhandler. I'll get a little spotted dog named Ruford. I'll hitchhike across the country. I'll cut my hair and call myself Juno. I'll join a ragtag band of musicians and we'll hop trains and dance on the beach until the cops drag us away."

"I'll get us Fazzoli's for dinner," she said.

I got up and grabbed my violin case. I pressed my hand to my stomach.

"Get me the tiramisu," I said.

* * *

"I didn't have a father either," my mom told me when I was younger, "Girls like us don't need fathers."

"Who was he?" I asked. "Do you even know?"

"It doesn't matter," she said. "You're mine, and I'm yours."

"That sounds like a cop out," I said.

"You're too young to have so much sass," she said, laughing a little.

"And yet."

We sat underneath the pink canopy of my bed, under warm fuzzy blankets. Our housekeeper had made us frosted lemon cupcakes — my favorite — and mugs of hot white chocolate. The Princess Bride was paused on the television.

I remembered that night clearly because I told mom I was sick and wanted to stay home from school. When in truth Veronica Rothburn, in her miniature blazer with the ruffled collar and her battered Valentino purse that she used as a lunchbox, had told me, "Girls with Daddy issues always become whores."

She pronounced the word like she'd just finished eating something sugary and had to dab the glittery crumbs from her lips. Whores.

I'd never given much thought to having a father before then. I already knew I wasn't like the other girls. I didn't try to be. My mother was the savior with angel skin. Everything she licked turned to glitter. She transformed tears into grateful smiles, diseased blood transformed into bubbly light.

But I couldn't stop thinking of the way Veronica's lips pursed. The haughty disdain. The slight smile. Whores. It was a word that made our lemon cupcakes and hot white chocolate and The Princess Bride all seem a little silly.

"Can't you give me a name?" I asked.

Something in my mom's face flickered and grew dark.

She knew. She actually knew who he was. She just didn't want to tell me.

"I can't," she said.

"Why are you lying to me?" I asked.

"I wouldn't lie to you."

"You're lying by omission. That counts as lying."

Tears welled in my mother's eyes.

I didn't know it then, but it was one of the last times we'd lay in bed together, the last time my pink canopy would feel like a sanctuary. Afterward, the lemon cupcakes would taste too sweet and the white chocolate too cloying. I couldn't find a spot on the bed that was comfortable anymore. The safety we'd found here hadn't been real, and the thin pink gauze that separated us from the world could be torn down at any time.

Whores. A whole choir of little girls chanting. A sneer that could burn down a state capitol. Whores.

Who was my father? What kind of man could make my mother cry?

* * *

Mischa told me that if I wanted to get better than anyone else I had to do more than anyone else. So long after the rest of the orchestra had gone home, I sat in the dark on the stage, underneath the gilded weight of the empty room, and I kept playing.

When I finished the auditorium thrummed with the echo of the strings.

I always liked the last second after a song ended the most. It was like the song itself poured into the walls. It shimmered in the air for a brief moment just before it disappeared, an alive thing beyond my hands, beyond the strings.

Then in the empty dark, a chair creaked.

My head went white with fear.

"Who's there?" I asked.

No response. I peered into the auditorium, trying to make out a shape amongst the pulsing shadows.

"Who's there?" I called again, already wondering if I'd imagined the noise. Still, everything in the theater had fundamentally changed. I now sensed the weight of another presence.

The light controls were backstage. It was only a few steps. All I had to do was run to the switch and throw it. Then I could be sure that I'd only imagined the noise.

I rose from my chair.

"Don't," came a soft, but clear voice from somewhere in the front row.

I sat back down.

It was a voice I heard in my dreams, dark as sap, warm enough to melt onto the back of my neck.

I wanted to ask, *who are you?*' But I didn't dare to even blink.

"Keep playing," he said.

Still, I didn't move.

The seconds draped themselves around us.

"Do you want me to say please," he asked. "Or would you rather I command you?"

I set my violin back in place underneath my chin and pushed the bow above my quickening heartbeat.

My instructor Mischa once told me that poetry was just the ugly imitation of music. "Music is the only real story. Words are just a cheap facade." He told me there was an ancient rhythm that pulsed from the heat of stars. It roared out of vacuums, out of dark matter, out of the quaking dance of atoms trying to smash themselves into new objects.

He made me press my face to a concrete sidewalk once and try to hear the music. The drumbeat of blood and glass. I only pretended to hear the music because I got tired and sore from crouching on the ground, and he knew I was lying, but he told me:

"If we could hear it, actually hear it, the music would tell us the ultimate story."

As I played for the stranger, I thought the story went something like this.

* * *

Beverly Sykes sold the world a prescription for happiness. She was the American Dream personified: Blonde and preppy, always willing, the eternal optimist. A pharmaceutical drug with nice hips and eager eyes. She became another icon for The Promise. And The Promise said:

You deserve to be happy. Happiness belongs to you if only you can find it. Self-actualization is the individual's ultimate calling. There's nothing more important than your own self-fulfillment.

But I'd been to the top of the towers where the men lived who'd swallowed my mother's promise. They said things like, "We're going to change how things are done around here," and "This city will never be the same." They still wore ugly smiles and stiff suits and laughed at their own unfunny jokes. They all wore the same perfume that smelled like rotting oranges. They all stared at their reflection in the darkening windows of their office, lost in their own eyes as they bled into the horizon line.

My mother didn't change anything, except that now everyone was so goddamn self-satisfied.

Once the mayor of Los Angeles took me out shopping with his daughter Claire for a photo-op. My mom warned me not to make a scene, but I never did take to the cameras despite all the coaching. I couldn't hide my disdain for Claire in her pink mink fur coat, eyelash extensions, and fake baby-doll pout. She walked like a lamb with broken legs and spoke in a cooing, gurgling voice without edges. If she'd told me this was the first time in her life she'd been allowed out of her room I wouldn't have been surprised.

"She looks so much like her mother, doesn't she?" the mayor said. "You're going to sink a ship someday."

Claire leaned forward, her training bra peeking out from behind her lace camisole, and stage whispered, "I just know we're going to be great friends."

I pulled my hand away from Claire's manicured grasp. "Oh, I'd love to be friends, but I won't be staying for long. I don't know how anyone stands it here."

She giggled. "Where would you go?"

I don't remember what I said, only that I kept thinking: There has to be more to life than this. There has to be more than strawberry gelato and cappuccinos in faux-Italian ice cream shops, picking out matching bracelets at Tiffany's, getting pedicures, and posing for blinding camera flashes.

Is this why my father left?

Because he couldn't handle the promise that was a lie?

The American Dream. Beverly Sykes: Blonde hotrod. Babydoll eyes. Take the curves as fast as you want. All you need is an appointment and a working dick. Happiness is all you want because happiness will keep you trapped in the amber of your own smug eyes.

I knew that the stranger who sat alone in the auditorium, listening to me play, would not be satisfied with mere self-satisfaction.

* * *

"I've never heard anyone play like that," the stranger said.

"Play like what?" I asked.

"So angry, and yet so tender," he said. "Like even your rage is something that should be loved. A fire that should be stoked with soft hands."

I said nothing.

"What?" he asked. "Why the sad face?"

"I'm not going to fuck you," I said.

His laughter somehow infuriated me more than the idea of him wanting to sleep with me.

I grew hot on the back of my neck and on the back of my hands like his laughter touched every part of me that was exposed. It probably could've curled the strings of my violin.

"What is it?" I demanded. "What's so funny?"

"Where would you be if you weren't the daughter of Beverly Sykes?" he asked. "Hmm?"

"Ugh, don't say her name."

"Why? Does it offend you?"

In a huff, I threw my violin into the case and snapped it shut. He stopped laughing.

I should've gone backstage and thrown up the lights, and pinned his image in the brightness, but I didn't. I knew if I did that I'd never see him again.

And somehow, for reasons I couldn't understand, like a spot in your brain disconnected from the rest of the wiring, I didn't want him to disappear.

"I don't care about your mother," he said.

"Then what do you care about?"

"You."

Then it was my turn to laugh.

"You don't know anything about me," I said. "Everything you hear online and in magazines and television. That isn't real."

"When I heard you play, all I could think about was that I wanted that moment to go on forever."

"You're full of shit," I said, but the words were hesitant.

When I went backstage to get ready to leave I found a present wrapped in my locker. Normally I'd throw such a present away. My mother drilled into my head from a young age to never unwrap presents from people I didn't know.

But I knew who'd given me this one - wrapped in gold with a black velvet bow.

I tucked it into my bag and I didn't open it until I was safely home and behind the locked door of my bedroom.

It was a floor length black dress with delicate lace sleeves and a satin bustier sewn into the fabric. A concert dress. Modest and tasteful, while still being modern.

I tried it on and it fit perfectly. I spun around in the middle of the room, letting myself imagine his eyes on me.

My entire life, nobody had ever seen me. They just saw the possibilities that turned my face into a mirror for their own unspoken dreams.

I let my fingers run alongside the neckline of the dress.

I always imagined if my father were still around, he'd give me a gift just like that dress.

* * *

Soon I stopped playing for anyone else. A concert hall full of unblinking eyes, wet and still, and yet every note belonged to him.

Sometimes the stranger was the man who sang through my violin, and sometimes he was my father. In my mind's eye, he sat in the front row of the auditorium in the dark, his gaze like antique silver, hands folded in his lap, as the darkness seeped into his eyes and mouth.

He needed me to play. He'd been in the dark without music for so long.

My sigh echoed across the room. My chair creaked as I leaned forward, my long black dress sweeping against the floor.

His invisible presence followed me. It hung outside the windows. It left stains on the sunrise. It crawled into bed with me, between my arm and the pillow.

When I practiced my violin my hands became more pliable, and my body carved a more familiar shape.

Mischa noticed the difference right away. "You are playing like a woman who has found God."

"That's a little dramatic," I said, but also secretly pleased.

"Don't get cocky," he said, rapping on the sheet music stand hard enough to make me jump. "It's harder to keep him than to find him."

HotLips Magazine released an article about "Ten Hot Teenage Boyfriends for Joanna Sykes!" A reporter accosted me after school and asked me if I had any candidates for my first. Gossip forums confirmed that I was going steady with a drama Youtuber named JezzSayYes, or alternatively, a male model named Julian Teagues who was definitely too old for me. Others claimed to have gone to my high school and seen me kissing girls in the bathroom. A "Physiognomy expert" released a sixteen-part video series dissecting my anatomy — from my scalp to my hips to my shoe size — in an attempt to pair me with the "optimal" partner for breeding. I got emails from "talent managers" and "executives" who wanted to sponsor me. They were just glorified pimps.

Even my mom asked me if I was "seeing anyone special" at dinner. I threw my utensils down in a huff and tossed my napkin down.

"Everyone is just so interested in who I'm fucking," I said. "Frankly, it's a little disgusting. I'm sixteen!"

"Joanna," she said, "I'm your mother."

"What does that have to do with anything?"

My mom pursed her lips and straightened her shoulders in what I could only assume was a posture of attempted authority. But Beverly Sykes was never good at being motherly.

"I'm concerned about you."

"You just want to know if I have powers like you," I said. "Why is it so important? You want to start selling a two-for-one special?"

"Joanna," she said, my name a warning.

"Why does everyone have to make love feel so cheap?" I asked. "What happened to a little mystery? A little goddamn romance?"

I ran to my bedroom. Mom shouted at me, but I didn't want her to see my swollen eyes. I opened my window and crawled out onto the roof, into the crevasse where I couldn't be seen from the street. The light-polluted sky, pale and muted at the edges, wrapped itself around me.

Every part of me felt shivering and haunted.

I hoped the stranger did not ever see me in HotLips Magazine or in Joanna Sykes's Physiognomy! Part 14. I would've died from embarrassment. The pouting girl forced into designer clothes and good angles wasn't me, but nobody had bothered to see otherwise.

Except for him.

If the world had its way I'd lose my virginity on a raised platform in the center of every screen, underneath halogen bulbs and camera flashes. They'd sell VIP tickets and over-priced water bottles. $30 for a t-shirt.

They'd hold me up by the legs and slap me on the back to make me cry just like a newborn. They'd turn me around, this way and that, until they rubbed out every spark inside me.

The stranger would not pry apart my legs in the light.

He'd come to me after my performance, after the auditorium expanded, heavy, with a perfect, shimmering story. He'd wrap his hands around me. Fingers on my chin. Arm around my waist. His silhouette would fill itself out around me.

I arched my back. I pushed my panties to the side.

He was as big as a constellation inside me.

* * *

We were not in the auditorium anymore. Not really. The stranger would not come onto the stage unless I closed my eyes, and when my eyes were closed we transported to a frosted valley outside of a country home. The ceiling gave way to a clear moon and an expanse of sky that'd never touched rusted skyscrapers. When the stranger exhaled on the back of my neck, it became the quiet warm air inside my fantasy.

"Touch me," I whispered.

"Not yet," he said.

My father would never have let my mother parade me in front of the world with all of those people trying to crawl underneath my eyelids like insects. He would have kept me away from the cameras and the satellites, inside the soft cradle of his arms. Instead of rotten oranges and cheap aftershave he'd smell of winter cashmere and pine.

Instead of teaching me "safe sex" and the importance of birth control, or the best way to apply natural makeup, he'd teach me Latin and show me the position of Saturn in the sky.

"What if I'm like my mother?" I asked, gripping my violin in one hand and the side of the chair in the other. "What if I had her powers? I could give you something that people die for."

"It wouldn't be enough," he said.

"Not enough?" I asked, although it was exactly what I wanted to hear.

His words lay across the back of my neck. "Do you think it's enough for you?"

No, I said. Or maybe I only mouthed it. No. Because I was imagining standing on a porch in the twilight dark, wearing the black concert dress. The violin case would be at my feet.

I saw my father sitting on the porch swing, his long legs splayed out, his presence like a weight. He wouldn't have a shotgun. My father wouldn't be that gaudy and crude. But his eyes would carry a warning for the stranger that climbed out of his car, a bouquet of roses in his arms, a hand extended for me to take.

There'd be no talk of my "powers," no mention of my mother's hungry thighs. As the stranger escorted me to the front seat of his car, there'd be no pleading look or sigh. No, "save me." No grasping of the wrist. No trying to lure me into the backseat for a quickie, fingers in my mouth, unzipping his jeans with one hand.

Between us, there would be a promise like a story without words, like the music that lured him into me and turned each ordinary moment into a painted romance.

"Why won't you tell me who you are?" I asked. "Why can't I see you?"

"You'll see me soon enough," he said.

"That doesn't answer my question."

He pulled my hair back, carefully, away from the nape of my neck. When his fingers brushed against my skin I shivered.

"I want to give you the one thing your mother never had."

"And what would that be?"

He barely made any noise as he bent to cradle me from behind. His touch, like his breath, felt invisible. His arms embraced me like an instrument, with just the right amount of pressure, fingers poised.

"A dream that's all your own," he said.

I set my bow to the strings once more. I didn't have to see him to know that he burned down onto me like a spotlight.

And I saw myself, from above and below. I saw myself in the audience of the theater and also in the rafters. I saw my father reach out from the dark with his smile dancing across the moment.

I started to play.

ACKNOWLEDGMENTS

Thank you to Robert who gave me a home and many late night talks about the intricacies of character and what it means to be a better human being. And thank you to my furry terrors — The Kid, Sunshine, and Pris. The many dog walks in the woods and trips to the beach and belly rubs always reminded me that being alive is worth it.

Thank you to John Skipp, who's been an inspiration, mentor, and a friend for the last several years. His sheer joy made me realize that yes, every day could be an adventure.

Thank you to William Marsden, a Bodhisattva who's almost always down to talk about story and interesting, complex ideas, and video games.

Thank you to Christoph Paul for seeing the possibility of this book and helping me bring it into existence. And thank you Leza Cantoral, for your editing, thoughtfulness, and encouragement.

And lastly, thank you to Dietrich Mateschitz, who invented Red Bull.

ABOUT THE AUTHOR

Autumn Christian is a fiction writer from Texas. She is the author of *The Crooked God Machine, We Are Wormwood,* and *Ecstatic Inferno,* and has written for several video-games, including Battle Nations and State of Decay 2.

    She blogs at https://teachrobotslove.substack.com/.

    Twitter & IG @teachrobotslove

ALSO BY CLASH BOOKS

PROXIMITY

Sam Heaps

WHAT ARE YOU

Lindsay Lerman

HEXIS

Charlene Elsby

GAG REFLEX

Elle Nash

LES FEMMES GROTESQUES

Victoria Dalpe

HIGH SCHOOL ROMANCE

Marston Hefner

ANYBODY HOME?

Michael J. Seidlinger

TRAGEDY QUEENS: STORIES INSPIRED BY LANA DEL REY & SYLVIA PLATH

Edited by Leza Cantoral

NIGHTMARES IN ECTASY

Brendan Vidito

WE PUT THE LIT IN LITERARY

clashbooks.com

FOLLOW US

TWITTER

IG

FB

@clashbooks

EMAIL

clashmediabooks@gmail.com

Printed in the USA
CPSIA information can be obtained
at www.ICGtesting.com
JSHW020807170124
55470JS00002B/13